ASHER
AND THE
PRINCE

✦ BOOK 1 ✦

THE APEX BLADE

Other Titles by

EVAN J. CORBIN

Atonement Camp for Unrepentant Homophobes

Atonement Camp for Redemption

ASHER
AND THE
PRINCE

❧ BOOK 1 ❧

THE APEX BLADE

EVAN J. CORBIN

ATONEMENT BOOK, LLC

For information about this title or to order other books and/or electronic media, contact the publisher.

Cover and interior design by The Book Cover Whisperer: OpenBookDesign.biz

978-1-7354385-4-2 Paperback
978-1-7354385-5-9 eBook

Printed in the United States of America

FIRST EDITION

ASHER

AND THE

PRINCE

The Witch

Asher Snow closed his eyes, cupped the dice in his hands, and rattled them together. He could visualize the cards. Seven high cards and nine low had been played. He held one of the two remaining low cards in his hand. He calculated the probability. The numbers implored him to pass on the bet, but he disregarded logic. Logic took too long for jackpots. It was a night to take risks. He held his breath and tossed the dice on the table. Double windens. His face burnt crimson as the dice came to rest on the table in their most dreaded configuration. With the deftness of an expert thief, Shafer appropriated Asher's last chips, sliding them across the board.

"Betting all your chips at once is a bold move," Shafer told him. "Big reward if you're lucky. Quick game if you're not."

Asher knew Shafer was right, but he had been counting on luck. More than that, it was what he had paid for. He retraced his steps: He bathed the night before, eating only roots for dinner. *As if there was a choice.* He took care to let the charm only touch cloth, never flesh. The charmed coin was in his left pocket with the dragon tail against his thigh, just as the witch instructed. He spun three times before going inside the tavern, drawing the most quizzical stares of onlookers. The witch, with no apparent regard for how ridiculous the ritual was, assured him that this was necessary to power the charm.

Asher's stomach knotted. His humiliation was a further indignity wrought upon him after purchasing the lucky charm with half his share of last season's profits. The other half of his profits now sat neatly stacked under Shafer's nose. Asher scowled as Shafer's meaty hand cupped the chips close to his chest. He recalled the carnival witch's face, her eyes alluring with the hue of a winter moon, smirking at him through the throng of fairgoers whose fingers were slick with fat from roast pheasant dripping through the trenchers. Feeling an uncanny recognition from the stranger, he pushed past stalls and vendors hawking their wares, surrendering himself to her trap—a trap so devious that its snare remained obscured until he considered it now. If there was any enchantment, it was only to part him from the coin he spent to procure the charm. Asher resolved to find her again that very night—to confront her and demand his coin back before his parents noticed his missing contribution to the month's expenses.

Rosen leaned back in his chair, resting his arms behind his head. "Let the young one learn the hard way. Bold moves may impress the ladies when they work, but temperance and discipline win the game."

Shafer grunted. "Asher wouldn't have an interest in impressing the ladies. But at least there aren't any young lads here tonight who may judge him foolhardy."

Asher was still taking a measure of Rosen, the newest addition to the Wednesday night boxtin game, forming an impression with the deliberation of a painter toward his new subject. Three of the last four times Rosen held high cards, he tilted his bulbous nose up, looking down toward his hand. Just as often, Rosen would signify a deck of low cards by scratching what remained of his hair under his diplomatic cap, a patchwork of burgundy and amber mosaics that mirrored Barbshire's royal crest. To Asher, the Crown's uniform illustrated the necessity of the oft-repeated warning to avoid slaying the messenger.

Asher's impression of the man was still only a sketch, so he forgave Rosen for his presumptions about what he might prefer in a companion. Even though Rosen wasn't a highborn, he was still the closest person to royalty Asher had ever met. He thought it best to mind his own presumptions of the man, lest he unjustly conflate Rosen with his employers, who merely added coin to his purse.

Invitations to the game were rare, as Asher knew too well. Shafer seldom missed the opportunity to remind Asher that he only earned his own seat for his skill with numbers. His aptitude for probability and chance made the adults marvel. At seventeen and without any formal education, Asher saw it as his only wealth.

"Ah," Rosen said, drawing Asher's thoughts back to the moment, "the magic of travel. Adventures and treasures. I've been to all the cities under our king's realm. Only the Eastlands elude the corners of my map."

Asher lifted his gaze over the brim of his stein. "The Eastlands?"

"A fabled land of plenty," Rosen explained, his voice tinged with wistful reverence as he recounted legends of a place where flowers always bloom and hardship never darkens a person's spirit. Asher groaned as Rosen spoke with the conviction of someone who had seen the land firsthand, deciding it was no more real than any of the other stories men told to nourish their souls when there was too little food to fill their stomachs.

"Without title or coin, I guess I'll never travel far enough to know for myself," Asher said, glancing at his lost fortune at the end of the table.

"You're in fair company, Asher." Shafer thumbed a coin between his fingers. "Coin is a rarity suffered by more these days. I've owned this tavern for twenty-three years, and this is the worst business has ever been. Not coincidentally, I can say the same of the harvest."

Timmons clenched a fist and leaned over the table with an eyebrow cocked the way it always was before a pontification. "What little I can take from the field is lessened by the gnomes. Caught three today, just before sunrise."

Asher shrugged. "My parents say the gnomes claim no more than any other year. It's just more noticeable when there's less to offer."

"We should thin their numbers," Timmons said, waving a finger. "Set fire to the brush patches just inside the Thicketwood groves. They nest there. Fewer mouths to feed mean they'll steal less from those of us who worked for what we have."

Shafer sighed and began to reshuffle the deck of cards. "The Crown won't tolerate another war with them. You know as well as I that you can never get them all—even if you tried."

It wasn't the first time Shafer had given Timmons this lecture, but Timmons was rarely in the state of mind to recall it. Asher could almost time it by now. After three pints, Timmons's cheekbones would flush plumb. Between the fourth and fifth, his admonishing finger would tick off the world's injustices and how he'd remedy each of them. The gnomes were always his preferred target, whether they deserved it or not.

"Gnomes pollinate the amber bushes in the spring. They claim the leaves we don't eat and pollinate the flowers at the same time. Whatever retaliation they would bring in another war, I bet it would be even worse for the harvest the next year without them," Asher said. "They do their part."

"Speaking of doing your part," Shafer said, "you should likely tend to the dishes in the back. At least you can earn back some of the coin you lost."

Bearers of defeat, Asher's shoulders slumped, as much a product of his weary spirit as the day's demands. He grunted as he trudged away from the mocking table, retreating through the battlefield of merriment, past the trenches of the bar, and seeking refuge in the kitchen's gloomy sanctuary.

The kitchen was a chaotic cornucopia of dented copper steins and chipped clay plates, all victims of voracious feasting. Asher considered the dishes to be his comrades, each a casualty of the nightly war Asher fought at the tavern. His mind worked as a diligent ledger keeper, meticulously weighing the paltry coin he earned against the invaluable, precious energy that his youth provided him in abundance. It was a lopsided transaction. He was paying with his golden vitality to earn his wage, an unjust trade that left his pocket light and his spirit bankrupt.

Asher would pass other teenagers on the cobbled path from the lower village to the tavern each night. Young men offered their arms for their ladies' fair hands. It was a world as unfamiliar to him as the deepest parts of the Thicketwood. *How do their lives afford such frivolity when coin is so rare?* Their diversions seemed as unattainable as the partners they so casually found in their arms. Work at the tavern and the mill left little time for Asher to find his own friends. Or so he told himself. In truth, he found little in common with his peers—their unexamined lives and petty dreams.

Condescension was jealousy's remedy. His lips pursed at the sight of poor peasants, barely more than indentured slaves to the Crown, imitating the regal lords and ladies with their play-acted formalities. Asher never believed that the royals and highborns warranted idealization. *Perhaps they don't even see the walls of their jail cell.*

Still, quiet moments of introspection forced Asher to confront his hypocrisy. He knew he was no more immune to the frivolity of a crush than anyone else. Prince Hunter Bracken, the only son of the king— the name itself was an incantation to Asher. Once in his mind, it never failed to quicken his heart. Hunter's straw hair was always blowing wild in the wind whenever Asher would see the young prince from afar at festivals. Even over the gates and heads of the crowd, the prince's untamed hair stood in lone contrast to the sharply buttoned burgundy vests and knee-high leather riding boots the prince conformed into. *Perhaps he doesn't see the walls of his cell any better.*

Born the same year and under the same moon as the prince, Asher counted those as but two of their similarities. Other similarities were more a thing of hope than fact, he'd remind himself. The prince's eye once caught Asher's a moment too long as he strode down the streets in the parade. His broad shoulders and fit physique were no doubt the product of feasts and training. No king would see his son slight or weak, Asher reasoned.

Despite his servitude, Asher thought he had more freedom than he would as a highborn or a prince, at least in some regard. To Asher's relief, the villagers took no more than casual notice of Asher's uncommon longings. He had no line to preserve, no expectation of marrying well or even at all. Propriety only reached so far into the village from the walled estate in the hills beyond.

Asher pulled himself back to the moment, standing in the kitchen amid the clanking of metal steins carried in their baskets by barkeeps and the stale stench of dried ale wafting through the air.

"One coin to Shafer for me to wrap a pound of chicken thigh to take home?" asked an older woman with a squat neck and food-soiled hands.

Asher's mouth began to water at the thought of giving his stomach something to do beyond its incessant grumbling.

Out of habit, Asher squeezed the empty coin purse hanging from his belt. "Not today, Marianne, but thank you."

Marianne crossed her arms and looked him over. "There's some scrap in a sack behind the kegs. Only a small one tonight. Shafer will know if there are too few sacks when he takes the rest to the stables."

Asher nodded. He glanced to the side, then pulled a dusty book from his satchel. "Here," he whispered. "This one is a bit more complicated than the one we worked through last week. Just sound out the bigger words. Do your best, and we can meet next week to review anything you don't understand."

Marianne gave a curt nod. No smile. Asher leaned around the cabinet of clean dishes, ensuring they were alone. He waved to her. She took the signal, tucked the contraband in her bag, and shuffled back to the pans by the stove. Asher scraped a clay plate with a stiff brush and flashed a half smile to himself. He took a measure of pride, knowing she could barely read the name she was given when they first started their work in the spring.

Books were rare, mainly on account of their illegality. At least for commoners. Asher couldn't decide which was the greater pleasure: saving his coin to purchase a book from a desperate gambler at the tavern or building a hidden library as a silent protest against the highborn and royalty with licenses to covet the volumes for their own.

With the last dishes stowed for the next day, Asher claimed the bag behind the kegs and strolled into the night. A breeze tussled his hair. His mother told him that the hue of his hair reminded her of autumn leaves—brown with hints of blond and auburn as if it never settled on a color. The faintest hint of the chill to come whispered in the wind. Summer was beginning to cede to fall, the nights a harbinger of the season's gallant last stand. His stomach grumbled—an omen of what would come from another hopeless battle. He gripped the bag of scraps tighter and made his way off the stone path, past the city's outermost walls surrounding the village, and up the hill to the edge of the Thicketwood.

Rustling leaves called out to him from the entrance to the blackened grove. The full moon revealed shades of hunter greens and pale ginger woven among the shadows. Asher thanked the moon, ever his ally, for brokering a concession with the darkness that night. Moss, dank with the scent of decay, cushioned his first steps off the trail.

From the unseen distance came an animal's call. A tortured, moaning whine. Asher thought of the warnings. Never enter the Thicketwood, villagers would remind him. Dark things. Evil things. Unknown things lie hidden under the shadows. Legends were shared in the tavern. Villagers' accounts poured out just as freely as the ale that inspired them. Trees and roots. Branches like arms. Leaves like stabbing nails on crooked fingers. The branches were said to be the temptresses of the forest, drawing one in and closing around fools who didn't take the warning.

Rage muted fear's bite. Death could find him as assuredly in the forest as he feared it would if he confessed his foolish gamble to his father. He cursed under his breath for letting desperation convince him to rely on magic instead of reason. He followed the path of broken twigs and flattened underbrush marking his familiar trail. The air grew heavier. The stench of death and rotting became harder to ignore. Asher wasn't certain whether it was the humid air or his sweat beading on his skin as he wiped his forehead with his arm. *Not much farther,* he whispered to himself.

"Go no farther or be torn asunder. Bring us vittles, and we won't plunder," a meek voice called up from below.

Asher broke into a broad smile and squatted down among the untamed leaves and cowered plants. "Lattice, my friend. It's just me. I brought all I could tonight."

"Our needs are few. We know it to be all you can do," the gnome said as his daggered teeth caught the moon's glint.

Asher could understand why Timmons and many villagers feared the gnomes. Large black eyes and sharp teeth. Fear was a deception—a justification that excused the obligation to learn about them. Asher was grateful for his grandmother's wisdom: Never presume good nor evil without evidence.

Asher glanced behind him and lowered his voice. "Careful of Timmons's land. With the coming winter, I don't want your clan to be cooked in his stew."

"War he seeks if he disrupts our sneaks," Lattice said, folding his arms under his cotton ball beard.

Asher chuckled. The gnome may stand only four palms high, but his pride towered above the trees. He unpacked chopped carrot ends and last week's bread from his bag. "Temperance, kind friend. Your sneaks need not be so provocative. Why antagonize him and provoke a war?"

Another howling cry pierced through whispering leaves and

fog. Asher jumped and looked as deep into the shadows as the Thicketwood would permit him to see.

Asher swallowed and steadied his resolve. "Lattice. I know the Witch of the Forest lives just beyond your nests. I need to find her. Tonight."

"Your advice is wise to take," Lattice said, placing his hand on Asher's weathered boot. "Unnecessary provocations, a grave mistake."

"Some provocations are necessary. She cheated me out of coin. Please, Lattice."

Lattice sighed, and a carrot cracked as he bit into it. "Persist if you must, from my safeguard you'll stray. Chase the trail ahead, as dawn leads to day."

"Okay. Take the trail to the east," Asher muttered as he stood from his squat in the moss.

Not waiting for Lattice to warn him again, he brushed aside branches and shimmied between bushes, taking care to avoid their prickled thorns. Rashes and swollen limbs afflicted too many who ventured too far, he recalled. The village had a lone apothecary. With his savings now exhausted, Asher took measured steps, recalling his lesson to be careful and not gamble chips he couldn't afford to wager in haste.

Closer now, the anguished cries grew louder. Faint whimpers came to his ear as an interlude between the crescendos of tortured pain. He made his way through a landscape of fallen trees, their branches contorted into unnatural shapes, resembling the blackened remnants of a fire long cooled. He squinted under dense leaves on high branches to find the trail cloaked in shadow.

Just as he began to regret not starting his long journey earlier in the night, he froze, still as stone. A rustle in the brush ahead. He considered whether it could be a wounded animal caught in a trap. Intuition urged him to see what his eyes couldn't. He caught his breath before his rising chest could betray him.

"Hey!" he yelled. "Are you hurt?"

Asher crept ahead. He came upon a slumped figure in a terry cloak. Startled, the figure thrashed under the weight of a tree, arching its body to face him. He recognized the silver eyes that caught the moonlight and reflected it to him. Asher gasped, the heavy air burning his lungs. With hair white like cotton tarnished with soot from smoke, there she lay—the trickster, the Witch of the Forest.

CHAPTER 2

THE SELFLESS PEASANT

Asher stumbled back, his chest tightening as if unseen tentacles coiled around his lungs. He gulped air into his lungs, his eyes wide with panic. He tried to escape, but his foot caught on a sticklebush hidden in the underbrush. He fell, and the bush's sharp thorns pierced his arm through his threadbare sleeves.

"Wait," the witch shouted. "Please. Don't leave me. I won't hurt you. I'm trapped."

Asher scuttled to his feet and brushed spined leaves from his shirt. As he stepped closer, the witch's plight grew more apparent. A heavy trunk lay over her hips, pressing her body into an indentation of mud and sticks.

"You cheated me out of my coin!" he yelled.

She rolled her eyes. "I would never. I'm harmless. You must believe me. Ages ago, I lived in the village. I sang popular ballads on stage at the tavern. I didn't force them to pay me. Back then, I was *beautiful*. I was entertaining them, not casting spells.

At least not in the traditional sense, darling. You must have tipped me in coin."

"I've never been to any of your cursed performances," Asher said, taking the most tentative step toward the fallen tree.

"Oh, forgive me. Yes, you're much too young. I had a whole routine, child," she said, waving her free arm back and forth over the brush with her eyes closed as if reenacting her dance. "Men adored me. They absolutely *adored* me. That isn't why they hate me, though."

"I can't imagine why they hate you. I'm sorry they do. But that doesn't matter now. I'm here for my coin back," Asher demanded, folding his arms across his chest.

She sighed. "A foul sickness befell the village. Years before you were born. They came to me for help. Dance was my hobby, but tinctures and remedies were my profession. I fashioned a face covering. It had lampen leaves tucked inside and shielded the body from sickness, but they didn't want to suffer the indignity of wearing them in public. Yes, a careful seamstress would have used a livelier pattern for a more tasteful covering, but time didn't permit."

"You're rambling," Asher said.

"Yes," she said, holding out her hand. "They turned on me. They thought the coverings were the cause of the sickness, not its cure. They exiled me. It wasn't the first time either. Probably not the last."

Asher squeezed his eyes shut and shook his head, trying to focus. "Exile or not, you snuck into the village. I found you at the harvest carnival. I was there with my grandmother. You wore a black shawl, but I remember your eyes. You sold me a worthless charm. I lost more coin at boxtin than I would have ever wagered but for your broken promise!"

She wrenched herself on her side and glared up toward him. "Show me," she demanded.

Asher took the coin from his pocket, pinching it in a cloth, and held it by her nose. She studied the charm in his hand. "It's not without *some* merit. You ate the roots?"

"Of course," Asher said, giving her his most practiced patronizing stare.

"And you bathed the night before?"

"Yes," he said, his patience dwindling.

She craned her head a few inches closer. "You're sure?"

Asher's face burned scarlet, and he tucked his arms tighter against his chest. "Yes, I bathed. It's just been a long day."

"Have you let it touch your flesh?"

Asher hesitated. "No, only cloth."

"Pick it up, then," the witch said. "With your fingers."

"You said not to," Asher said.

"You were also told it was a magical charm, dear boy."

Asher studied the coin. The witch wrenched her body forward, taking her eyes away from Asher and fixing them on the coin. Asher gingerly pinched the coin's edges between two fingers and turned it in his hand.

"Now what?" he asked.

The witch smiled. "Look closer. The dragon."

Asher's eyes focused on the back of the coin. The dragon began to move. Its wings slowly flapped down and back up as if it were flying. Startled, Asher dropped the coin and backed away.

"Relax, child," the witch said. "I've seen such a trick of the eye before on many coins, not unlike this one. Best to keep the charm. Bad luck to discard it. Wishing good luck doesn't necessarily mean any charm would guarantee a good roll on a round of your boxtin game. Luck is elusive. May not find its way to where you hope."

"I don't need *luck*. I need my life savings back," he said, picking up the charm.

The witch groaned and let her head fall back onto the ground. "Help me move this tree. Then we can talk about it."

"How did you end up under a tree?" Asher asked, examining the splintered trunk across her body.

"Picking mushrooms. They illuminate at night. Didn't see the rotted tree. If I were so evil and powerful, wouldn't you think I could just free myself?"

Asher reasoned that if the gnomes could be misunderstood, the witch could be a victim of the same slander. Still, he approached with caution, knowing that even a tame animal could lash out and bite when wounded.

Asher grunted and pushed the trunk with all his might. He heard the wood crack and snap as his full weight set into it. His flat boots started to lose traction, sliding in the dirt. The witch pushed and moaned, digging her meaty hands into the ground like a ship's anchor, and pulled herself free. Asher coughed and slumped down on the tree, fighting for breath.

"Not so bad," she said, standing and shaking bark from her cloak. "Nothing's broken. It'd just heal right back up if it were. You'll need amber water for that scratch on your arm. Can't let you rely on some fool apothecary in town. He'd just as soon amputate it as cure it."

"Amputate?" Asher asked, gulping.

"My house is just beyond this clearing."

Asher froze in place. Visions of him trapped in an iron cage, being fed fatty broth before being cast in a boiling pot, warned him to resist the invitation.

"No need to fear," she said, hobbling away. "If I were to kill you, I would have. I have more to worry about than you."

"I just saved you. Why would you need to fear me?" Asher asked, anchoring his hands on his hips.

She turned. "You saved my life. Not only do I need to give you the amber water for the injury you suffered before you saved me, but I'm also magically bound to grant you a wish. If I don't, I'm cursed. Nasty curse. I'd grow older. Warted nose. Green skin."

"*A wish?*" Asher asked. "You propose to refund me for a worthless charm by offering me another?"

"There," she said, pointing into the fog in front of her. Asher crossed an unseen line on the ground, and a stone hut materialized from the fog. Bright yellow and orange flowers grew in beds illuminated by flickering gold light from the windows. A chimney smoked, reminding him how cold it had become since he first passed into the Thicketwood.

He rubbed his shoulders for the warmth it may provide. Her

offered amber water seemed enticing, but his mind screamed caution. It could be an elaborate trap. Perhaps the meat wouldn't taste the same if the animal tensed before the slaughter, he considered.

"Yes, yes. I know," she said, turning back to him at her door. "I don't blame you. Based on what you've no doubt heard, it would be insane to follow me into my home. Wait here for the amber water if you'd prefer. Haven't cleaned for guests inside anyhow."

Before Asher could say anything, she disappeared into the golden light. The door closed behind her. Through the window, he watched her riffling through a cupboard, taking this and that. A moment later, she returned, stepping through the light and back into the shadow.

"Here," she said, handing him a vial. "Put this on your arm. Hands as well. Nasty things, sticklebush thorns. It's just amber water, I promise."

Asher accepted the vial, uncorked it, and held it to his nose. It smelled like amber water. Holding it toward the window, he saw the telltale pale yellow hue. It was identical to what he'd seen the apothecary charge a dozen coin for. His arm was already starting to sting. In proper light, he imagined he'd see a scarlet rash. The mumps would come soon behind. Not having much time or any coin for another alternative, he doused his arm and hands with the water. Instantly, the burning subsided.

"Keep the rest of it. Use it once more in the morning, just to be safe," she said. "Now, what's your wish?"

"My wish?" Asher asked. "I wish you would refund my coin for this worthless charm!"

"You said you were at the festival, yes?"

"I was! You were in this slanted shack with a table full of other worthless charms I had the good sense not to buy."

"Did you see the sign?"

"What sign?"

The witch rolled her eyes. "The one that said *no refunds under any circumstances*? Not to mention, you haven't proven it to be defective."

Tears welled up in Asher's eyes. "Please. My family is not wealthy. We're just peasants in the lower village. The harvest yielded little this year. I made a mistake. I'll give it back. It's hardly used." Asher held the charm toward her, and his voice choked with sobs. "Please—my father will kill me if he finds out what I've lost."

"There, there, child," she said, shaking her head. "I can give you something better than coin. I can whip up a batch of stilt wax. Burn it in a candle, and you'll grow another few inches. Where and in which direction? I cannot promise. Perhaps a necklace to gift a fair lady."

Asher huffed and folded his arms.

"Oh," she said, squinting her moon-gray eyes, "a noble lad, then, it seems. Or have you already found one?"

"I haven't," Asher said as he wiped his sniffling nose on his sleeve.

"Surely, you must be lonely... longing for a companion. Isn't there anyone in the entire realm who you think would be inclined to fancy you? Perhaps with a magical nudge?"

"I wish for the coin I lost," he insisted.

"I'm a witch, not a bank. If I could make my own coin, why would I risk execution by sneaking into the village to sell my charms?"

"If you won't refund my coin, then I wish the harvest had been better this year," Asher demanded.

The witch laughed. "Child, they call me a witch, not a deity. The harvest is already in the past. Not to mention, I told the farmers ages ago that they needed to alternate their crop each year with legging beans. Let the soil grow strong. They didn't listen then; they won't listen now."

"Okay. How about peace with the gnomes? I don't want to see another war."

"Child," she sighed. "A noble wish. However, my curse won't be broken unless you wish something for yourself. *Only you.* If another could benefit from it, the wish is impossible. Not to mention, I'd be much more concerned about the prospect of war with Bishop Falls than a skirmish with the gnomes."

"What war?"

The witch lowered her voice. "Surely you've heard the rumors?"

Asher shook his head and shrugged.

"I suppose someone in your station may have the luxury of ignorance. Forget I mentioned it."

"If you can't prevent it, I guess it's just as useless as my other wishes anyway."

The witch rubbed her chin. "What about an enchanted cat? It can speak."

"A cat that talks? What would it say?"

The witch looked to the stars. "I said it *can* talk. It just never chooses to. Agreed. Bad wish. I have some mushrooms," she said, holding up a crooked finger as if the idea just came to her. "They let you see colors you never knew existed."

"I don't see the point in a wish that wouldn't help people."

She looked at him with a puzzled expression. "Curiously valiant. Sadly, I have no cure for that ailment either. Go home. Take the day to think about it. Come here tomorrow night with your wish." She looked around the clearing and whispered, "Please do come back. It would be cruel to save my life only to condemn me to an agonizing death worse than the one I would have suffered under the tree."

"You said you'd just grow old?"

"*Exactly,*" she hissed. "Tomorrow. You'll return?"

Asher stuttered. "Yes... I'll come back."

"Please do hurry back," she said. "I can already feel crow's feet starting to settle in."

Asher squinted in the dark, but he thought her face was just as gruesome as before. Pale skin blanched by the sun's neglect. Strong cheekbones, more familiar on the face of a man than a witch, he thought. Still, he looked closer. Her puffed white hair rested unnaturally on darker hair just beneath. Asher darted his eyes away, certain that she must be afflicted with the most unnatural of spells.

Gripping the bottle of amber water tightly, Asher scurried away from the house. He vaulted over fallen logs and soon found his familiar path of broken twigs and bent grass, which led him out of the forest and back into the clearing. He took a deep breath. Unburdened by the Thicketwood's weight, his lungs filled with a refreshing lightness as if they had grown buoyant. As the fog lingering in the air lifted, the haze obscuring his mind began to do the same. Senses no longer dulled, fear returned. His jog became a breakneck run.

Panting and with a cramp aching in his side, he didn't slow down until he came upon his parents' rowhome. Each house was bunched against one another like misshapen puzzle pieces forced to fit. The most neglected homes were only supported by leaning against those in scantly better shape. *How long could even the strongest walls hold carrying the weight of another?* Such was life under the Crown's tax and subjugation, he thought. The wealthiest among them in the lower village, still poor. Only rich by virtue of having a few more bones to boil in their watery broth.

Powerless to bend destiny with any meaningful wish, Asher's stomach growled with growing anxiety over an impending war. The last war with the gnomes came to mind like pressure on a forgotten bruise. Fires raged through the village each night as the gnomes repaid the brush fires set upon the Thicketwood. Villagers perished in such numbers that strangers mourned their dead together at mass funerals. Asher was too young to remember the horrors, yet too old for his parents to protect him from the fear. Despite his parents' assurance that all would be well, he was old enough to see the evidence it wasn't. The suffering. The sleepless nights in shelters within the castle's keep.

But war with Bishop Falls—the largest city under the kingdom's rule, with its own knights and archers. He couldn't fathom how much worse that would be.

The weight of his own helplessness slowed his pace to a shuffle, his shoes scuffing the ground as he walked. Some may see war as a chance to throw off the yoke of oppression, but Asher knew the reality. They were but pawns in a game played by those far more powerful than themselves. Even the thought of resistance seemed like a luxury he could not afford. Regardless of the victor, the poorest among them had already lost.

CHAPTER 3

THE FORTUNE

Asher sank deeper into the wooden barrel tub behind his parents' house. Steam wafted from the water's surface to greet the crisp morning air. With his nose just above the water, he watched lilac petals float like lazy ships on a placid lake. He caught his father's glance as the man shook his head.

"You bathed yesterday," he grumbled. "Sometimes I think you were switched at birth with the son of a highborn."

Asher longed for the theory to be true. A striking resemblance to his parents was enough evidence to dissuade him from the fantasy.

Even though the sticklebush scratches were all but healed, he thought it prudent to rub his body down with the family's bar of scented lye soap and bathe once more before dousing his arms with the last of the amber water, just in case any dried berries still stained his skin. The family's soap was so potent with lye that Asher feared it would necessitate its own remedy, but he took the chance. And the lilac petals did nothing for his bath, but they added a certain ambiance. He believed it was fitting to make the occasion as special as possible, to ease the uncertainty of when such an opportunity might arise again.

His mind wandered as he carefully soaped up his newly healed arms. He considered the burden the witch referred to as a wish. Perhaps he could wish for wealth to find him eventually if the witch could not procure a bag of coin on demand. He immediately dismissed the idea. Undue fortunes would make his family the target of disdain, disrupting their perilously balanced social order. Or maybe he could wish for a modest sum, no more than what he lost on his worthless charm. The idea enraged him. *Even if the witch were true to her word and I could wish for anything, why would I cast it away for something so small? Are even my deepest hopes so... hopeless?*

Another idea came to him as a petal drifted off on a different path on the water. His eyes widened, and his mind raced. He jolted up. Water sloshed from the tub to the ground. *Rosen.* He knew he needed to speak to him. Asher knew quite little about their newest boxtin player, other than that he was a royal carrier and diplomat. Well-traveled. Asher needed to learn more. He was the only person Asher had ever known to have the ear of royalty. If anyone could substantiate the witch's rumored war, it would be him.

"Longer you're in there, the longer your day," his mother said as she walked by carrying a bundle of clothes from the line draping across the yard.

Asher groaned and lifted himself out of the tub, grabbing the burlap towel next to him. His back tensed in anticipation of a day shoveling grain into storage before resuming his duties that night at the tavern, but his mind was preoccupied with a heavier burden.

"Minced root pies are on the stove," his mother said. "Growing boy. I added a bit of steamed frog to yours. Don't tell your father."

"Thanks, Mom," Asher said, trying to hide his revulsion with gratitude. Frog was a rare *treat*. Asher knew meat was never something to turn down, but he was grateful the frogs hid themselves well enough to avoid his plate as often as possible. Rabbits and chicken were rarer still. Either would be better than the gamey frog meat that was never enough and too much at the same time.

Asher hesitated at the door. He considered his mother as she bustled around the kitchen, cursing herself when she absentmindedly dunked a sudsy plate into the waste bucket instead of the rinse water. It was an important day for her. For the first time in over a month, she had a housekeeping client—a young highborn family just moved into their first home in the upper village. Her hair was tucked under her nicest bonnet, and Asher thought she was nearly unrecognizable with her lips pasted plum, offering the closest rendition of a highborn woman that her wage could afford. Like the laundry she would wash and the shirts she would press with the iron, Asher appreciated how she could restore beauty, no matter how deep the stain.

"Should I take anything to Grandma Rose?" he asked.

"Oh," she gasped. "It's out of your way. Are you sure? It would mean the world to me. I can't be late today."

It was unnecessary for her to remind him that punctuality was essential. In Asher's estimation, the sun was already too high in the sky. Another errand would burden both of them, but Asher knew his feet were swifter.

"It's no problem at all," he said.

"Bless you," his mother said, pushing a small sack of leftover food to his chest. "Your grandmother always says—"

"That I'm going to grow up and serve as a map to lead the kingdom into its future." Asher completed the mantra she had been reciting to him for as long as he could recall.

Asher held his breath and looked away from the bag to avoid gagging at the smell of frog juices seeping through it. He began preparing his excuses to dodge aimless conversation with his grandmother. Her stories would snare him better than the sharpest sticklebush in the Thicketwood. His grandmother's age had long been a thing of local speculation. She couldn't recall her age any more than she could reliably remember his name. Nonetheless, her kind temperament endured beyond the reach of her years and memory.

Asher buttoned the last remaining button on his vest. His mother looked him up and down with a thoughtful smile before gently stepping over and placing her hand on his chin.

"My dear son," she said, nudging his head to meet her eyes. "Burning from both ends, trying to save the world by yourself. Slow down. Take it from me. Have as much compassion for yourself as you have for others. Most importantly, you can't save everyone."

Asher rolled his eyes. "I'll be home tonight."

Asher rubbed his tongue against a molar, hoping to dislodge a bit of frog meat lest he be cursed to taste it in his mouth a moment longer. Bag in hand, he left his home and ended his journey a few blocks later, climbing the four broken-stone stairs leading to his grandmother's door. He rapped on the door three times, finding a spot on the decayed wood least likely to impale him with splinters. Drooping shudders clung to the windows, held together by the force of habit rather than nails. Asher took comfort in knowing that his visits ensured the occupant was at least spared her home's neglect.

"Over here, over here!" his grandmother yelled, stomping through her garden with her nightgown sagging over her boots. "I'm coming. I'm coming."

"Don't rush! Take your time," Asher said, fearing she'd fold like parchment if she fell.

"Have you seen a yellow tabby?" she asked, sounding frantic. "White patch on her chest? Tail broken and mended at a sharp angle?"

Asher scrunched his eyebrows, pretending to give the question his most sincere consideration. "I'm so sorry, Grandma Rose, I don't believe I have."

"She got out last night. Such bad weather. Must be half-starved. I posted signs in the square. She's gone missing!"

Asher took one of the hand-drawn posters his grandmother offered. He squinted and then turned it upside down, thinking the sketched rendition was as likely to recover a hamster or raccoon as it was a cat.

"I'll keep an eye out for her, I promise," Asher repeated the same script he performed almost every time they met. His mother once told him the poor animal had been missing since before he was born.

Huffing along the way, she climbed the stairs. Asher frowned, noticing the dirt stains on her nightgown, which crept ever higher toward her waist. He made a mental note to ask his mother to borrow the soap next time.

Hand on the door, she looked up to meet his eyes. "You've been to the Thicketwood?" she asked, bracing herself on the rail.

"Yes," Asher admitted.

"I fear that the time is soon near. Winds carry warnings from afar—warnings that cannot be ignored. Your line will end with you."

"I just came to bring you some food," Asher said, eager to change the subject.

She blinked and steadied herself. "Thank you for the food, Asher," she said, offering him a slight bow. "Your kindness rivals your mother's. Please give her my thanks. Cupboards are barer this year than those that came before."

More grateful for her lucid interlude than concerned for her delusions, Asher took the opportunity to part ways before she invited him inside. Not even her esteemed jams were any remedy to the biscuits he assumed she baked with mortar and stone. His stomach grumbled. He thought it was less from hunger than the frog.

Asher's mind was free to wander as his feet took him along the path to Grayson's mill, as they had done each day since he was old enough to lift the shovel. Cullin Creek flowed beside the watermill with its typical vigor, yet the mill's blades didn't turn. A rogue plank, wedged at the mill's foundation, appeared to be the culprit. Asher reached out to dislodge it but stopped short. It was placed too deliberately to be an accident.

Experience had taught Asher that Mr. Grayson was uncommonly particular about his mill's workings. The line between fixing and sabotaging something was always too difficult to reliably discern. The prior summer, Asher made an improvement to adjust the millstones, aiming for a finer grain. Mr. Grayson squeezed his temples and stopped Asher before he could demonstrate the improved contraption.

Mr. Grayson's eyes had been wild as he pleaded, "Why didn't you ask me first?"

"I thought you'd tell me no—that it was a waste of time," Asher had said, withholding mention of the unlicensed book he purchased that inspired the idea for fear of compounding his crime. "I wanted to prove that it would work first."

"Did you think to petition the town magistrate first?"

Asher folded his arms. "Well, no."

"And what would have happened if there was an inspection, if the magistrate found an unlicensed improvement?"

Asher struggled for an answer. "We could always just take it down if they didn't like it."

"*Take it down?*" Mr. Grayson repeated. "I'm no highborn. They'd tell the regent. My license to run the mill would be revoked, and I'd be lucky to avoid the shackles. The magistrate has never approved any new turn of gear or substitution of a stone. I doubt the committee even convenes to consider a petition before issuing a rejection and hassling me with questions as punishment for asking."

Forcing himself to focus on the present and avoid lingering in the past, Asher hiked up the steep hill, dotted with rocks and patches of grass that weren't sacrificed under the carriage wheels hauling grain from the mill. Mr. Grayson's family lived in the homely cottage at the top of the slope. Asher always admired the small dwelling, if for no other reason than that it stood alone. No shacks leaned against it, and it was far removed from the carriages and boisterous neighbors in town that kept him awake longer than he'd ever prefer.

"Good to see you, Asher," Mr. Grayson said as he opened the door, a forlorn look on his face.

"Mr. Grayson," Asher said, pointing to the watermill, "the wheel is wedged. Where are the carriages and everyone else?"

"There's no more grain to mill. That means there's no more grain for you to shovel. Harvest was poor this year," he said.

Asher pitied the man. His face looked like clay left to harden in the sun. Normally gregarious and quick with a laugh, the man looked to the mountains beyond, not meeting Asher's eyes as he spoke. How hard must it be to tell so many young men the same thing all day, Asher thought. Mr. Grayson was just the first domino to fall in what would soon come. Famine. None spoke the word. Instead, the villagers would tend more earnestly to their gardens. Festivals would be canceled without explanation, but Asher knew none need be given aloud. The word brought fear.

Asher didn't fear the hunger. He dreaded what would come next. The gnomes would be easy targets. Legend purported hidden food stores buried in gnome holes beneath the damp moss and shrubs in the Thicketwood. Asher knew the stories to be embellished, confirmed by his nightly trips as much as common sense. They were so small, after all. How much could they truly eat? Hunger made men do desperate things. The thought made him tremble.

"I understand, Mr. Grayson. If I can do anything to help your family, please let me know," Asher said as his mind turned to his pressing need for coin to help support his own family.

The mill owner ran his hand over rugged wooden rails on his porch, paint chipping off as he did. "Any help I need would be charity I fear I could never repay. Go home, Asher," he said, turning hollowed eyes to him. "Any help you could offer would only distract you from your family. They need you more."

Asher bid the man well and took uneven steps back down the hill, nearly slipping down the slope before he caught his footing. Each step was a tenuous reprieve before he knew he would slide again. Near misses and close calls were nothing new to him. Such was his life. This, like anything before, would pass. Just so long as he kept his footing and didn't stop trying.

CHAPTER 4

The Tavern's Tales

He arrived at Shafer's tavern hours early, hopeful that an odd job might await him. Soot was easier to shovel from the hearth than grain from the mill. Once, an errant hoof from a horse unwilling to take its shoe in the tavern's stable led to a boy's injury. Asher owed his brief occupation as a substitute stable keeper to the boy's misfortune. The boy's leg eventually healed, but Asher was still glad to add the trade to his assorted record of odd jobs that would pay enough to survive.

Asher's own stint in the stables taught him that experience and wisdom were not so easily interchangeable as a worker's shift on Shafer's ledger. Asher insisted upon shoeing a wild and untamed foal. He thought that the other stable boy on his shift was too young. Barely any older himself, Asher had at least tamed the beast enough that it would take a carrot from his hand. The boy protested, but Asher insisted, letting his confidence substitute for experience. *I know what I'm doing,* he had shouted.

Asher flinched at the memory of the horse kicking dirt before it smashed its hoof into his arm after he drove the first nail into the shoe. Throbbing pain and swelling grew beyond Asher's ability to hide it under the length of his sleeve. Asher snuck into the stables each night for a week, shoveling manure with his other arm doing the work of two. Once certain he had contributed enough extra labor to justify the apothecary's fee, the arm nonetheless healed on its own, sparing him the further injury of begging for the owner's charity. A scar traced the length of his forearm. For a time, Asher thought the scar was a daily reminder of his hubris. Over time, he noticed it less often until the wound was nearly forgotten.

Asher took a deep breath and walked into the tavern. He took comfort in knowing that no matter how the world outside shifted and changed, the tables remained steadfast in their well-worn positions, like old friends. The regulars, too, were reliably early, already settled in their usual seats as if they were highborns holding deeds to land.

"You're here early," Shafer said, tucking a rag in his pocket after wiping down a table. The lunch patrons had all but left, and it was the only time in the day when the owner had a moment to catch a breath.

"Mr. Grayson's mill was shut down for the season. No grain," Asher said, taking a seat at the empty table.

"Sooner than I expected," Shafer said, shaking his head.

"I have extra time. Have anything for me?" Asher asked. "The oven is more soot than stone lately."

Shafer sauntered to the bar and poured two steins, handing one to Asher and sitting across from him. "Won't be needing the oven anytime soon," he said, taking a long sip. "Price of food is more than the patrons can pay. Ale, on the other hand. Ale was made from last year's harvest. Won't run out of that soon. Cheers," he said, holding his stein across the table.

Asher tapped his stein against Shafer's and took a sip, apprehensive to ask an obvious question. "Without food, I don't imagine you have much use for someone to serve it and clean the dishes."

"You've always been my brightest employee," Shafer said, taking another gulp, longer than the first.

As his hardships grew, Asher began to dread going home that night. Looking his parents in the eye and explaining he lost both jobs in a single day. He imagined his father's lecture about punctuality and blaming his morning bath for his misfortune. Worse, he dreaded his mother would say nothing, too fearful to speak of the family's sacrifices that would inevitably follow.

"Rosen," Asher said. "Have you seen him today?"

"You're in luck. Back room. Quieter back there. He was going through some maps."

"Excuse me," Asher said, leaving his stein at the table. "I need to speak with him."

Asher walked to the back room, a reserved space for special events. Cabaret shows and the like. It occurred to him that the room had sat neglected for most of the last year. As promised, he found Rosen pressing the wrinkles out of parchment maps with frayed edges. The musty scent gave him the impression they were ancient.

"Going somewhere?" Asher asked.

Rosen smiled and leaned back. "Good to see you again, lad.

I'm always going somewhere or finding my way back. Sometimes I'm not certain which."

Asher leaned forward to gaze over Rosen's frothing stein at the weathered parchment sprawled between them. The map, a tapestry of ink and ambition, captured his eyes with its meticulous detail. At its heart lay his home, the capital city of Barbshire. Its proud castle nestled securely within the embrace of a formidable keep. Around it, like loyal subjects to their sovereign, sprawled the bustling villages. The upper village encircled the castle with its highborn, and the appropriately named lower village meandered beyond it with homes like his own. These were all cradled within the grand embrace of the capital city's towering outer walls, a testament to the kingdom's impenetrable might and majesty.

His gaze wandered northward, tracing the verdant expanse of the Thicketwood. Beyond the forest's shadows, the majestic Blue Mountains rose like ancient guardians, their peaks veiled in mist, obscuring their mysteries. His eyes followed the map's journey north toward Bishop Falls.

Intersecting lines, delicate as spider's silk, wove a network of trade routes from Bishop Falls to the surrounding cities. Asher's gaze wandered toward the edges of the map, where the ominous expanse of the Poisoned Fields surrounded them like the world's edge. Its presence needed no labels, for the smudged ink that ringed its borders spoke of a land forsaken, a realm of whispered warnings and unspoken fears.

In corners of the tavern lit by flickering torchlight, young men, fueled by ale and bravado, would often recount tales of daring ventures into the forbidden expanse beyond. Their voices, boisterous and brimming with the folly of youth, fell deaf upon the ears of older men, who sipped their ale in silent skepticism. For despite the vigor of their claims, an unyielding truth hung heavily in the smoky tavern air—no soul brave or foolish enough to traverse the horizon within the Poisoned Fields had ever returned to tell a tale.

"Where this time?" Asher asked.

"Crown business. Can't discuss," he said.

"Last night, you mentioned the Eastlands. Where are they?"

Rosen laughed. "They're not on any map I have."

Asher slouched his shoulders, crestfallen. "Have you met a royal? The prince?"

Rosen looked around the empty room and leaned across the table, his voice a whisper. "Speaking about them would put my head in a basket. Your head would join my own if you ever acted on your intuitions with the prince, however astute they may be. Don't think I can't tell how your eyes widen when you speak his name."

Asher gripped the arms of the chair to prevent himself from falling out. "What's he like?" he asked with what words he could muster.

Rosen's smile soured, and he took another long swig from his stein. "The farther you are from the castle, the happier you will be. Dark times are on the horizon. A poor harvest just makes things worse."

"Like a war with Bishop Falls?" Asher asked.

Rosen slammed his stein on the table and swung in his chair, eyes wild. "How do you know about that?"

Asher took an evasive tone. "I hike in the Thicketwood. Many secrets are whispered among the trees. I'd rather hear it from you. Better that you tell me the truth than risk having me spread rumors."

"Ale lubricates the tongue like oil on the wood, I suppose," Rosen said, setting his stein before him next to its empty companion. "I've said too much."

"Rosen, please," Asher said, placing his hand on the map. "If such things come to pass, would you leave us alone in the dark, unable to prepare?"

"I grew up here in Barbshire—in the lower village. Resiliency is a way of life," Rosen said, sighing and taking another sip of ale. "Still...our king conceded to Bishop Falls's governor's demand to trade double our ore quota for their usual grain shipment. They had a bumper crop this year, unlike us. I fear their governor recognized our grain shortage and our king's concession as an act of desperation. Opportunity often arises from another's despair. Hunger demands satisfaction—whether for want of food or power."

"An insurrection?" Asher asked, his mouth suddenly dry.

"The Crown doesn't believe so," Rosen said. "Your prince has been ordered to take the governor's daughter's hand in marriage as a part of the trade deal. Until then, no grain imports."

"He must be devastated," Asher said.

"To the contrary. He's elated," Rosen said. "Whatever personal concessions he may make, I think he's cunning enough to realize the accommodation will bring the kingdom closer, increasing their combined wealth. Maybe quell rumors of strife within the kingdom as well."

Asher looked down at the unswept floor. "I guess that makes sense. Bishop Falls is the largest city in the kingdom."

Rosen's eyes narrowed. "In that case, you're just as misled as the Crown," he said, his voice seething. "Bishop Falls is plotting a trap. They seek to draw the city's guard down. Strike us when we're least suspecting—likely in the spring at the wedding itself."

"What evidence do you have?" Asher asked.

"Couriers and diplomats like me pick up many rumors, some more credible than others. They fit together like a puzzle. Yet no one heeds my warnings. Our king is too desperate, too narrow in his view. Already, Bishop Falls keeps its garrison within its walls. They should have been deployed to take the watch for bandits on the trade roads to Fool's Keep and Graycott. Why? It's obvious. They save their men to spill their blood at our gates. The prince mustn't marry the governor's daughter, Asher. It's imperative."

"With no one willing to listen, how could anyone stop it?" Asher asked, his hands clenched into tight fists.

Rosen shook his head and peered into his stein. "Only if the king could be made to reconsider, which seems impossible."

"It must be more than that," Asher said, rubbing his temples. "I've been to Bishop Falls once. They didn't seem to harbor any hatred toward the capital."

"Asher," Rosen said, and then paused as if he were gathering his thoughts. "It wasn't always this way. The king's grandfather held the peace. Since then, the distance from Barbshire to Bishop Falls has grown further than this map would suggest."

"So what is it, then?"

"There *is* more," Rosen began. "Our kingdom has... withheld something from Bishop Falls, along with all the other cities under the king's rule. Something to which they believe themselves entitled." Rosen swirled what little was left of the ale in his stein, watching as it sloshed in circles. "I fear I may share some of the blame. My best intentions don't always lead to good outcomes."

"We withheld ore?"

Rosen's face flushed scarlet as if scorched by the summer sun. "No. I've said enough! Enough to be executed not once, but twice over," he said, his voice trembling. "Guard this secret with your life. Just... be safe. Please, stay safe."

Asher staggered from the tavern, his senses numbed. Flickering torchlight painted his elongated shadow onto the cobblestone street, stretching his dark silhouette farther down the road than he expected. From where he stood on the hill, the distant walls surrounding the city and its villages appeared vulnerable and low. Powerlessness gnawed at him. An extra work shift or a lucky hand at a boxtin game could fix most of his problems, but not this.

His influence on royal affairs was as insignificant as a pebble in a river. Such lofty concerns were reserved for those unburdened with day-to-day survival. Asher's thoughts drifted to his promised wish, a desperate hope offered by a dubious patron.

Asher thought it possible that her promised wish would be no more reliable than before. Burdened by the prospect of war, the scant hope that she might be sincere began to justify the risk. Seeking a selfless desire would be futile, especially if it crumbled along with the city's walls in an impending war. His wish had to be transformative—not just a temporary fix, but something powerful enough to avert war and shield his family from unbearable hardship. His small intervention in the river of fate had to be a boulder that redirected the entire current.

With boxtin, math and probability often determined the winner. But it wasn't always enough. Players less skilled than he sometimes triumphed more frequently. Their secret? Bluffing. They used bold risks and unwavering confidence to instill doubt in those with stronger hands. Asher sensed the witch had the upper hand as arbiter over what wish she would grant. He decided that he needed to employ a similar tactic—a daring bluff to disguise his intentions enough to fit within her game's narrow rules.

If he could disguise his true intentions, he might be able to turn this dangerous gamble to his advantage. Sometimes, asking for one thing could ensure another. Like he had learned from his long nights shuffling cards in the tavern, the best rewards followed the highest stakes.

CHAPTER 5

Asher's Lie

Candles flickered inside the homes along the winding stone street that led down the hill to the house in the lower village with the red door and lilac flowers on the windowsill. Asher quickened his pace. A somber quiet took the early evening. By this hour, he was accustomed to dodging mule carts that gathered too much speed going down the hill. He learned to weave around crowds that walked too slowly down sidewalks that were too narrow. But not tonight. Absent a drunkard stumbling home from the tavern and arguing with himself, he was alone.

He found his parents sitting silently across from one another at the table by the hearth. An oil lamp burnt low, casting as many shadows over their faces as it did light.

"Where is everyone?" Asher asked, taking note of the bone protruding from the pot on the stove. He caught a whiff of the boil as he walked past. No buttery marrow or scent of meat. *At least it isn't more frog.*

"Same as you, I presume," his father said as he stirred his broth.

"Everyone heard about the mill. That impacted the market. The tavern. Livestock won't be fed much longer. Slaughtered too young, so there won't be much meat."

"I wasn't hired for the house in the upper village," his mother said, stirring the thin broth in her bowl with a spoon. "Rains from yesterday flooded the river bridge, but I crossed anyway. Mud and silt caked on my shoes and ruined my dress. The highborn took one look at me and dismissed me. Didn't want to risk having me ruin their floors."

Rage flushed Asher's cheeks as he ground down on his teeth. The highborn would dismiss his family with disapproving glares and conversations that would stop when they passed any of them on the streets, their eyes not perceptive enough to discern the working poor from vagrants, nor would their leather-shoe aristocracy have the grace even to recognize the difference.

Asher sat between them, relieved that his misery had company, but gradually coming to terms with the enormity of the plight. "What about the quarry?" Asher asked.

His father shared a glance with his mother. "The Crown called up double shifts until the next new moon. Every able-bodied man is to take shifts to mine more ore to trade for food. You'll be sent down to the caves. The small ones always are."

"Simon!" his mother hissed.

Simon churned his soup with his spoon. His fingernails were outlined in a stubborn black soot that the harshest soap could never remedy. "It's good work. Honest work. A real man's work.

Not foolish games of chance or stable boy labor. The boy should follow in my footsteps."

Asher lost his appetite. He knew the caves more from stories of young men dying in a collapse or from foul air than by any personal experience. Thankless, dangerous work. He imagined himself climbing out of the cave, caked in dark ash that would resist the harshest soap, squinting at the sun, and being thankful to escape. He feared becoming nothing more than a story told by men at the tavern blessed (or cursed) to live long enough to recount the tale. And if death didn't find him first, he would become like his father, seeing life as only a brief reprieve from his labors.

Asher held his tongue, quietly acquiescing to his fate. Experience taught him that work was no more negotiable than the price of meat at the market. His mother would always boast to the neighbors that he was never sick a day in his life. It was a blessing to one degree and a curse to another, as he never had an excuse to avoid work. Guilt overcame him, knowing he had to make another choice, even if it would cost the family his labor. He knew he could get lucky and perhaps work for days or months, but the caves would eventually claim their toll. They always did. *What then?* He considered his best contribution no more than a fleeting one. Perhaps tragedy would at least gift them with one less mouth to feed.

Sipping the soup in silence, he gazed at his mother. If he were to go missing, it would at least be better than being crushed by stone. At least then she would have hope—a commodity suddenly rarer than coin.

"Headed to the tavern," Asher said, rinsing his bowl in a pail of water mixed with wood ash and lard in the kitchen. Its acrid, burnt stench was at least as harsh as any soap the tavern had.

"Work?" his father inquired, rising to clear his dish. He limped, one leg trailing stubbornly behind—a constant reminder of the mine's peril. The curve of his father's spine was pronounced, a testament to the countless hours he had spent hunched in the mine's oppressive darkness. Even here, in the supposed comfort of home, his father never truly escaped the mines.

Asher nodded. "Schafer may have some work tonight in the stables."

His mother met him by the door, whispering in his ear, "Don't tell your father. You know how he gets. But if you could part with a few coin from your savings to pick up salted ham tomorrow, it would help. Before the store goes bare."

Asher nodded. Stomach tight with guilt, he left and closed the door behind him.

He sprinted farther down the hill, away from the tavern and toward the Thicketwood. He ran through the grove leading to the forest edge, indifferent to the weeds that whipped his shins.

Asher deliberately avoided the dense thicket where Lattice nested as he found the path he had taken the night before. His mind was focused on the only path he could see, and he couldn't risk Lattice dissuading him from the choice he had to make. Whatever dangers lurking among the splintered trees and the rotting stench of death's decay would be far safer than the fate he ran from.

When he reached the clearing from the night before, the hut

with the warm lights and smoking chimney was nowhere to be seen. With measured steps, he inched closer. As if stitched together from the fog itself, the house came into focus. Faster now, he ran up the stoop, his hand hitting the door with the rest of his body close behind.

A latch clicked on the other side of the door, and it creaked open. Wafts of perfume came from the home, bringing the scent of his mother's lilacs mixed with sweet berries. He stepped back and caught the witch's gray, moonlit eyes from behind the door.

"Asher!" she greeted him as warmly as if they were reunited friends. "I'm so glad you came! A moment longer, and I would have succumbed, my dear." She pressed the back of her hand to her forehead.

"You seem fine," Asher said, squinting to see the lines she claimed had settled in her face.

"I can feel life evaporating from me—beseeched with the curse. Moisturizer and dollops of swine lard can only help so much. A new gray hair just this morning! I see hideous lines around my eyes when I squint," she said, demonstrating the act.

"The same thing happens when anyone squints," Asher said. "How long until the curse would actually kill you?"

"I have no idea," she said, pacing the room and blotting her nose with a brush of floral powder. "It's been so long since I've been mortal. I'm not sure how quickly the aging process happens."

Asher cocked his head. "Wait. How did you know my name?"

The witch waved dismissively. "I wouldn't be a good witch if I couldn't figure that out now, would I?"

"What happens when you grant my wish?" Asher asked, abandoning his hesitation to step inside from the cold and following the scent of onion and beef from the pot on her stove.

"I won't get a day younger, but at least I won't get a day older," she said, taking a bowl and ladling stew from the pot. "You're famished. Eat."

Too hungry to ignore precaution, he took the steaming bowl from her blanched hands and slurped two spoonsful of the broth.

"Do tell me you have a wish," she said, pouting her lips and taking the seat beside him.

"I do," Asher said, swallowing more than he should have without remembering to chew. "I want you to make Prince Bracken fall in love with me."

"How unexpected," she remarked with an eye roll.

"Did you know I'd ask for that?"

Whatever color remained in the witch's cheeks faded before his eyes. "*Love*? That is the oldest of all magic. No spell, tincture, or ointment for that. Oh no. That requires as much from him as you."

"So, you can't do it?" Asher asked, his plan starting to fade as quickly as the hue on her face. The prospect of it all had begun to sound ridiculous, but Asher had come too far to stop now. Make the prince fall in love with him and abandon his ambitions for the governor's daughter, and then somehow prevent a war. His face flushed as reality cast its light on his naive desperation.

"I didn't say that," she said, holding her hand up. "I can help. Yes, let's see." She spun around and began pulling vials and jars from the cabinet. "Sage of the Wilma. Dog's root. Complicated spell. Won't last more than a few hours. Love needs nurturing. Love needs to grow from a spark to a bonfire."

"Sounds like you can't do it," Asher said, stirring the stew with his spoon.

She froze and turned to face him. "You don't even know the prince. What makes you think you'd want him to love you? Or you, him? People rarely live up to our fantasies of them."

Asher hadn't considered being pressed on the matter. She was right, but he couldn't share his whole plan—only enough to convince her the wish was for him alone. He drew inspiration from the fairy tale books he read before he grew old enough to see young lovers as mere figments of fiction, no more real than the dragons and monsters they battled. These young lovers, so eager and reckless in their affections, were like drunkards in the tavern, buying an ale, no matter the price.

"With the harvest so meager, I will be sent to mine the caves. If he loved me, he'd rescue me. Take me away from here. To the Eastlands, perhaps. We'd both be safe."

"Here," she said, setting a bottle next to his bowl.

"A potion?" Asher asked.

She rolled her eyes. "No. Oregano. For your stew."

Asher sprinkled it on the stew, improving the taste slightly, not that it would spoil his appetite without it. Another ladle refilled his bowl. Eyes fixed on the first true meal he could remember, he still felt her gaze upon him like a snow owl perched on a hidden branch.

"First," she began, "I will give you an amulet of protection. The charge will last no more than a day. It can at least give you time to survive one shift in the cave's depths. I will see to it that the prince finds you before the sun next sets."

Asher set down the bowl. "That soon? He'll fall in love with me by then?"

"No," she said, fidgeting with a towel. "It takes... time. Yes, it takes quite some time for this particular spell to manifest. You will need to be patient."

She pulled something from a jar of mint leaves and then pressed a ruby amulet in his hand. Its gem was held in a copper brace upon a chain. He stared at it as it reflected the candlelight from the table, calming him instantly. His pulse slowed to a restful beat, and any lingering anxieties about the mine seemed to fade into memory.

"Best not get too used to the feeling," she said, eyeing him. "Far too many men have grown addicted to that charm, unable to adapt to any life without its protection. A day under its influence won't be quite so dangerous."

"What happens if I use it for more than a day?"

The witch scraped her fingers through her hair and sighed. "Just use it in the mines. Not before. Not after. This charm's power will fade—even faster the more you use it. After a day, it will be a harmless rock. Were it to last much longer, you'd risk your life. Few things in this world give without taking."

"Thank you," he said, hands shaking as he slipped the charm in his pocket.

The witch smiled and closed her eyes. "I can feel it. I feel the aura. Life is returning. Faintly. The curse will be fully lifted if I attend to my bargain."

Asher studied her and could perceive no aura nor magic, just the drifting steam from the half-empty pot behind her. He made another attempt to thank her and excused himself while she sat transfixed in her chair, eyes closed and humming a song to herself.

Asher began his journey home, each step heavy with thought and trepidation. Above, the moon, coy and reticent, shrouded itself behind a veil of thin clouds, casting a pale, diffused light over the land. Tall grasses whispered secrets in the gentle night breeze, their silhouettes swaying like specters. The occasional rustle in the underbrush hinted at gnomes concerned enough to follow him, yet unwilling to grant their company.

Asher navigated through a dense patch of sticklebush that seemed to guard the exit of the Thicketwood like a natural barrier. The thorny branches sprawled across the trail, intertwining with the broken twigs and stones that littered his path. With cautious, deliberate steps, he weaved through the maze of prickles, mindful of every movement to avoid the sharp embrace of the bush. As he edged around it, the sticklebush seemed to sense his presence, its branches subtly recoiling as if granting him passage.

A smile cracked across Asher's face as a rare feeling of delight, like finding something under his bed that he thought was lost, filled him. This smile blossomed into a soft chuckle, which grew into a hearty, full-bodied laugh echoing through the quiet woods. For a fleeting moment, Asher's shoulders rose as if unshackled from the fears that had long clung to him. Light-footed and carefree, his steps became like a dance.

He quickened his pace. His cautious walk broke into an

exuberant jog. His feet barely touched the ground as he darted through the night, each step lighter than the last. Approaching a small creek, he leaped with newfound confidence, only to misjudge the landing by mere inches, almost certain to stumble upon reaching the other side. As he sailed through the air, an unexpected gust of wind pushed against his back, guiding him safely to solid ground.

Exhilarated, Asher's mind raced with the possibilities for his new charm. Yet, as quickly as the thrill had come, it was tempered by sober practicality. He remembered the witch's words—the amulet had a limited charge. Worse, he could thirst for it like a drunkard spending his last coin to swallow down poison, promising it to be his last. His mind drew a parallel to a horse strained under the weight of an overloaded wagon, a reminder that he shouldn't squander this precious gift on reckless whims. Somberly, he slowed his pace, intending to avoid addiction to the power and save its charge for the truly perilous moments in the day ahead.

Still, a lingering curiosity whispered to him. An unremarkable detail from an enigmatic night tugged at him as if fighting for his attention—its voice growing louder and more insistent. *Why was the amulet nestled in a jar of mint?*

CHAPTER 6

THE WITCH'S LIE

The Witch of the Forest tapped her walking stick against the moss, making sure there was firm ground beneath before she took a wide step and lunged up the hill. She couldn't recall the last time she was awake early enough to see the rising sun torch the trees with shimmers of blanched yellow and gold. A new day was an uncommon thing to observe. Now she made strides through the forest as the year's end fast approached.

She took a deep breath of crisp air, noting the scent of fig and wet bark. Uncertain whether the smell was the telltale sign of the gnomes' work, she took careful steps, mindful of a newly covered hole that could hide whatever so-called treasure they might have recently buried.

Gnomes were curious, but she respected that they were even more eccentric than her. She once watched from the branches of a tree while a small family of gnomes painstakingly buried an odd-shaped cone from a bush. Another time, her curiosity dared her to risk a grave transgression when she dug up a particular mound, certain that the gnomes had buried her diamond-studded shoe, only to unearth a dingy shirt she felt best left buried. Even the villagers would sometimes encroach on the Thicketwood to find their buried treasures. Their footprints would be even more evident in times of hardship when necessity made men bold. She knew they would soon trespass into the forest once again.

Treasures were in the eye of the beholder, and stories told at taverns had a way of taking on truth mixed with greed and hope. Such stories were never her cocktail of choice. Still, she knew that not every story was myth—not all the gnomes' treasures were so unremarkable. If anything, the pedestrian trinkets they buried were wise decoys designed to disappoint the villagers and discourage them from seeking what must be kept safe.

"Buried in tasks throughout the day. Let this meeting be worth the fray," said an impatient gnome sitting on a stone. She wore a golden coned hat with a beaded shah over her shoulders.

"Governess Wintery," the witch said, bowing and twirling her hand with a flourish. "I met with the boy. Asher. Rosemary was right. He is the one we seek. Please guide his journey."

"Forgive my caution, your word aside. This treasure, in our keep, must reside. A trial for him, we must conduct. Then his journey we can instruct."

"Fine," the witch said. "I convinced him I could grant a wish. Took him some time before he came up with something I could work with. I'm headed to the palace. I need to recruit a traveling companion for him."

Wintery slid off the stone and walked toward the witch. "Asher, in the forest, a name held dear. Brother Lattice deems his friendship sincere. But this power is a jealous flame that burns too bright to share. Is bringing another to this journey wise to dare?"

"Who's to say?" the witch asked. "It's a bit of a gamble, but I did promise the boy. More importantly, if the prince can be persuaded to join the quest, it could present another opportunity for success."

Wintery rubbed her chin and bowed her head before walking deeper into the forest. The witch watched her leave before planting her walking stick into the ground and hoisting herself onto higher terrain.

She followed the rising sun through the forest until she came to the clearing at the foot of the hill leading to the royal palace. There stood the prince, taking repose in the shade of a pale bark tree. A twinge of guilt came to her, noting his tranquility, nose buried in his book. It was, after all, a place he likely came to avoid tutors and servants, chores and duties. If royalty gifted any autonomy, she knew this quite clearing was the only place he could truly rule.

"Prince Bracken!" she called to him from where the forest met the field.

Startled, he dropped the book and bolted to his feet. "Witch of the Forest! Take one step into the clearing, and I'll have you hung for breaching our treaty!"

"Calm down, Hunter," she said, leaning against a tree. "I sneak into the city all the time. You need more than a wall to keep me out. I'm not here to harm you. Actually, I can help."

"You will refer to me as Your Highness, Prince Bracken," he said, gripping the sheathed dagger on his belt.

"I rather prefer *Your Heinie*. It rolls off the tongue so much more casually," she said, giving passing recognition of his form in the tight riding pants he wore. "Does the family call you that? Heinie? I rather think they should."

"Treasonous, witch! What help could I take from one who only lives by my father's compassion?" the prince yelled back.

"A...prophecy has come to fruition. A young man born under the same moon as you came to me, delivered by fate. The gnome's greatest treasure, the lost sword of your line, has revealed itself," she said.

Hunter loosened his grip on the hilt. "The Apex Blade? Where have those pests taken it?"

She sighed. "The gnomes never stole it. Not exactly, anyway."

"Traitors, nonetheless," he said, glaring at her, yet frozen in place like the boulder beside him.

"They merely safeguard it," she said, giving a dismissive wave. "Until the prophecy is fulfilled, it's too dangerous to be in the hands of the unworthy. Your great-grandfather would know that well."

Hunter folded his arms, his brow furrowing into a deep scowl. "Prophecies," he spat as if the word were a curse. "Legends and lore. How can I trust such fables spun by a witch?"

The witch twirled her walking stick in her hand and casually paced about, a refrain from a staged rendition she memorized long ago coming to her mind. "One person's prophecy is just another's well-structured plan coming to fruition." She paused, waiting for the prince to react and frowning when he didn't. "I don't consult the Watchers or the olden deities. I speak the truth. Would you risk having the blade escape, or is it better to see for yourself on the scant chance that I'm being honest?"

"My father will take an army and reclaim it. Where is it? Tell me honestly, and I may weigh upon the king for his mercy for your insolence!"

The witch smiled. "Dear prince, the prophecy hasn't deemed your father the heir. It's you. You're the one to whom the prophecy bequeaths it."

Hunter's jaw went slack, and she delighted in watching his grimacing face as he struggled to understand. "You mean, I'm... I'm worthy?"

The witch shrugged and tugged at her woven red shawl. "I'm just as surprised myself. Yet so it seems."

"Where may I claim the blade?" Hunter asked, his voice softening.

"The gnomes have hidden their most prized treasure far away. Far from the villagers and their greed. High in the Blue Mountains to the north," she said. "There's good news, I must report. I have a map."

"Then give it to me," he said, pointing at the stump at the edge of the clearing. "Place it there but come no farther into the field."

"It's not an ordinary map, I fear. This one has a name: Asher Snow."

He sneered and his face turned the same hue as her shawl. "Bring this man to me. By my knife, he will tell me where it is."

"He's barely a man. Only hours younger than you," she said. "Quick mind. Handsome as well, not that such things matter to you." She paused to watch his eyes dart to the grass, thinking him wise not to let her see into them. "You can certainly torture the poor peasant all you'd like, but it won't work. He doesn't know that he knows. He won't know until he does."

Even over the rising sun's glare, she could see his cheeks flush again. "You speak in riddles. Tell me plainly," he said.

The witch rolled her eyes. "It's simple. Find him tomorrow at the mines. Take him through the Thicketwood to the Canopy of the Elders. That leads you to the base of the Blue Mountains. Then climb. You'll find what you need along the way with Asher's help. I know no more."

"How do you know this?" Hunter asked.

The witch smirked. "There are many tools to gain knowledge in this realm. I'm blessed to know some of them."

Hunter pushed out his chest. "I'll take my servants and a contingent from the palace guard to join us."

"Really?" she asked. "Once the king learns of your quest, do you think he'd cede to the will of the prophecy? Let his son claim what he thinks is his own?"

She delighted in seeing the prince's smile fade. His silence let her appreciate the dawn finches as they sang their song in the background without competition. The prince looked up from the ground to meet her eyes. "With this blade, we wouldn't need to kneel before the governor of Bishop Falls and trade treasure and honor for their patronage. We could claim it."

"Imagine your father discovering how worthy you are. You would claim that which he has long sought. You would give him a reason to be proud of you." She smiled as her words soaked in like water in arid soil.

"My father *is* proud of me."

"Then why do you say that as if you're trying to convince yourself?" she asked with a velvet voice, enchanted by a potion of empathy mixed with compassion. "Has he shared all his secrets—trusted you with knowledge? Or has he kept it to himself, insisting that you are too young to learn—merely a child, still unworthy of the Crown?"

Hunter looked at his feet. "He has shared some of the world's mysteries with me. He says others are too dangerous for me to know. How can I rule one day if I'm not prepared?"

The witch extended a hand, palm open. "All the better reason to follow this quest, Hunter. It is your proving ground. Emerge from the shadows of doubt and step into the light of your own strength and wisdom. Your father's pride, yes, but more importantly, your self-worth awaits you at the end of this journey."

With a breath that drew courage from the very air around him, Hunter steadied himself and brought his eyes, both brave and young, to face the witch. "Fine. I will go."

"There's one other catch," the witch said, almost as an afterthought. "A detail I thought prudent not to share with the lad but feel obligated to tell you. While two may ascend on the quest, only one shall return from the mountain."

A flash of fear passed over his face, leaving it as swiftly as a cloud racing past the sun before a storm. "I understand what I must do," he said, swallowing.

CHAPTER 7

THE RESCUE

"Asher!" a voice called down to him. "Asher, climb out of there right now!"

Careful not to tip over the oil lamp beside him, Asher thumbed a sharp stone in his hand, certain it was diamond. Finding the rock among the ore would grant him a week's wage, at least. He gripped it tight as he snatched the bucket of rocks beside him and carefully followed the rope to a woven ladder. It creaked, and several frayed tethers snapped as it took his weight. A warm intoxication flooded his muscles from the amulet tied around his neck. He gave the fractured rungs on the ladder only passing concern as he began his climb.

He squinted in the light as he approached the surface, and hints of fresh air soothed the acrid burning in his nose from lamp oil vapor and pulverized rock. Nearly tipping over his harvest of gem and ore, he found his footing and met a hand that helped him out of the ravine. After rubbing his eyes on his soot-stained sleeve, he finally saw the quarry master's face. The man's weathered face, typically as unyielding as the rock he mined, now mirrored the helplessness of wet linen at the mercy of a storm's winds.

"I found a diamond among the stones," Asher said, holding out his bucket.

"Then give it to me," another voice demanded.

Asher turned to find the voice, and his knees nearly buckled. Prince Bracken stood mere feet from him, wearing a brilliant white riding vest that made Asher feel even filthier than the dirt and soot that stained his flesh. He dared meet the prince's eyes, finding them butterscotch brown. From afar, he had never been able to tell.

"I will take it to the palace," Hunter said. "It remains to be seen whether its cut and clarity warrant any value. Many stones appear to have promise, only to end in disappointment."

Asher reluctantly held the stone before him, forcing himself to loosen his grip and let it fall into the prince's hand. He glanced at the stone and could only think of his family. A leg of pork for the pot. Wood for the stove. It vanished before his eyes as the prince closed his fist around the diamond and shoved it into his tunic.

"You are the one called Asher?" the prince asked.

Asher stuttered, finding the sound of his name unfamiliar from the prince's lips. "Yes. Yes, Your Highness. Asher Snow." Asher carefully observed the formalities he was taught to use when referencing royalty. Keep your hands in plain sight. No sudden movements. Asher knew the rules well. Such customs were to be memorized but not in anticipation of some joyful day when any of them would be invited to a ball. Stern warnings always accompanied such lessons. If a villager should have the occasion to speak with a royal, he could be assured his life was already held by a frayed tether.

"Fine," Hunter said. "I need you for a special task for which you are uniquely qualified."

"Your Highness," the quarry master said, lunging between them and bowing his head, "I assure you this boy has no unique qualities. If Your Highness seeks a knight, may I suggest my own son? A few seasons older and taller than this one. Certainly stronger. I assure you."

Hunter studied the man. "My business with this one is my own. For the Crown."

Asher battled the urge to give in to astonishment, attributing his unusual stroke of luck to the witch fulfilling her part of the agreement. He chanced another look into the prince's eyes but decided he knew little of love if it was to be seen in the prince's expression. Loathing. Disgust. Yes. But love? Asher's head sank.

In a breeze, Hunter mounted his horse, its hair just as brilliantly white as the prince's vest. Asher squinted, not from the sun but from the glare shining back at him.

"Peasant," the prince said, spit leaving his lips with the word as he stared down at Asher. "Follow me to the horse trough. Neither this horse nor my clothing shall be stained by your filth."

Numbly, Asher stumbled behind the prince as the horse led the way to troughs in the distance. The prince gave curt nods to passersby, his posture perfectly set on the saddle.

Far enough removed from the crowd behind them, the horse

stopped. "You will need to wash in the trough," the prince said, nodding to the wooden structure that held water barely cleaner than the ashen animals that drank from it.

Asher dipped his hands in the gray water and splashed his face, doing his best to take more dirt from his skin than he had added.

"No," the prince said, sighing. "Disrobe. The clothes cannot be saved."

Stunned, Asher gaped at the prince, then back across the field to the crowd of his neighbors, watching him like the marbled statues that stood guard at the palace entrance. The prince glared down at him from his horse. Hands trembling, Asher unbuckled his belt and slid what was left of his stained and torn trousers to the grass. A chilly wind gusted, making the hair on his legs stand on end.

Turning his back to the prince, desperate to hold on to whatever dignity he could, he carefully slid off his shirt, catching the necklace with the charm in his hands as he pulled it and the shirt over his head and let them fall to the ground. He shivered as the charm's influence waned, like stepping away from a fire into the cold night air.

Asher heard chuckles behind him as he dipped his forearm into the trough, scrubbing his arm against the splintered wood to wash away a filth that so deeply stained his skin it had practically become part of him. He splashed water on his chest and neck, smearing grime into a greasy paste that clung to him like paint on a canvas.

"We haven't all day," the prince sighed. "Remove the loin as well."

Asher's teeth chattered as the slightest breeze was like a

knife piercing his wet skin. With his ashen back to the prince, he untethered the underwear around his waist, having no dignity left to protect. The laughter behind him mixed with taunts and insults, none of which he could distinctly hear. As the water made his flesh numb, he ignored the onlookers behind him, splashing ever more over his skin. He sank his legs in the trough, submerging one and then the other, watching the black char darken the water like ink being spilled from its well.

He turned his head to see the prince riffle through a bag on the horse, pulling out a clump of beige and white clothes. He tossed them toward Asher. The pile landed a few paces from where he stood, just beyond the puddle of mud he made.

"Put those on," the prince said.

Covering himself with his hand, Asher shuffled to the pile of clothes, exposing himself for the instant it took to pull up the underwear. Then he slid on the trousers, wondering whether the prince himself wore the same. The fabric held a scent of flowers. He fit his arms through the linen shirt, its sleeves and neck drooping over him. His shoulders were barely broad enough to hold the garment on his chest. He shuffled back to pick up the tattered clothes he had discarded.

"Leave them. Just the shoes," the prince said.

Asher met the prince's eyes and swallowed his contempt. Carefully, he hid his hand in the clothes and snagged the amulet, slipping it into his pocket while using the clothes as his shield. Then, mindful of the witch's admonishment not to discard the carnival coin, he dug it out of the pocket and added it to his own, alongside the amulet. Instantly, the amulet's influence returned to him like a warm cloth pressed against a swollen bruise.

Hands now trembling so fervently that he struggled to lace his shoes, Asher stood and faced the prince, unable to lift his eyes to see the face he felt looking down upon him.

"Mount the horse and hold on," Hunter said with a revolted tone that Asher couldn't ignore. The prince took his foot from the stirrup, and Asher lunged his foot into it, gripping the skirt and hoisting himself up with a grace he knew he wouldn't possess without the aid of the amulet in his pocket.

"Well done," the prince mumbled before pulling the reins.

The horse took his command just as compliantly as Asher had done moments before. Together, they rode at a brisk gallop toward the edge of the village.

"Where are we going?" Asher dared to ask.

The prince was silent, but Asher couldn't decide whether he heard the question and chose not to answer. Asher dared not ask again. The horse came to rest, and the prince started digging in his side satchel. Asher's eyes widened at the familiar sound of coins clanking against one another in the bag.

"Here," the prince said, turning to hand him a fistful of coins, more than Asher could ever remember seeing, even more than the tavern would earn in a full month. "Take this to the store by the road. I can't be seen there. I need provisions."

"What kind of provisions?" Asher asked, unable to take his eyes off the golden coins that sparkled in the midday sun.

"I'm going on a journey, and you're to follow me. Tell no one if you mean to live. Get food that will not spoil nor rot. Get amber water. Shoes for us both. They must be fit for climbing. I'll need a change of clothes, considering you've already cost me my own. Scented soap—two bars, at least. A bottle of sandalwood cologne."

"Your Highness," Asher said, interrupting, "the village store wouldn't have sandalwood cologne, not at any price. The peasants are unfamiliar with such refinements."

The prince twisted farther in the saddle to meet Asher's eyes. "Not even a small bottle?"

Asher shook his head.

"Fine," the prince said, sighing. "Get whatever you deem necessary. I don't know how long the journey will take. At least a week, I'd say. We may not be able to travel by horse. Bring no more than you can carry."

Asher slid down from the horse to have his feet meet the ground, wondering whether the prince meant to say *we*, only to resign himself to the more likely interpretation.

"Tell no one why you are buying these things, and don't mention me," the prince reminded him as Asher jogged through the brush to meet the road leading to the village's general store.

The coins clanked as he ran, their weight forcing Asher to hoist the trousers up to his waist every few steps. He slowed to a casual walk as he found the street, careful not to let the coins' melody betray him to those who had so little and needed so much. With a small fortune weighing him down, Asher thought of running— taking the coins to his family and escaping into the Thicketwood. The fantasy was doused by the realization that the angered prince, joined by the palace's best knights, would no doubt find his innocent parents before sunset.

He opened the door to the market, giving a nod to the butcher. Asher had visited the market countless times, yet he felt just as much a stranger to the shelves as the prince would have been. Asher had no cause to walk down the aisles in search of fine soaps and clothes that had not known others before him.

"Can I help you?" the store owner asked. Asher thought the question was more a warning than an offer.

"Yes," Asher said, drawing out the word long enough for his brain to decide what to say after. "I need two pairs of your finest travel shoes. A fitting of clothes. Preserved meat as well."

The store owner slinked to the aisle from behind the counter, close enough to lower his voice. "Asher, you're a fine lad. You helped my daughter learn to read. I won't forget your help, but these things will cost more coin than you have to spend."

"Not true," Asher said, holding several coins drawn from his pocket. The store owner's eyes grew large. "Boxtin," Asher said. "I played boxtin at the tavern and finally had some better fortune."

"Well, well," the store owner said, smiling. "It looks like we both have good fortune. Let me show you what just came in. Tan polished leather, but flexible. Smell," he said, holding the shoe under Asher's nose.

He took a deep, albeit cautious sniff. "That's what new leather smells like?" he asked.

"Now, two pairs? Your size?"

Asher tried to remember the prince's foot in the stirrup. "Yes, that's right. My size."

The store owner whistled as he filled a burlap sack with everything on Asher's list. Asher let his eyes wander, feeling a sudden chill. He thumbed his pocket. The amulet was still there, but it grew the slightest bit colder. The witch was right. Only so much of a charge. Then he spotted something else to add to his list.

"There, the sprig of mint," Asher said, pointing. "Two strands of that as well."

The store owner nodded and added it to the bag. Asher counted out the coins to pay. Twelve in all. By Asher's count, he still had another dozen coins in his pocket.

"Here," he said, handing three more coins to the owner. "Please put two more legs of the salted ham on hold for the next time my mother comes here."

"Why not bring it yourself?" he asked.

Asher shrugged his shoulders. "I guess I can only carry so much."

He saw the store owner's eyes run up and down his body, no doubt deciding not to dispute the point. Asher regretted not asking for more—paying for all he could with his coin. Still, he didn't want to risk the prince accusing him of stealing from the Crown. He returned to the clearing, hoping the prince wouldn't ask for a receipt.

CHAPTER 8

THE GOOD GROUNDSKEEPER

Asher shifted the weight of the burlap bag full of provisions from his weary left shoulder to his right as he crossed the sun-dappled clearing. Ahead, an ancient oak's massive, gnarled trunk loomed, its sprawling branches casting intricate shadows on the rolling hills. Though the formidable oak hid the prince, the flick of his horse's tail, twitching impatiently, betrayed his cover.

"Your Highness," Asher said, letting the bag slip off his shoulder, "I have the provisions. You have change," he said, taking out a fistful of coin.

The prince looked down at him, scrunching his nose and lifting an eyebrow as if repulsed by the sight of it. "Just keep it. Get on the horse. We need to get as far as we can before nightfall."

Asher let the coins fall back into his pocket, stomach dropping with regret for not leaving the rest of the coin for his parents to use on credit at the market. He consoled himself with the thought that having Hunter fall in love with him could save the kingdom and avoid the looming war. All the meat and wood at the store would do little to help his family if a war were to occur.

He slipped his foot in the stirrup, only to have it slide out. He tried again, this time finding a fit. He grabbed the saddle's skirt and tried to heave himself up, only to fall back down after making it halfway up. The prince glared at him. Cheeks burning red, Asher took a breath and used all the strength he could muster. He heaved himself up, nearly falling over the other side of the horse when the bag's weight swung like a pendulum with his momentum.

Hunter sighed loud enough that Asher thought it certain he meant it to be heard. The prince pulled the reins to the left and squeezed his legs against the horse. The horse leaped forward so quickly that Asher, not daring to touch the prince, almost lost his grip on the saddle.

Finding improvised handholds, Asher strained to maintain his balance on the saddle as the horse charged off in a wide arc over the open fields toward the Thicketwood. He groaned as his arms strained to pull himself back to center. He imagined that the prince would take him to the castle. Asher considered what curse the witch must have called upon to drive the prince toward such madness.

"You're no use to me dead," the prince yelled back at him over the rush of wind. "Hold on properly to my waist."

Timidly, Asher checked to ensure the bag of provisions was securely tied to the saddle and then slid closer to the seat, wrapping his arms around the prince's waist and grabbing his fist with his other hand. With his face closer to the prince, he noted scents of the same flowered soap on the prince's clothes mixed with sweetened sandalwood.

The horse bounded over a log, and Asher instinctively hugged Hunter's waist tighter, feeling the prince's body heat against his cheek. His every twist and turn caused a cascade of muscles in his back to swell. At last, the horse slowed to a trot, and Asher loosened his grip, sitting slightly farther back on the saddle.

"We've come to the Edge of Ruin," the prince said, bringing the horse to a halt, eyes fixed on the dense wood beyond the clearing's edge.

Asher couldn't recall ever seeing the Thicketwood from this far to the west. The trees, warm and welcoming back home, took on an ominous, imposing guise, their inky silhouettes standing as vigilant sentinels. They resembled tar-black obsidian, hardened and eerily beautiful under the gaze of sun and shadow.

In the wood to the east, Asher would sit by the gnomes' den and watch deer and other creatures of the wood rub their antlers and bodies against the trees, stripping the trees of their spires and carving their existence into the woodland's long memory. Here, the trees were unblemished. Dark, jagged spires of wood-like daggers lurched from their trunks. The autumn sun neglected the leaves, rendering them wilted shades of brown and yellow. The wind gusted through the forest, its breath charting a journey from east to west. Asher could hear the soft rustling, the leaves narrating the wind's path, their susurrus filling the woodland with an eerie symphony.

"Why are we here?" Asher asked, interrupting the silence.

The prince pulled the provisions from the horse, handing Asher the sack. "There's a path just beyond. It will take us deep into the forest, toward the Canopy of the Elders. My horse can go no farther."

"What's the Canopy of the Elders?" Asher asked.

The prince delivered a sharp slap to the horse's flank, sending it galloping across the field toward the village. He turned a disdainful gaze upon Asher. "Look at you. Pathetic," he scoffed as Asher struggled to hoist the heavy sack back over his shoulder, his shirt slipping down in the process. "Did you manage to find even two pairs of proper shoes?"

"Yes, Your Highness."

"Then put on a pair," the prince said. "Yours are barely more than stockings. You won't make it a mile."

Asher did as instructed. Leaving his old shoes behind, he jogged to catch up to the prince as he approached the threshold separating the fields from what may come from within. His feet bounced as he stepped, barely feeling the ground beneath him. The prince strolled assuredly into the brush.

Asher reached into his pocket, yearning for the amulet's lost charge. He missed the intoxicating warmth and safety it had so recently provided. Now only the rough edges of a cold charm met his touch. Their pace slowed as the wood grew denser. The prince twisted and contorted his body to navigate through a nest of sharpened spires. Asher followed suit, ensuring his baggy shirt didn't snag on the wood.

Above, the sky was painted with flames of burnt umber as the sun began to set. The view of the sky was eclipsed by a flock of ebony-feathered birds, each just as dark as the tree bark. A chill passed through the trees. It was not heralded by the rustling of leaves or the playful whistle of the wind, but it arrived stealthily, seeping into the marrow of the woods, tracing the length of his spine like icy tendrils. Ahead was a small clearing, a circle of moss and dead leaves where no trees dared to plant their roots. Leaning against a dying tree, Asher inhaled the sour decay of its damp bark. It was pungent and acidic, with a rich aroma of rot, the unmistakable scent of life inseparable from death.

"Stop, Your Highness!" he yelled just before the prince stepped into the clearing.

Hunter turned and scowled. "What? Can't keep up?"

"No, Your Highness," Asher said. "The clearing. It's not safe. It's bog sand."

The prince regarded him with a puzzled expression, as if Asher were a riddle he couldn't quite solve. Hunter stooped to pick up a fallen branch, tossing it casually into the center of the clearing. For a few moments, nothing happened; then gradually, the branch began to sink. The surrounding leaves shifted subtly, creeping over the wood until it was completely engulfed, leaving no trace of its presence.

"How did you know that?" the prince demanded.

"I've seen it before. On the eastern edge of the Thicketwood. Just like here, there's an unnatural clearing. Always a perfect circle. The bark on trees captures the scent. I've smelled the rot before," Asher said.

"You've been to the Thicketwood before?" the prince asked. "Brave. Few villagers live to tell the tale. Snared by beasts in the forest or befallen by gnome traps."

"I... I go there often," Asher said, looking away from him. "It's peaceful. Not like the village. I bring the gnomes food as often as I can, especially in times like these."

"You *feed* them?" he asked incredulously.

"Why are we here? Why am I important to you?" Asher asked, ignoring the prince's question.

The prince looked up to the sky. "We need to keep moving. Suffice it to say, it's unclear to me that you offer more value than the service of your back and arms to carry the provisions." The prince looked him up and down. "Such as you can, it seems."

Confident that his worth to the prince would be enough to stave off a blade to his throat, Asher chanced letting down his façade. He sighed and glared at the prince, urging him to elaborate.

"Fine," the prince said. "I met the Witch of the Forest, whom I believe you also know. She told me a great treasure can be reclaimed in the Blue Mountains. It was stolen from my line, and I intend to reclaim it for my kingdom. She insists that you can be of service in my endeavor."

"Service?" Asher asked.

"Our path is uncertain. She says you hold a map, though you aren't aware of it. I hope the truth will make itself known to you when circumstances demand it," he said, walking around the bog sand's perimeter. "You should hope she's right."

Asher swallowed and wiped the sweat from his brow, following behind. His mouth was dry, but he dared not ask the prince to stop for water. He strained to understand why the witch would promise something he couldn't offer.

At last, Asher hopped over the stump of a bush and met firm ground. He looked down at his shoes, caked in mud with dead leaves and small twigs. Shame and guilt snared him like an unseen thorn from the brush. His first pair of true shoes were defiled so quickly. His feet were dry, and he knew he could clean the shoes in the waters of the first brook they should find, but it would do little to wash away his simmering rage. The coin he spent on the shoes could have fed his parents for weeks, yet Asher suspected that the prince had no interest in value—not of the shoes, his parents, the kingdom, or especially the companion that trotted behind him in the mud.

They paced in silence as the moon lit their path. The clear night permitted the moon's gift to pass through a latticework of leaves from trees towering above them; each flicker was like a distant wax light, giving them just enough but no more.

"Why do you hate me?" Asher asked the darkness.

The prince sighed and brought his march to a halt. "I don't hate you. I distrust you."

"Have I been disloyal?" Asher asked.

"No," the prince said after a moment of thought. "You could have let me walk into the bog sand, but you didn't. I distrust you because of what you represent. Peasants. Illiterate, thieving, conspiring, demanding. The Crown seeks peace and order, but we impose it on barbarians who only learn from the blade and the whip."

Asher's jaw went slack. "I don't know whom you're describing, Your Highness. Villagers suffer the tax and barely have enough to survive. And that was before the coming famine. I know how to read. My mother taught me. More perhaps would as well if the Crown shared the royal library."

The prince scoffed and turned back to the trail.

Asher jogged behind to close his distance with the prince and raised his voice. "If the groundskeeper for the royal gardens didn't tend to the pedal bushes, would they not turn brown and decay?" Asher asked. "Then would that groundskeeper deem the flowers unworthy of his attention when he's also the cause of their rot?"

The prince stopped and whipped around, drawing the knife from his belt. "Insolent swine! The slim prospect that you may be of some value to me is the only thing staying my blade from your chest. Don't question my father's fidelity to his people!"

Asher dropped the sack of supplies by his side and spread his arms. "If my life is no more valuable than the service I offer, then murder me now! Slice my throat and leave my body to be reclaimed by the forest. Give me the chance to be loyal and consider my criticism a gift that helps you better understand your people. Or I will not help you find this treasure, and I'll save you the indecision over my worth."

The prince lowered his blade. "If the groundskeeper tended to a thorned bush and was cut each time he tried to tend to it, could you pass judgment on him for neglecting it?"

"Perhaps the groundskeeper would need to adjust his approach. Learn where the thorns are and adapt to wait for it to reveal its beauty," Asher said.

"Perhaps," the prince said reluctantly. "We should make haste. This part of the wood is called The Madness. Its foul air leads men to insanity. You feel it? The chill? Anger swelling within you?"

Asher nodded, considering the origin of his sudden, seething rage, weighing how much brewed from within and what portion was stirred by the sinister whispers in the air.

"Then hurry. If we linger too long, we'll succumb," the prince said, stowing his blade with a sigh. "I should not deem you accountable for your people's transgressions. Just because I can't see the thorn doesn't mean I'm not apprehensive to find it. I will try to adjust if you submit yourself to your role."

"Yes, Your Highness," Asher said, bowing slightly as he had seen the villagers do in their reenactments of royal propriety.

The prince rolled his eyes and looked at the trees above. "Enough with the propriety. We're the only ones here. There's no need to impress me, and the formality stings my ear. For so long as that's so, you may call me Hunter."

Asher nodded, catching himself before thanking *His Highness*. Together, they quickened their pace. The chill bit Asher's skin, and his lungs burned with the smell of sulfur. He pressed his shirt against his nose, and his rage began to subside.

"It helps to breathe through your shirt," Asher offered. Hunter gave him a quick glance and began to do the same.

Legs burning and nearly overcome by thirst, Asher jogged

behind Hunter with the sack bouncing against his back. The forest carried shrieks from unseen beasts cloaked in shadow from afar. Birds cawed above them, desperate warnings for those who would not heed their calls. Nearly stumbling over a graveled stone, Asher regained his balance and ran faster to catch up. Thick, humid air settled on Asher's skin. He saw a pond nearby. Toads croaking in their chorus with insects were nearly deafening.

"Hurry," Hunter said, his voice muffled through the fabric in his shirt.

Asher ran faster to catch up. Now in a breakneck sprint, his heels scraped against the new shoes, making each step more agonizing than the one before. He took deep gulps of air, filtered through the flower-scented shirt, but was still unable to catch his breath. Ahead, was a tunnel of weeping trees arching over the path. They lined the path like an honor guard of knights holding their spears at royal weddings.

The species was unfamiliar to Asher—not pine, maple, nor any other he could recall. Even in the dim light of the moon above, he could see dark green leaves drooping from the trees. They were large, like the leaves of an oak, but still as vibrant as the first foliage of summer. More than just the glistening in the moonlight, the leaves shared a luminance of their own.

"We're here," Hunter said, gasping. "The Canopy of the Elders."

THE CANOPY
OF THE ELDERS

Asher stepped across the threshold under the towering arch of trees, dense enough to block the sky, yet the tunnel still dimly lit their path. So thick were the leaves that he first thought they were the craftsmanship of a master spinner's loom. Moving the thick vegetation aside, he found branches intricately intertwined. This barrier hid the death and decay from The Madness just beyond the fecund veil.

"Have you been here before?" Asher asked, staring up at the cathedral's ceiling, tall as four men.

"No," Hunter whispered as if to avoid disturbing the solemnity of the guardians in their slumber. "My father has. Told me stories."

Asher peered down the tunnel, unable to see the end. "It feels so..."

"Safe?" Hunter asked. "The Thicketwood is a contrast. A foul air brings madness behind us. This is an undisturbed oasis. No harm can find us here. Not even a snake or wasp."

Asher's cheeks flushed warm, a radiance emanating from within, reminiscent of the amulet, yet different—like words that rhymed. His pace slowed, and he touched a leaf to inspect the wavy veins on the underside of its waxy sheen. As he did, he marveled at his hand as its small scrapes and cuts knit together, leaving his skin healed and unblemished.

"My hand!" Asher yelled, holding it up for Hunter to see.

"It is a place of healing. A place of life," Hunter said as he started to walk ahead.

Asher caught up with him. "Why would anyone leave this place? Pilgrimages of people could come to recover from sickness."

"Many have tried," Hunter said, his voice softer. "Most never make it through The Madness. Or worse. Generations ago, my father said crowds would do as you suggest. Yet, the Elders cannot help too many. We rob them of their power the longer we stay. Too many people at once would drain them. Leaves would turn brown and dry, and it would be decades before they'd bloom again and share their power."

"Where does this power come from?" Asher asked, almost to himself.

Hunter stopped and shrugged. "Same as anything unnatural, I guess. Believe the stories of ancient times?"

"Books on the subject, or any subject, are rare," Asher said, rolling his eyes.

"There are ruins. Ancient cities. Then the great war. They

killed almost every living thing. Not all that survived was the same as before. Changed somehow. Imbued with enchantments," Hunter said.

"Where are these ruins?" Asher asked, sitting on the mossy path.

Hunter crouched down next to him. "They're cursed. Far beyond the Poisoned Fields. Expeditions have gone for generations to explore them in the far north, past the Blue Mountains and Bishop Falls. There are some to the south, a week's travel from Barbshire's edge, as well. It's said those who go get sick and die. We know little about them because no one ever comes back. That's why travel into the Poisoned Fields is prohibited."

Asher began to clear a space amid the grass to unpack his satchel. "I've read enough to know that the old clerics said many things, but it takes more than fervent speeches of forgotten times to make a thing true."

Hunter glanced at Asher with a thin smile. "Perhaps you're wiser than I assumed."

Asher dug in the sack of supplies, pulling out a copper bottle. "May I offer you water?" he asked.

"No, but thank you. I have my own," Hunter said, drawing a bottle from the sack he carried from his horse. "You should drink."

Asher took a long swig from the bottle, greedily swallowing several gulps before forcing himself to stop, unsure when they could refill their supplies.

"We should eat something as well. We can't rest here though," Hunter said, sitting across from him.

"Why not?"

Hunter traced the edge of a leaf on the wall of vines beside him. "It would be foolish for us to drain the Elders' power for the sake of those who do not need their blessings."

Asher handed Hunter dried meat and took some for himself. He dug deeper into the bag and found two apples. Hunter accepted one with a slight smile. For the first time on the journey, Asher saw a glimpse of the same charm that would inspire his fantasies when he saw the prince from afar. Under the enchanted luminescence of the Elders, Asher thought he saw behind the veil of nobility and into the person hidden behind his title.

"The canopy is beautiful," Asher said, squinting to spot a gap in the canopy to glimpse the stars. "Shame, though. I always like catching the Watchers at night. Despite anything that happens here, they're so constant."

Hunter looked up as if searching for the same window toward the sky. "They chase one another seven times a night this time of year. What meaning do the villagers ascribe to them?"

Asher shrugged, giving up on his attempt to see through the leafy shroud. "Some say little. With enough ale, others become philosophers with tales taller than these trees."

Hunter flashed a casual smile. "And what do *you* believe?"

Asher looked up again, mostly from habit. "They don't move as stars. I don't believe in the gods of old. Temping though—the idea that someone cares enough to watch down on all of us."

"It's been generations since the last clerics had followers," Hunter said. "Echoes of their myths linger in people's hearts. Faith is a stubborn thing to banish, no matter how hard we've tried."

"Faith and hope seem to travel as a pair—just like the Watchers in the sky," Asher said. "I fear that you could never banish one without risking the loss of the other."

Hunter answered with a contemplative hum, his gaze lifting to take a second look toward the veiled expanse. "Aside from all the suffering and starvation, what's life like in the village?" Hunter asked, biting into the apple. "Are you married? A girlfriend waiting for you?"

Asher blushed. "I've never had any interest in girls, at least not in the romantic sense. Except, there aren't any other young men my age who appear to share the same interest."

Hunter sat straighter. "I meant no offense. It must be incredibly hard to carry that shame."

Asher relaxed into a smile. "The villagers never mean offense either. It's not something I've ever been ashamed of. People don't care about those things. If someone works hard and keeps the peace, that's all that matters."

Hunter's face softened into speechless shock. Asher dared not say more, thinking it enough to establish his preference. The witch said the spell would take time. Asher couldn't see any alternative than to hold on to the slim hope that she would keep her word. Slimmer still was the hope that he'd want to return any such love, no matter how flawless the prince's skin or sweet the smell of his shirt.

"We should get some sleep," Hunter said abruptly as he picked up his bag. "The other end of the tunnel should open into a field. I had the foresight to bring a small tent. I have a spare sleeping bag for you, but the moss rivals my mattress in comfort, I suspect."

Asher followed the prince as they crossed through the canopy and exited into the sleeping forest. As he stepped away from the last of the enchanted trees, a wave of anxiety came over him, like being startled and waking from a dream. It passed as quickly as it came. He turned back to the Elders and marveled over their peace, protecting him from every harm or fear.

Once the prince decided that they were far enough away from the canopy, he dropped his bag in the moss. Asher looked on with a certain bemusement as the prince assembled his tent. Hunter's hands moved with practiced intention as he erected the poles and unfurled the cloths on his makeshift fortress. A miniature version of the Crown's triangular flag adorned the top of the tent. Hunter finished the project by rolling a burgundy sleeping bag over the cloth tent floor. With a quick glance to Asher, the prince knitted the buttons on the sheath to close the partition into the tent.

Asher sighed and took another drink of water before finding a soft patch of moss not far from the tent. He pressed the ground with his hands, and it bounced back like a dry sponge. Satisfied, he rolled out the sleeping bag, removed his shoes, and slipped inside. On a hunch, he took the mint sprigs from the store, wrapped them like twine around the witch's ruby amulet, and tucked it into a cloth pouch. Deciding it was wasteful to consume any charge it would take from the mint in the night, he tucked the pouch inside his shoe, an arm's length away.

He inhaled deeply, savoring the fragrance of the scented blanket. His back, aching from tension, gradually eased as his muscles relaxed. Accompanied by the melodious chorus of cicadas chirping in the woods, he drifted asleep.

DROWSILY, ASHER BLINKED HIS eyes open. Bird songs called to him from above. He drew his hand over the sleeping bag, damp with the morning dew. Feeling more rested than he could ever recall being, he found the prince meticulously disassembling his tent, taking care to pack it just as Asher recalled seeing him assemble it.

"We have a long day ahead," Hunter said, not turning to him.

Asher laced his shoes and stowed the pouch with the amulet in the sack of supplies. He caught up to the prince as they walked in silence. Asher struggled to think of something to say. He considered asking how the prince slept before deciding it was foolish—a trivial question whose answer had no value beyond obligating the prince with the burden to answer. Still, the silence gnawed on him like the blister growing on his heel.

"What kind of treasure are we looking to reclaim? How was it stolen?" Asher asked.

Hunter walked ahead of him in silence just long enough for Asher to regret asking the question. "It's the Apex Sword," Hunter finally said. "Have you heard of it?"

"I haven't," Asher said.

"My great-grandfather was the last to wield it," Hunter said.

"It's enchanted with fearsome magical powers that can slay entire armies. With it, we can unite the kingdom once again in peace."

Asher ran a hand through his hair, combing twigs out in the process. "That's it? Some awful weapon that will instantly make them settle their disputes and live in harmony under the threat of death?"

"Myth and legend can fuel loyalty as much as fear," Hunter said. "The sword bearer cannot be harmed, and the blade will never break. The blade can cure the ill and bring fire from the sky."

Asher squeaked the first syllable of a question, but he caught himself before the sound could become an offense. Hunter adjusted the strap on his shoulder that carried his royal bedding and hiked ahead. Asher took long strides to keep pace.

"There's a clearing ahead," Hunter said.

No more than six paces from end to end, a wooden bridge spanned modestly over the chattering stream below, its waters tumbling over stones rounded and smoothed by time's relentless toil.

Past the humble crossing, Asher could see the trail emerge as if drawn by some unseen hand. Earth gave way to a path haphazardly strewn with pebbles and gravel at its start, meandered to grow in definition, where distant stones were laid as if by the will of the land itself, leading toward the distant Blue Mountains. These mighty peaks, shrouded in mist and lore, stood as ancient sentinels, their summits kissing the sky, beckoning to those souls drawn to wander beneath their heights.

As they neared the bridge, Hunter's steps became measured until he abruptly stopped, hand reaching for the hilt of the blade on his belt. Asher saw a figure of diminutive stature, scarcely taller than three hands placed one atop the other. The gnome, enigmatic and small, stood resolutely in the middle of the bridge, her arms folded defiantly against her chest.

"Into this sacred realm, what journey do you take? For power, for glory, or is it merely a mistake?" came the meek voice. "But no, O prince, I fear to know the path you undertake. Ahead lies despair, only tormenting heartache."

Hunter stopped at the edge of the bridge and put his hands on his hips, looking down at the gnome standing in his way. "Stand aside and let us pass. We have urgent business ahead."

Asher's eyes widened in amusement as the gnome theatrically mimicked the prince's stance, resting her arms on her hips and squaring her legs in place. Her golden hat signified a family Asher hadn't met. Hunter groaned and rested his hand on his knife's hilt.

Asher took a cautious step toward him. "Hunter," he whispered. "Let me try."

The prince huffed and glared at Asher, his eyebrow arched.

Asher swallowed and knelt by the edge of the bridge. "Dear mistress gnome, we mean you no harm. Blessings to your family, and we promise not to disturb you. Our path will be quick. We only aim to follow the trail ahead."

"I won't hinder your path through our domain," she said, relaxing her arms to her side. "Many squander their hours in vain. Yet this legend lacks a solid base. A legend woven from falsehoods is naught but a wild, fruitless chase."

"Legend?" Hunter asked. "What legend do you speak of?"

"You know it well," the gnome said. "The story is not mine to tell."

With that, the gnome shrugged and pranced back across the bridge, disappearing in the brush with only a ruffle of grass in her wake. Hunter gritted his teeth and told Asher to follow as he stomped across the bridge, turning to take the path. Asher sensed the incline as he marched ahead, certain that the gradual climb proved they had found the right path.

As they followed their route around trees and climbed over larger rocks that acted as natural stairs, they came to the top of a hill with a plateau leading to the base of the mountains. Asher rubbed his eyes to adjust to the light in the clearing. He blinked twice, not certain what he saw ahead. Peering through the mist that languished within the glade, the contours of a market emerged. Nestled beneath a canopy of pristine white linen, myriad stalls unfurled like petals, each a vibrant splash in a tapestry of hues. Festive pennants and banners of orange and blue fluttered in the gentle breeze.

"What madness?" Hunter whispered.

Asher shared a glance with him, just as perplexed. Cautiously, they made their way to the tent market. As they got closer, Asher recognized pointy hats of red and green bobbing just beneath the tables.

"It's a gnome market," Asher said. "Looks like two families. Each family has hats with a color of their own."

"Stupid vermin," Hunter said, shaking his head.

Asher glared at him, making sure the prince's hand was far

enough away from his blade. Flags danced in the air with images of long swords, broad swords, and others with intricate designs or slender shapes. The homage to the blades bled over to tablecloths, bathing towels, and logo embossing on steins.

Hunter picked up what appeared to Asher to be a child's toy—thin, rectangular cuts of wood joined together with twine to form the shape of a crude sword. "What is this?" he asked the nearest gnome.

An older gnome with a beard huffed as he climbed on top of a stool to look over the table. "Those are on sale today. Perfect for the young ones seeking to take the way. If you want them in gray, we're all sold out, I am afraid to say."

"What is this place?" Asher asked.

"This place?" the gnome asked, looking confused. "You've arrived at the gift shop for those who take the quest. Most return quite eager for a rest. Some begin here, but I don't think it best."

"What quest?" the prince asked, placing his hands on the table and leaning toward the gnome.

The gnome stood statuesque. "The quest for the Apex Blade, of course. Travelers come all days of each season, up the mountain, then back down, sad with remorse."

Wild-eyed, Hunter glared at Asher. He saw the prince's fists clench as if the act squeezed blood into his red-flushed cheeks.

"Esteemed gnome," Asher said. "What path do the travelers take on the quest?"

The gnome pointed to a trail leading toward the east end of the mountain's base. "Easier climb over there. The path to the west, none often dare."

Asher picked up an ink pen shaped like a sword. He tossed it in his hand to estimate its weight and flipped it over to inspect it further. He picked up a commemorative shirt; its fabric was rough. *The Legend is a lie, but this shirt proves I didn't die*, it read. He sifted through a few of them, looking for a smaller size.

Asher groped through the trinkets and wares on the table, catching a familiar golden glint of light. *It can't be.* Asher picked up a coin identical to the one wrapped in his pocket. Once again, the dragon's wings etched into the coin began to move as the gnome watched on.

"This one's not for sale," the gnome said. "Its value is only to keep the wind at bay and the shirts from sail."

Asher seethed with a newfound indignation, dropping the coin back on the table. "The wings flap. Nothing more. I know this trinket well."

"No, they don't," Hunter said, holding the coin into the light and squinting at its markings.

"Probably broken and just as fake as everything else here," Asher said as Hunter tossed the coin into the gnome's hands.

"Come on," Hunter said, spinning on his heel and marching toward the east path with his shoulders hunched before him.

Asher stole one last glance at the gnome before jogging after Hunter. The gnome twirled the coin in his hand and held a toothless smile as he returned the glance.

"The Witch of the Forest has deceived me!" Hunter bellowed. "She will pay for this with her life!"

"Hunter," Asher said, daring to grab the side of his arm. "Something's not right here."

CHAPTER 10

THE ONLY PATH

Asher took the lead and stopped by the eastward trail, staring down at the path ahead.

"We're here," Hunter said, his voice a blend of impatience and condescension. "What's so amiss about my public humiliation back there?"

Asher took a deep breath, letting it out slowly. "Hunter, have you had much experience with gnomes before?"

"Thankfully, none," he said, folding his arms across his chest.

"The gnome said people come here daily on this fool's errand, but have you seen any of them today?"

"No," Hunter said. "Perhaps they got an earlier start of it than we did, not taking as much rest as you to stop and wheeze along the way."

"Were there any brown leaves in the Canopy of the Elders? Is that not the only path?"

The prince looked away from Asher's eyes, shifting his weight from one leg to another. "I don't recall."

"It was green and lush," Asher said. "This eastern path, the one most traveled—why is it overgrown and not at least as trodden as the path before?"

The prince studied the path. "That's... a good question."

"The pens on the table back there—only the ones on the top of the pile had swords painted on the side. Why were the others blank? The same thing happened with the shirts," Asher said.

Hunter huffed and turned back to face the trail behind them. "You think it was a deception?"

"I'm certain of it," Asher said. "I just don't understand why. Gnomes only deceive to hide their treasures."

"The gnomes have held this blade as their most prized treasure ever since they stole it," Hunter explained.

"Is that why you hate them?" Asher asked.

Hunter grunted and shifted his camping bag from his left shoulder to his right. "The blade is a powerful weapon. There is some merit in keeping power away from those unworthy to wield it, but I blame them for deciding among themselves to be the arbiters of valor."

"What makes you think we can find it?" Asher asked.

The prince turned to him and planted his foot on a rock. "The Witch of the Forest told me I was destined to find it. A prophecy wills it. You are my guide."

"You trust her?" Asher asked.

"I know little of myth," Hunter said. "The kingdom of Barbshire is in more dire need than you may know. Famine will claim more lives than any invading army. Bishop Falls knows this. They hold our people and our honor to ransom, seeking to turn our plight to their advantage."

"How?"

Hunter turned back to the path. "I am to wed the Bishop Falls governor's daughter, bringing our kingdom closer together. The alliance is a wasted opportunity. I could marry into stronger territories with more robust trade opportunities. Bishop Falls trades just enough grain for us to survive this season in exchange for far too much of our precious ore, forcing people like you to risk their lives in the mines."

"Are you certain that the marriage will prevent a war? People in the village," Asher began, "they say the marriage is a ruse to send their armies within our gates."

Hunter laughed or perhaps coughed. Asher wasn't certain. "You must be kidding. For all their bluster, Bishop Falls would never actually attack."

"How can you be certain? Do you even love the governor's daughter?"

"Love? I've never met her. And I can be certain because my father says it's so."

"What will you do with the sword?" Asher asked, jogging to keep up with Hunter's stride. "Defeat them in war? Plunder their city?"

"When my great-grandfather held the Apex Blade, none would dare risk rebellion. I would cut them down to remind them, if necessary. There was peace until the blade was taken from him," Hunter said.

"War is never won, not even by the victor," Asher said, his voice barely more than a whisper. "Wouldn't the certainty of their defeat by the blade force fair trade and alliances? You have the chance to unite the entire kingdom in peace. Innovation, science, prosperity. Those are the fruits of peace and stability. And you wouldn't have to marry her."

"If there were truly an alternative, I would take it. I must do my duty, regardless of whether I'd prefer another."

"Do you prefer another?" Asher asked, tempting his fate.

"Order is purchased with sacrifice, not indulging in whatever I may prefer," Hunter said after a long pause. "Anarchy is the alternative. Leadership is not easy. Resources are limited. There isn't a single council meeting where the local governors don't start and end with concerns for our people. My father listens, and we do the best we can."

"Why not at least open the libraries to the people? What cost would that incur?"

"Knowledge is a dangerous thing, Asher. An educated population leads to uprisings. Calls for change. That time may come, but not now. It would be like harvesting food before it's ripe. You think of us as monsters, but we're only trying to keep our people safe."

Asher scrunched his eyebrows together. "How do you know these things? You seem so... certain."

Hunter studied him before he spoke. "There are many secrets in this realm. Knowledge of the past. Potential futures. Far more than you'd find in all the libraries of the kingdom combined. My father would say that those secrets should not be shared."

"What of your mother?"

Hunter bit down on his teeth before composing his answer. "She may be more accommodating to your perspective on literacy. As to the dangers, she would still agree."

"I think we should take the western path," Asher suggested, eager to divert the conversation from a topic as perilous as the terrain before them.

"Why?"

"The gnomes will try to trick us. Send us on the path where we'd be least likely to succeed."

After deliberating and concluding that one path was just as deceptive as the other, they agreed to take their chances with the western path. As they returned to the field, the scene had transformed; the festive displays and tables had vanished, and not a single gnome who manned them remained. A steady wind rushed over them as they passed the deserted market, and neither of them spoke. Contours of the other trail, a path of rock and mud amid the high grass, began to take form in the distance. The western trail, with its gentler incline, seemed more inviting at first, but Asher could only see part of it. Trees and the mountain's natural curvature hid the rest, shrouding their chosen path in mystery.

As they trudged silently up the winding path, the mountain's first bend revealed itself, a gentle curve that heralded the start of their ascent. The trail, initially clear, soon became a mosaic of rocks and pebbles. With each step, the path became more treacherous, the loose stones beneath their feet shifting and crunching, making every stride a challenge.

The mountain tightened its hold on the trail, stony fingers stretching over the path with a determined grasp. The autumn sun began its descent toward the west, casting long, serpentine shadows that wove across their way.

The air grew cooler, and a steady breeze meandered through the trees, sending a shiver down Asher's spine as he wrapped his arms around himself for warmth. The wind carried the crisp scent of wilting leaves, a reminder of the season's change, and the faint, earthy aroma of damp moss clinging to the rocks and trees.

After what Asher estimated to be an hour's journey, Hunter halted abruptly. Asher looked up from his careful watch of the path. Before them, the trail ceased abruptly, giving way to a formidable stone wall. It rose before them like a natural fortress, stretching upward as if to rival the height of the royal gates back home. The cold and unyielding cliff bore the marks of time and weather, its texture rough and uneven. Asher felt the mountain was daring them to find a way forward, a natural guardian for the secrets that lay beyond.

"How are we supposed to get up there?" Hunter asked, looking for some unseen way around it.

Asher stepped into the clearing. "There," he said, pointing to a rope coiled up behind a stone.

Hunter picked it up and studied it before tilting his head back and squinting to measure the height. "Look—the top of the cliff. It has an anchor protruding from it. Someone must have left it there for climbing."

"Odd that there's a rope here," Asher said, tugging on the rope and testing its strength.

"You think it's a trap? Another way for the gnomes to thwart us?"

"No," Asher said. "It's sound. We just need to find a way to tie this to the anchor up there."

"I can climb," Hunter said, taking the end of the rope and wedging his foot between rocks on the wall. With a burst of energy, he lunged toward his next step. His foot slipped, unable to find traction. He slid back down with a cloud of broken gravel and dust billowing around him.

Asher took the opportunity to dig through his bag while Hunter dusted himself off with his back to him. He snatched the amulet from its pouch and slid it into his pocket. The charm's influence washed over him like sinking into a warm bath. The mint was all he needed to recharge its enchantment after all.

"Let me try," Asher said.

Hunter arched his eyebrow and looked Asher up and down. "I train with the finest knights. I've climbed higher walls than this."

Hunter took to the cliff again, making it one step higher before losing a handhold and sliding back down, landing harder than the first time.

Asher took an end of the rope and tied it to his waist. He found a solid hold on a jutted stone above his head and another place for his foot. He pulled himself up to find another foothold thereafter. Slowly, he scaled higher than Hunter had managed. One wary step after another, he continued his climb.

"Careful! Not so fast," Hunter called up to him, his voice strained with a concern Asher thought unfamiliar.

Asher's hand groped above his head, scraping over a slate of stone to feel for any crack to hold his hand. As his nails scratched across the rock, it disintegrated to powder with his touch, but only enough for him to wedge his hand within the stone and hoist himself up again.

Methodically, Asher shimmied up the cliff, finally hoisting himself on solid ground. He crawled to the metal hook and tied his end of the rope around it, testing it to ensure it would hold.

"Tie the bags to the rope, and I can hoist them up before you climb," Asher shouted to the prince.

After Asher pulled up their supplies, Hunter held the rope in both hands as he approached the wall, pulling himself with each step.

"I didn't know you could climb," Hunter said, breathing heavily.

"I'm small. Less weight to lift, I guess," Asher said with a shrug as he picked up his bag and avoided the prince's eyes.

"It looks like the trail has only given us one path," Asher said, pointing to the cave.

Hunter studied the opening and squinted to see into the darkness. "The witch assured me of that," he mumbled as he picked up his gear bag.

Asher shuffled behind the prince into the cave's mouth. He ran his hands over the rough, gray stone laced with moss trails. Jagged boulders lined the walls, and the ground was slick from water, leaving a path of mud that caked his shoes. The damp, moldy odor grew stronger as they wandered deeper into the darkness.

As they trudged through the mud to a bend in the cave, a bright prick of light beckoned to them. Asher let out a deep sigh and fixed his eyes on the exit as they took careful steps, trying to avoid slipping. A cool breeze of fresh air met them on the other side of the cave, where a narrow path led from the cave to higher points along the mountain.

Hunter stepped to the ledge and looked out across the valley. "Look," he said, pointing. "Bishop Falls is in the distance. Likely a two-day ride from here."

Asher stood beside him and held his hand to his forehead to blot out the setting sun. He looked out over rolling plains of straw-hued grasslands leading to the sprawling city that followed the Great Laden River's winding bends. "Why do they have all of those tents?"

"What tents?" Hunter asked. Asher pointed to the left of the city's gates.

Hunter's face flared violet. "They're assembling ranks."

"Ranks?" Asher asked.

"War, Asher," the prince said, voice low and rumbling. "They're camping out to raise their army. An army to take Barbshire."

"The village isn't prepared for war," Asher said. "They barely have enough to feed themselves, much less knights."

"The witch deceived me," Hunter said as his voice quivered. "She tempted me on this fool's errand. If the diplomats from Bishop Falls noticed my absence, they could assume I've absconded from my obligation to marry the governor's daughter. It would be an act of war. We must warn my father. We'll have to come back for the sword," Hunter said, returning to the tunnel.

"Can we make it in time?"

"We will run with the wind," Hunter said.

Asher grabbed his bag and jogged as fast as he could without slipping on the stone. He followed the prince back to the other end of the cave.

"Where is the rope?" Hunter asked, his eyes wild with accusation.

"It... it was here," Asher said, pointing to the now unencumbered iron rod jutting from the cliff's edge.

"Your knot was feeble!" Hunter yelled as he knelt to look out over the cliff. "I could have fallen to my death."

Asher dropped his bag and dove to the ground, peering over the steep drop. "Hunter, the knot was sound. Look, there's no rope below!" he pleaded.

For a long moment, the prince sat frozen, looking down at the empty path as dusk began to encroach. "You're right. It's not there. Who would have taken it?"

Asher struggled to answer. "Maybe the same person who left it for us to find?"

"It's too far down to climb without a rope," Hunter said. "One slip, and we'd fall to our death."

"What do we do?" Asher asked, sensing the amulet's charge subsiding like a neglected fire burning to embers on a cold night.

"The only thing we can," Hunter said with a sigh. "There truly is only one path now. We must hope the witch spoke the truth. We reclaim the sword and return to Barbshire before they ride."

CHAPTER 11

THE PRINCE'S FOLLY

King Bracken, cloaked in his highest regalia of burgundy robes and a heavy golden crown, leaned forth from his gilded throne and roared with an urgency that echoed through the ancient stone hall, "Are you not the vanguard of my royal guard?"

The knight, a seasoned veteran of countless battles, bowed his head in acquiescence. "Yes, my king."

"Is it not the purpose of your sacred vow, the sole duty of your sworn oath, to ensure the prince's safety? To keep constant vigilance over his movements? To guard his life with your own?" the king bellowed as his words shook the very stone on which he sat.

"Yes, my king," came the knight's response, more uncertain than his prior affirmation.

"Yet you come before me, daring to admit that the prince has been missing for two days? That you are as ignorant of his whereabouts as the lowest of my court? If the whole of my royal guard is riddled with such blatant incompetence, how shall I replace you once the shackles have been fastened about your wrists?"

"Reginald," the queen whispered from her seat to her husband's right.

King Bracken looked at his queen with resigned weariness. She drew in a measured breath, closing her eyes in a futile attempt to summon some semblance of tranquility, a solace as elusive as her missing heir.

"Honored knight, what clues have you managed to unearth thus far?" the queen asked, her voice as smooth as she could muster to hide the dagger she felt piercing her chest.

The knight lifted his head, betraying his weary, troubled eyes to the queen. He cleared his throat. "The quarry master reported seeing the prince astride his steed, which later returned to the castle riderless. He mentioned that the prince demanded the company of a commoner, a peasant boy. He asked for this boy by name."

"And what have we learned of this peasant boy?" the queen pursued, her brow creased with worry.

"The boy, Asher Snow, is a peer of our prince in age but from a family neither influential nor notoriously defiant. The quarry master, believing our prince was seeking a squire for knighthood, offered his own son, hardened and strong from his toils in the mines. Yet our prince insisted upon Asher, the frailest and youngest among them."

Queen Verity pursed her lips in contemplation. "Where did my son take this boy?"

"According to a village shopkeeper, the same day our prince disappeared, this boy visited his store, lavishly equipped with more coin than his station could ever justify. He purchased hiking gear, clothing, rations, and other provisions. We surmise our prince sent the boy on his behalf."

"And the boy? His family?" the king asked.

"We visited their dwelling," the knight said. "His parents claim to have not seen their son since the day he vanished."

"Detain the boy's family," King Bracken said. "Our dungeon's hospitality may encourage them to speak more freely should they know more than they are willing to say."

The queen flashed a worried glance toward her husband, hoping to calm his hand. He met her eyes, and she recognized the expression. It was the one she saw more often than she preferred—that of an enraged man who warned her not to push the issue.

"Yes, Your Majesty," came the knight's reply.

The king rubbed the unshaven stubble on his chin. "Send a team of our knights toward the Blue Mountains. If the boy's foolishness led him as far as you say, the mountains would be the most sensible extension of his folly."

"Your Highness," the court's counsel interrupted. "A delegation from Bishop Falls was received only a hour ago. They would like to speak with the prince in preparation for the marriage. If he's not to be found..."

"They will assume that he's absconding from his responsibilities," the king said. "Or that we have changed our position on our agreement."

"I believe so," the counsel said. "Either conclusion could escalate tensions. Rosen was negotiating with them."

The queen raised her finger. "Perhaps we will explain the

circumstances to the delegation and request they join our expedition to find him. We can assure them there is no deceit and gain the benefit of an expedition from the other side of the mountain."

The court's counsel darted a glance at the king. "How would that assure them our prince has not absconded his duties?"

Verity leaned forward to speak before her husband had the chance to answer. "Our son has a fertile imagination, reading books about adventure. Taking expeditions with the knights when time affords such luxury," she said, smiling dismissively. "It is his prerogative to have one last adventure before he assumes his royal obligations, is it not?"

The king grunted his approval. "Sensible. Dispatch Rosen now. Let the governor of Bishop Falls hear the request before his delegation returns from Barbshire."

"Yes, Your Highness," the counsel said, bowing his head.

"I will speak to Rosen myself," Verity said, not wishing to risk any reckless instruction given to her diplomat by any other.

"Let me take my own counsel with the queen. You are dismissed," the king said, shooing the knight, his counsel, and the other assembled highborn in the royal court toward the door.

The king sat beside his queen in silence until the great door to the hall closed, and the footfalls surrendered to silence. "Verity, I fear less for our son's departure than for his destination."

The queen removed her ceremonial crown and let it clank onto the table beside her. She frowned as the effort failed to relieve any of the weight that burdened her. "Your grandfather's sword? Why would you ever expect that he'd seek it out? Surely the stories you regaled him with these past seventeen years would not tempt such a quest in our time of need?"

The king looked out over the empty court. "It's not the sword I worry about. There are much worse things for him to find in those mountains. Things both more valuable and more dangerous than a blade."

"Reginald, such things are not for him to find. My bloodline guarantees that," she said.

"Can you say the same of this Asher boy?" the king asked, turning back to face her. "Once the boy's parents are here, we must test the mother."

Verity nodded. "Naturally."

"I don't like his company either."

Verity laughed. "You've never met the boy."

"Don't be coy, Verity." The king squirmed in his chair. "Our son does not need distractions, lest he consider his royal obligations less favorable than other alternatives."

"I'm certain he already does, but it hasn't stopped him yet." Verity smiled and gave her husband's arm a playful poke. "Whatever his interests, he's his father's son. Wouldn't he at least find a lord? At worst, a knight?"

The king looked to the cathedral ceiling above as if to find answers among the mosaic of fabled heroes from the past. "You think I'm too harsh and aim to soften my mood. If only you knew how precariously we sit on fate's edge—one break in our line, and we stand powerless to prevent the darkness."

Queen Verity pursed her lips and took a deep breath as she stood, smoothing her dress and taking one last measure of her husband's eyes before making her way out of the chamber. She marched down the torch-lit passage toward the diplomatic wing. Her eyes narrowed with the thought of this boy's parents being shackled for the crime of being her son's victim.

She thought herself the quiet muse who whispered disarming enchantments in her husband's ear to distract his temper in the vain hope that it may make room for whatever nobility was bestowed upon him. She laughed to herself. *Enchantments?* She was no mystic, muttering arcane nonsense. She favored logic, even when her efforts were just as useless as a charlatan's incantation.

Gathering her resolve, Queen Verity glided gracefully toward the imposing doors of the castle's diplomatic wing. These massive, ornately carved doors, bound in iron and aged oak, stood as silent guardians to the myriad hushed secrets and delicate negotiations that unfolded within. With a determined push, she entered the chamber, a sanctum of strategy and statecraft.

Inside, the room was a hive of clandestine activity. Walls lined with shelves of ancient tomes and scrolls whispered tales of old alliances and forgotten feuds. In the center, Rosen, her most trusted advisor, sat hunched over a cluttered table. It was a chaotic landscape of maps, each detailed with the intricate topography of neighboring lands and stacks of missives, reports, and diplomatic correspondences.

The flickering light from the wall-mounted torches cast long, dancing shadows across the room. Rosen, absorbed in his work, was surrounded by the tools of his trade: quills, inkwells, and various seals for all types of royal correspondence. The air was thick with the scent of parchment and wax.

As Verity stepped farther into the room, the soft rustle of her gown against the stone floor broke the silence, causing Rosen to look up. "Queen Majesty," he said, bowing his head.

"Should our kingdom be assaulted by parchment, I fear for our survival, dear Rosen. Your papers appear as an enclosing army around you," she said.

Rosen returned a sheepish smile. "Fear not, Your Majesty. Paper cuts are mere distractions when our enemies plot sharper conflicts."

"Bishop Falls?" the queen asked, sitting opposite him.

Rosen narrowed his eyes as his face grew stern. "Their messenger came last hour. I assured them that our prince has not reneged on his duties and that his absence was no more than a miscommunication with his scheduling clerk."

"My son doesn't have a scheduling clerk," the queen said.

"They don't know that," Rosen said, reprising his smirk. "Naturally, the clerk will be punished."

"Naturally," the queen said. "Did it help?"

"Not at all," Rosen said. "They are determined to take advantage of any slight to strengthen their cause for outrage. They tell their citizens that Barbshire has long held them back and treated them poorly. Now, at the time of our need and greatest weakness, they seek retribution."

"Amendments to the trade agreement?"

"Won't do," Rosen said, crossing his arms. "They see us as having no claim to rule them beyond the words on these papers. Rebellion. That's their aim. For months, our spies have told us how speakers gather in their square and blame us for not permitting them to use the iron plow. Even as they plan for a marriage, they conspire to make their own citizens despise us."

Queen Verity massaged her temples with her head resting on her palms. "The king will never permit that plow to be used."

Verity refused to continue the discussion, having lingered on it for too long. "Would they join us in a search party? Prove to them that we aren't trying to hide anything?"

"I asked the messenger," Rosen said, lowering his voice. "He says the governor would accuse us of pretext. They would likely see it as a plot to murder their best knights in the deepest woods. There is another... complication."

"Complication?"

"It appears that the governor's daughter is also missing. They're preparing an official inquiry to be sent to the Crown. I believe they suspect that Barbshire abducted his daughter as leverage for the trade negotiations."

"Absurd," the queen said, jolting up in her chair.

"Your Majesty," Rosen whispered. "The hour is much later than our king may be willing to realize. Even if the prince returned this day, it would be too late."

The queen looked away from Rosen. "Speaking of my son. He was last seen with a peasant boy known as Asher Snow. It's an enigma. A commoner somehow captured my son's attention. He seems an unlikely companion for a royal. Do you know anything about this boy?"

Rosen bit his lip. "He works at the tavern. Bright young man, I'm told. Never spoke to him."

Verity studied Rosen's expression, listening for what was unspoken. "Go to Bishop Falls. Speak to the governor. Do your best," the queen said.

CHAPTER 12

GERTRUDE

"How long do we have?" Asher asked, trying to steady his shaky voice.

Hunter took a deep breath. "It looked like they'd just begun amassing their army. It will take no more than two days before they're ready and another two before they arrive at the city's gates. Much beyond that and there won't be much of a city left for me to protect."

With nothing to say, Asher followed a few paces behind as Hunter marched ahead. The path on the other side of the cave was more treacherous than before. Each step required careful negotiation to avoid slipping off the ragged boulders that made some semblance of a trail up the side of the mountain. Crawling as often as he stood, Asher kept up with Hunter's relentless pace as best he could. His knees and legs burned with each step on the path, lit by slim glints of the moon's light.

Adrenaline substituted for food and rest as Asher gulped in breaths of air. His mind kept replaying the encounter with the witch. Even if she were true to her promise, Asher panicked that his concealed wish would doom his family. Having the prince's love would mean nothing if there was no kingdom to save together.

Asher considered it again, and his thoughts narrowed on the witch. He had never asked to have the prince abduct him in secret. He just asked for love—a love that would prevent a marriage and stop a war, not one that would be its seed.

"What have we here?" a woman's voice called behind them.

Asher turned to see two young women, neither much older than himself, each burdened with oversized satchels draped over their shoulders and metal water steins tied at their waists. The bottles clanged together like bells as they hiked toward them.

Hunter placed his hands on his hips and pushed out his chest. "I am Prince Hunter Bracken, son of our sovereign, King Bracken. Under pain of my father's wrath, come no closer."

The taller of the two women came to a stop and let her bag slip from her shoulders and fall to the ground. She huffed and mirrored the prince's stance. "I can assure you that I have no interest in coming near you."

"Who are you?" Asher asked.

The woman glared at Asher, raising an eyebrow. "Your Grace, is it a new custom in the capital to permit your servant to speak?"

Hunter lowered his voice. "It is not, but the question stands."

"I am Gertrude Wicker, daughter of the governor of Bishop Falls, and commanded to submit myself to you in marriage. This," she said, motioning to the woman beside her, "is my hand-maid, Ruth."

Asher turned to see Hunter's face flush. "I beg your forgiveness. We have yet to meet," Hunter said. "Nonetheless, I hardly expected to see you hiking this high in the Blue Mountains."

"Likewise. I assume you are part of the search party?" she asked.

"What search party?" Asher asked.

Hunter glared at him. "You will do well to mind your station and not speak unless asked to."

Asher turned away from the price's stinging glare. His harsh words and scolding expression broke whatever accord Asher had reached with the prince. Suddenly aware of his folly—the delusion that they could find love, much less friendship—Asher stepped backward and looked down to find kinship with the gravel and dirt that muddied their path.

"Lady Gertrude," Hunter said, his voice steady, "what is the cause for this search party?"

"My escape, naturally."

"Escape?" Hunter asked. "Why would you be escaping as your city's knights and archers form ranks outside your city's gates?"

"I can only assume that my father believes the capital took me prisoner," Gertrude said with a shrug. "What's your theory?"

"I assumed that they thought I absconded from my duties by..." Hunter began and cleared his throat. "By going on an unannounced camping trip."

Gertrude folded her arms and gave a knowing look to Ruth. "A camping trip? You didn't mean to flee the realm and escape your obligation?"

"I will do what is expected of me. You must return to

Bishop Falls immediately and let them know you haven't been captured."

Gertrude laughed. "Why would I return if I'm trying to escape?"

"And why, exactly, are you trying to escape?" Hunter demanded.

"Because," she said with a sigh. "I have no intention of submitting myself to a man."

"It is your duty!" Hunter yelled. "Would you prefer to see rebellion—a war that would claim lives in both cities? I mean no disrespect, but it isn't my preference either. My desires are trivial when balanced against the greater good."

Gertrude turned her satchel on its side and sat. "I don't want to see anyone die. I don't want to see anyone suffer," she said, her voice carrying a tenderness that contrasted with the determination in her eyes. "Some may say it brave to sacrifice my will for the greater good. But I would see myself as a coward for denying my love to another and living a lie to serve men who put their interests above my own."

"You don't even know me," Hunter said. "We've only met. How can you condemn me before I can answer your charge against me?"

"It's not you, Hunter," she said, looking at Ruth. "I said that I had no intention of submitting myself to a man. Not you. Not any man."

Asher saw a faint smile on Ruth's face as she met Gertrude's gaze. He recognized their fortitude—a confirmation that neither men nor their armies could ever break a bond forged in love. Humbled by their admiration and resolve, Asher's heart swelled as it yearned to share any measure of the same love for another.

"I... I don't understand," Hunter said. "I could never put my desires above those of the kingdom. You should just choose. Suppress whatever longings you feel and obey your father's command."

"It's obvious that you've never known love, my prince," Gertrude said as she stood. "Our decision is final. We won't return to Bishop Falls. I will not marry you. Yet, I pray to the Watchers that you can still find a way to avert this war, whatever its cause."

"Where will you go?" Hunter asked. "There will be no refuge in any city."

Gertrude heaved her satchel over her shoulders. "We know. Our journey lies to the west—through the Poisoned Fields, toward whatever may lie beyond."

"The Poisoned Fields?" Hunter asked. "You'll not survive."

"No one has survived before, but that's only because I haven't been among those who've tried. If death should nevertheless find us, then that end would be far better than a life lived denying who I am and whom I love," she said. "If the heir to the throne can't understand that, then I fear for our realm far more than any war."

Asher watched as Gertrude and Ruth walked past them toward the west, taking their own path—away from either city. In them, Asher saw the witch's cruelest curse—the denial of love's promise, coupled with the torment of beholding its purest form just beyond his reach.

Once the two women passed out of sight, Hunter grabbed Asher's arm. "When we're around other people, you need to mind your station. You could have betrayed our intentions!"

Asher could not bear to lift his eyes. "I was only trying to help."

"Help?" Hunter scoffed. "If I were to be perceived as weak by the governor's daughter, can you imagine how that could be used against the kingdom?"

"I've lived a life where I don't care how others perceive me."

"You may have the luxury of being at the mercy of people's judgments—but I don't. What must they say about you? You, who seeks the company of gnomes over his peers. You, who prefers to be gay and consign himself to loneliness and despair."

Asher pulled his arm from Hunter's grip. "I don't prefer to be gay. I am. So are Gertrude and Ruth. And, no, I don't languish over how people see me. I'm no chameleon who changes his colors to blend in so often that he forgets his true nature. I'd rather someone hate me for who I am than admire me for someone I'm not."

Hunter combed his hand through his hair and sighed. "It is wrong of me to expect you to understand such things."

"Don't confuse my position for ignorance," Asher said. "You start with the presumption that your version of strength is the only way to find respect. My version of bravery and strength comes from authenticity."

"Gertrude walks her path—choosing to be authentic at the cost of her life."

"Exactly," Asher said. "And that makes her the bravest person I've ever met."

Hunter shook his head and looked toward the path they chose. "I shouldn't take my anger out on you. Sometimes, it's hard to discern bravery from foolishness."

"It's like playing boxtin," Asher said. "The most reckless players are ones with nothing left to lose. Gertrude and Ruth have no more cards to play. Their gamble is the only choice they have left to make."

CHAPTER 13

CROSSROADS OF FATE

Asher heard the slip before he saw it. Ahead, Hunter's leg fell through the shadow into a gap between two boulders. He screamed in pain, and Asher scurried over the rocks to reach him.

"My leg," Hunter groaned, trying to pull it out of the gorge.

Asher knelt beside him and dislodged a rock that had anchored his foot. Slowly, Asher helped the prince pull his leg back onto the rock.

"Is it broken?" Asher asked, not daring to touch the blood-streaked leg.

"No, I don't think so," Hunter groaned. "My ankle is twisted, but I can move it."

"I can wrap it," Asher said, lunging for his bag.

"No time," Hunter said before wincing as he put some weight on the foot. "We have to keep going."

Asher swallowed hard, his throat suddenly parched as his gaze followed the prince. After two labored paces up the mountain,

Hunter's ankle gave out under his weight, and he crashed back down to the stone.

"Hunter," Asher said, voice as low as he could make it. "We can't see. It's dangerous. If you get hurt worse, we have no hope of making it. There's a landing below. Let's camp."

"There's no time," Hunter said again, pulling his leg against his chest with his eyes squeezed closed.

"I can wrap the ankle. I can make a malyeast tea from the leaves in my kit. It makes the swelling subside. By morning, it could be better."

"How do you know these things?" Hunter asked, his voice calmer.

"I picked up a small medical kit with our provisions," Asher said. "Villagers find cures in nature all the time. Apothecaries are too expensive. I know what I'm doing. I promise."

Hunter looked into his eyes. His expression granted the behest even though Asher thought he'd never speak it. With the prince's arm around Asher's shoulder, they navigated one deliberate step at a time back down the mountain to a clearing large enough to accommodate them for the night.

As the prince assembled his tent, Asher took his amulet and wound the mint around it more tightly than the night before. He stowed it in a pouch. Without the sun's warmth, bitterly freezing wind blew against the mountain. Asher's fingers grew numb as he pinched dry leaves into a cup. He knew the recipe well. For it to work, the tea required his own water ration to be added to the prince's cup. With a thirst growing into a hunger, Asher considered taking a drink for himself, only to dismiss the idea—he only had enough for the prince.

A small fire was quick to warm the cup. Warm in his hand, he offered the tea to the prince. Hunter took the cup in both hands, his eyes narrowing slightly, lingering on it with a trace of wariness. He brought it closer to his lips, allowing the rising steam to waft around him. His nostrils flared as he took a cautious sip.

Without more wood than he happened to pick up along the trail that day, the fire wouldn't last the night. Asher retreated from the prince's side, dug into his pocket, and unfolded a small knife. He sifted through chunks of splintered oak from the kindling in his bag to find a suitable lump of wood. Absentmindedly, he sat on a stone and started to whittle, shucking off wood shavings. Light from the fire danced across the cut wood, revealing layers untarnished by nature's severity.

The fire's light dimmed as Hunter crossed by the flame to sit beside him. "She's right, you know."

"Who?" Asher asked, not taking his eyes off the wood in his hand.

Hunter looked toward the sky. "Gertrude. I've never known love."

"Given the circumstances, I assume you're relieved of the obligation to find it with her."

"So it seems," Hunter said, chuckling. "I mean, it terrifies me—the idea that an emotion could be so strong, corrupting a person to become so selfish."

"I see love as selfless. It's about caring about someone else so much that you're willing to sacrifice for them."

"Well, yes," Hunter said. "But what makes love between two people so important that they forsake their duties to society?"

"Love doesn't always demand that," Asher said as he accidentally cut a gash too deep in the wood. "I think Gertrude and Ruth just ran out of options. I suspect they would have stayed in Bishop Falls if there was a way to balance their obligations with their love."

Hunter was silent, and the crackling fire was the only sound between them. "But what if you get hurt? What if it all ends in despair?"

"That's the risk," Asher admitted, "but it's also what makes love profound enough to be in the bards' refrains and all the poems. It's the courage to be vulnerable, to open yourself to the possibility of pain for the chance of experiencing it. Love can hurt, but it also heals. It's a force that drives us to be better—to ourselves and each other."

Hunter's gaze shifted from the fire to Asher, a softness in his eyes. "And you believe it's worth it?"

"It has to be," Asher said. "I haven't experienced it either, but I want to. Otherwise, there's no meaning in life—no cause to fight for."

Hunter let out a long breath. "What are you making?"

"Just whittling. A hobby, I guess. I used to make animals. Sheep. Horses."

"I did the same thing when I was younger. I probably made

an army of knights on their horses," Hunter said, waving his arm across an imaginary battlefield.

Asher chuckled at the thought of the prince, high in his castle, carving under the same light of some shared moon from their past. "I think I like making something out of nothing."

"Exactly," Hunter said. "I would never start with anything in mind. I'd examine the wood first and let it guide me—telling me what it should become."

Asher handed the wood and the knife to the prince. "I thought I'd carve a gnome, but it looks a bit more like a toad. What do you think it should be?"

Hunter stroked his thumb along the freshly cut grain and hummed as he squinted. "I'd reason that it could be a most valiant knight."

"Does the wood always want to be a knight, or is that just the only thing you know how to carve?"

"Maybe a whittle of both," Hunter said, his eyes twinkling with a wry smile.

Asher groaned and shook his head. "I had no idea that you were so punny. Maybe you should *branch out* and carve something *yew*."

As their laughter echoed around the fire, Asher was lost in thought, contemplating the prince's true shape. He wondered if Hunter, like the wood he carved, bore a rough exterior, masking a tender soul beneath layers of weathered bark. Or perhaps he was repeating his mistake by presuming to force the shape into his own desires. He cautioned himself to proceed with deliberation, to avoid letting his desire to create his vision misguide him, sculpting not the knight he envisioned but yet another toad.

The fire grew dim, and their conversation trailed to silence. Winds circled and howled through the cave below, whipping the small flag on Hunter's tent from one direction to the next, bending its mast in surrender to the strongest gusts but never blowing it off its mooring. Asher ran his hand over the gravel, hoping to make the softest spot for his bag among the rocks.

Hunter set the empty cup down and tugged at the wrappings Asher had placed around his ankle and foot. "It's too cold tonight. You'll freeze out here."

Asher looked up and saw him holding the flap to his tent open. The invitation sparked a surge of revolt that warred with a rush of excitement. He considered committing an act of defiance—insisting on sleeping within the thin layers of his blanket rather than risking some fresh ridicule in the night, but he knew the prince was right. The temperature on the mountain would plunge. The same voice that persuaded him to abandon logic in favor of a lucky coin at the tavern urged him to accept the invitation and see what shape the carving could eventually take.

Asher hesitated. He held his head low and climbed into the tent with his blanket, pushing his body as far against the edge of the tent as he could, taking up no more space than he was forced to. He thought himself more unforgivable than a moth drawn to the flame. Unlike the moth, he appreciated the danger from the outset but gave himself to it, nonetheless. Hunter mated the buttons to close the skirt on the tent. Asher felt a shiver passed over him. The prince's warm back pressed against his. Too fearful to move or sleep, Asher lay motionless, listening to his pulse pound in his neck as the winds gusted around them.

He forced himself to calm down as Hunter's breathing softened to an even rhythm. Asher moved his arm from underneath his side just enough to find a sliver of comfort. He wasn't certain whether he lay for minutes or hours—whether sleep found him for brief moments or not. Hunter snored peacefully for a time, then stopped. At last, Asher succumbed to the twilight that blended his thoughts with dreams, unable to discern where one began and the other ended. He gave himself over in surrender, letting sleep conquer him.

———

HE HELD BACK A gasp and jolted awake as Hunter rolled to his side, draping his arm over him and pulling him closer. The faint scent of sandalwood on his skin wafted to Asher's nostrils as Hunter cupped his body around him. Face flush, Asher's body burned like a fever. Gradually, he began to relax—loosening the muscles that knotted his neck and arms like they were braced for a fight.

The prince breathed against his neck. Hunter stretched out his hand, finding Asher's palm. Frozen in fear, Asher went numb as Hunter's fingers wove a pattern with his own. Asher's mind worked to make sense of it like nimble hands trying to loosen a stubborn knot. Hunter could have reached to him reflexively, like an instinct. Or maybe Hunter considered it the making of a perfect ruse. The prince could hold him through the night and wake to an alibi, insisting that sleep could justify that which the day would not.

Asher's neck tensed with the thought that the prince would wake and blame him for the crime. After a few moments of feeling their heartbeats dance in time with one another, Hunter's untamed hair came to rest as it tangled with his own. Enveloped in a wave of peace even stronger than the amulet's protection, Asher ceded his thoughts once more to the twilight.

GROGGILY, ASHER ROLLED OVER. The light of a new morning blazed through the thin cape of fabric surrounding him. A divot in the blanket where Hunter slept was the only trace of him. Blurry-eyed, Asher saw the unbuttoned flap of cloth fluttering with the wind. Beside him, a roughly carved knight on his horse. Asher picked it up and examined it approvingly, finding it remarkable that Hunter could see potential in something he thought he had ruined.

"There you are," Hunter said as Asher crawled out of the tent. "I was just about to wake you. We need to make double time today."

Asher groaned and stumbled to his bag, taking a handful of nuts from a pouch and wishing they could refill their water. "How's your ankle?"

"Stiff, but I can put weight on it. I believe the tea and wrappings helped."

"Keep the wrappings tight until tomorrow," Asher suggested as he held the amulet in his hand, spun with mint. Before unwinding the plant from the charm, he reconsidered. Perhaps the charm would never deplete if he kept the mint wrapped tightly around it all day. He hesitated, recalling the witch's warning. *I can quit tomorrow*, he assured himself as he considered what dangers may find him the next day.

He slipped the charm into his pocket, and the pang of hunger and thirst seemed to subside, lending support for his decision. Other longings were not as easily quelled. He wanted to ask Hunter about the night before—Hunter's hand intertwining with his own. He held back, certain the question would be met with disdain. Perhaps the prince was right, he thought. Some truths were too dangerous to know.

"We should find water soon," Asher said.

Hunter reached into his bag and gave his water bottle a shake. It made no sound. "Are you out as well?"

"I used the last of it for the tea."

Hunter held a stoic expression. "These mountains are bound to have streams. We'll resupply as soon as we can. Hurry," he said, gripping the back of Asher's arm and urging him forward. "We've already wasted enough time."

Asher lunged his leg to the top of a bolder and hoisted himself up. After two stones, his legs began to burn. After a half-hour, their hurried pace slowed to such progress as they could make by draping their arms over boulders to lift while straining their legs. Even in the cold, Asher was hot with exertion. He groaned each time he hoisted himself atop another stone. Weary-eyed, Hunter glanced back at him in solidarity.

Each time Asher thought his legs would fail him, he found a sudden boost of energy. Before the sun reached its highest point in the sky, Asher had taken the lead. Hunter's groans grew louder as he surmounted the stones.

"There's a clearing!" Asher yelled down to Hunter. "Just a bit farther."

Adrenaline mixed with the charm's enchantment, and Asher hoisted the prince's gear over his shoulder to carry it with his own. Nimbly, Asher scaled the last haphazardly fallen boulders on the trail and stumbled to his feet on a clearing. His smile grew weak. Instead of finding the mountain's peak, the clearing merely framed the majesty of the range. Snow-capped peaks reached even higher into the sky, surrounding them like impenetrable walls.

Asher turned to see Hunter's face, his expression one of defeat. The prince's lip quivered on the precipice of sobbing as he looked at the surrounding paths. Unimpeded by the mountain, a steady wind gusted, giving them no reprieve.

"I count two paths," Hunter said. "Each leading to no certain end."

Strength returned to Asher's body as he rested to orient himself. "What's that?" he asked, pointing to a mound where the trails diverged.

Together, they limped toward the mound. Two weathered wood slabs hung on a pole, pointing toward each path.

"It's gnome scribe," Asher said, reading the writing on the wood. "One points to a cave. The other says *easy path*."

"That must be the other mountain path the gnomes told us about," Hunter said. "It looks like we have another way back."

"We could still get back to the kingdom," Asher said as his heart pounded faster.

Hunter frowned. "I don't know which path to choose. We risk coming back too late with nothing to help. Or we continue on a dubious path toward a scant hope of finding the blade."

"It feels like we should take the path to the cave."

"Without water and winter ever closer at these heights, our lives and the lives of everyone in Barbshire are at stake. We can't gamble our kingdom on a feeling."

Asher turned to face him. "It's not a gamble this time. If we go back, we're certain to fail. If we go forward, at least we have a chance. You said I was a map, but I wouldn't know it until I did. My grandmother said the same thing. My whole life. Now I know why. It has to be."

"If this is the path you choose," he said, "then we follow it. I trust you."

Asher's heart swelled at the prince's words. His legs found strength from a power greater than the charm around his neck. With each step forward, the ground grew firmer beneath his feet as though the mountain had given him its approval.

CHAPTER 14

THE QUEEN'S RESOLVE

"That's reprehensible," Queen Verity said, her eyes narrowed into slits as she spoke to the guard. "They are our guests and shall be treated as such."

"It was our king's orders," the guard said, half stepping back to the wall behind him.

The queen took a deep breath and closed her eyes. "Just take me to them."

"The dungeon prisons?" the guard asked.

"That is where they are kept, is it not?"

"Yes," the guard said hesitantly. "It is hardly a place for the queen."

"It is hardly the place for *any* mother," the queen said. "It's exactly why you should take me to her immediately."

The guard unlatched a torch from the wall behind him and led the way to an iron gate leading to a stairwell that plunged into the depths beneath the castle. The gate's lock clanked to the stone, shrieking a final warning as the rusted hinges relented and the gate opened. With a final look back at the queen, the guard lifted the torch slightly higher and stepped into the abyss of shadow kept at bay just beyond the light's reach.

Queen Verity followed behind, instinctively holding her arms close to her chest to avoid soiling her finest-sleeved regalia on the mossy stone walls lining the narrow, winding stairs. As they descended, the stonework on the walls transitioned from smoothly sanded blocks to smaller, jagged, and mismatched stones of varied sizes. The air grew heavy and smelled of rusted chains and mold. If fear and hopelessness had a scent, the queen was certain it wafted into the stairwell at each floor they passed as they descended.

When they reached the third level beneath the castle, the guard left the stairwell and proceeded down a hall lit with too few torches. In the shadows, vermin scampered away amid the steady percussion of water dripping into unseen puddles. The queen forced herself to focus on the guard ahead of her. She reminded herself that fear was an unwelcome guest upon a queen's visage. The irony did not escape her: The royal theater troupe, who performed grand plays for her and the king, were blissfully unaware that they were not the sole masters of drama in Barbshire. Their most captive audience, the king and queen, were, in fact, the most skilled thespians. Confident in her craft, the queen raised her chin and clenched her jaw, embracing her role.

"Here, Your Grace," the guard said, pointing his torch at a cell beside him.

Queen Verity stepped into the torchlight and found two figures huddled on what barely passed as a bed. One figure stood and moved into the light. The woman met the queen's eyes for only an instant before she fell to her knees on the ashen stone.

"Queen Majesty," she whispered, bowing her head.

"Rise," the queen said. "Are you the mother of the child named Asher?"

The other figure leaped to his feet and stepped into the light. "If my son has disgraced the kingdom, let me punish him!"

The queen frowned and studied the man. "Dear sir," she began, "he has done no such thing. He is merely missing. I fear I owe you my apology as it appears that my son is responsible for Asher's disappearance. My son took yours against his will, and they've traveled into the mountains."

"My son would never seek to insult the Crown," his mother said, her voice little more than a whisper.

The queen took in Asher's parents as the light flickered within the cell. His mother's dress was patched in various places, worn down and threadbare. In royal circles, the queen would hear the court ridicule the villagers for wearing mere rags. The queen studied the dress as closely as the light would permit. It was stitched with determination and resourcefulness. This earnest beauty made the queen feel revulsion for the royal tailor's dress on her shoulders, tattered by comparison. Asher's father carried an expression the queen too readily recognized. Duty to the Crown before family. Covered in soot, he wore the same loyalty he professed.

"We have treated you most unfairly," the queen said, failing to catch a quiver in her voice. "We are two mothers in search of our sons. On my authority, you will be treated as guests. This guard will escort you to the guest wing. There, you will find fine food and water from the royal aquafer. The royal tailor will be at your disposal. In one hour's time, I would like to speak with you," she said, eyes fixed on Asher's mother.

"Will there be frog?" Asher's father asked. "Frog stew?"

"Simon," his mother said, jabbing his side with her elbow. "The kingdom is on the brink of a famine! How could you ask for such things? Would you take food from the queen's own table?"

The queen had enough light to see the man's face flush. He bowed his head and took a small step back, letting the shadows consume him.

"It's quite alright," the queen said before her guilt could object. "We will gladly share what provisions we have. Would you do no less if I were a guest in your home?"

"We would—anything you desire! We would make an entire vat of the stew," Simon said, eagerly promising to slaughter a hog and offer fine spices.

"Then you won't object to me doing the same," she said. "Guard, please escort our guests as I have promised."

Queen Verity enjoyed watching the guard's face contort from confusion to shock, finally resting on a resigned assent to follow her orders. Perhaps it was easier to assert her authority in the company of the very cells a guard would find himself in for insubordination, she thought. She walked ahead, taking no torch, eager to intercept the chef and avoid overwhelming her guests with the feast she first envisioned.

After ensuring her guests were settled, the queen returned

to her chambers. Looking at herself in the mirror, Queen Verity decided her handmaid succeeded in her mission—making the queen appear as unassuming as her wardrobe would permit. Gone were the blouse with its flowing sleeves and her sash emblazoned with the kingdom's royal seal. These were the armaments she normally chose—the ones that would command as much respect from her subjects as she could hope to find over her husband's booming voice. Here, subtlety was needed.

At the last moment, she decided to let her golden hair flow over her shoulders in a manner exclusively reserved for quiet nights with the family. With only her handmaid at her side, she made her way to the guest suites in the nearby tower.

Three raps on the door, and it gently opened. Asher's mother was hunched over as she pulled the door open as if uncertain about the protocol for the simple act. The queen found Simon seated at the table, ravaging the presentation of sliced meat and cheese before him.

"Dear mother," the queen said. "I should properly introduce myself. Please, call me Verity."

"Oh," Asher's mother said. "Lily. It's a pleasure to meet you."

"Would you mind joining me in the study across the hall? We should talk. One mother to another," the queen said.

With Lily at her side, the queen entered a room filled with books, tightly squeezed into every shelf and extending in stacks toward the ceiling. Lily scanned the room, gasping in a quick breath before breaking her trance and walking to the nearest shelf. She feathered her fingers over a book's spine and squinted at the title.

"I've always loved reading," Lily said. "Asher would never leave this room if he were here."

"Asher can read?" the queen asked.

"Oh yes," Lily said, still transfixed on the book spines. "I taught him myself. Now he teaches others. So few books in the village, though."

"I would imagine there are none. Is it not a crime to own a book without a license?"

Lily blushed and stuttered. "Heirlooms. Nothing that would require a license."

The queen sat at a table. "For as long as you're here, please feel free to read any book you would like. We can have this fire kept for you here. Please, join me.

"Tell me," the queen said as Lily sat, "have you heard from Asher, or do you know why my son would have wanted to take him?"

"No, Your Grace. We have never known anyone highborn, much less royalty. He was at his first day in the mines. Our king required every hand in the mines, and the tavern and the mill where he worked both closed. Times like these, naturally."

The queen absentmindedly twirled a coin in her hand, lost in thought. "Does he have any special skills that my son may have sought out—beyond reading and a heart surely as pure as your own?"

Lily looked quizzically at the table, her eyes moving toward the coin. "He is quite bright," she said slowly. "I say I taught him to read, but that gives me too much credit. It felt like I merely reminded him how. At seven years, he was already reading anything I could find. Taught himself numbers."

"Is that so?" the queen asked, leaning closer.

"We love the kingdom," Lily said, meeting the queen's eyes. "But despite the kingdom's blessings, coin is difficult to earn. For a time, Asher had quite the fortune with boxtin games. He could remember the cards and calculate when the numbers told him he'd be more likely to win. I never told his father when he won thirty silver and four gold the year prior. Stashed it away."

"His father wouldn't approve?" the queen asked.

Lily laughed. "No. Simon would think gambling just as foolish as reading and numbers. Forgive the man. I can't expect him to understand the value of anything not earned by suffering."

"Perhaps stash this away as well," the queen said, offering Lily the coin.

"I couldn't," Lily said, blushing.

"Please," the queen said, holding it out farther.

With a timid reach, Lily accepted the coin. She fumbled with it between her fingers, her movements clumsy. Verity observed as she tried to twirl the coin through her fingers as she did a moment ago. The queen concluded that Lily's attempted manipulation was far less deft than the finesse she had first demonstrated. "What do you think of it?" the queen asked.

Lily looked closely at the metal as it caught a glint of light from the fireplace. "It's beautiful. I haven't seen this before. Is it gold? Copper?"

"I'm not sure," the queen said. "What do you see on it?"

"I see a lion on one side. A dragon on the other," Lily said. "Wait..."

"Yes?"

"My eyes must be tired," Lily said. "The wings. The dragon's wings appear to move on the coin."

"Yes," the queen said, smiling. "A clever illusion. Please, keep it. My gift to you for enduring that awful cell."

The queen selected a few books she thought Lily would appreciate and bid her good night before returning to her chambers. There, she met the king's disapproving glare from where he sat at his writing desk by the fire. No books or ink sat before him. An empty glass rested by his hand, its sides still slick with ale.

"Guests of the queen?" he asked, his voice laced with skepticism as his fingers tightened around the glass.

"Indeed. I insist."

"The queen's mercy must not offend the king's command."

"Suffering and indignity. Do you intend to wring out truth like water from a rag?" she asked. "Far better to invite it with a smile and a glass of wine."

"And?" he asked.

The queen turned away to face the mirror as she twisted her hair back into its usual bun, her movements practiced and deliberate. She caught her own reflection—not of a queen, but of a woman who dressed the part and memorized her lines. She clenched her jaw as she lifted her chin, her voice as intentional as her reflection. "Nothing. She doesn't have the blood. The coin did not move."

CHAPTER 15

INTO THE HEART
OF SECRETS

Asher grimaced each time he swallowed, waiting for the sharp pain in his throat to subside. His thirst was indistinguishable from the pangs of hunger. He imagined drinking deep gulps of clear water from a mountain creek and promising never to want anything else again. He clutched his shirt with the charm underneath, begging for its intervention. Its embrace grew colder each time he reached for it. Asher debated whether the mint had gifted all it could to the charm or whether his circumstances were beyond the token's mercy.

His hand trembled as he withdrew it from his chest, his fingers grown numb and ghostly pale. He was tempted to blame the ailment on his need for nourishment and rest, but he knew both were unjustly accused. Asher's thoughts darkened with the realization that the charm was now exacting a heavier toll than the gifts it bestowed. Though rationality demanded he tear the charm from its chain and cast it aside, his craving for its deceptive promise gnawed at him more fiercely than hunger. Like long shifts at the tavern, he again found himself exchanging his vitality for necessity.

"Your path is leading us to the face of the mountain," Hunter said. "I don't see another trail leading around it."

Asher squinted in the setting sun at the mountain ahead. Hunter was right. Asher couldn't imagine climbing a mountain with such a sheer incline. Still, he looked closer—his eyes focusing on a blemish on the mountain's face. He quickened his pace.

"Two stones," Asher said, forcing the words from his dry lips. "Right by a cave. That's where we're going."

"You're sure?" Hunter asked.

Asher nodded.

Hunter's eyes widened, and he took bold strides. Asher found the strength to keep up. As they approached the cave, they found warped metal sheets bolted into the mountain, punctured by holes and rusted through. Faint letters appeared on the metal—too few to make out words. As he stepped into the cave, a humid gust of air breathed over his face. Dirt covered the ground, but Asher nearly lost his footing over it.

"What is this?" Hunter asked, scraping the dirt away with his shoe.

Asher stood over what Hunter uncovered. The floor had a dull sheen—as if it were made of the same metal as the sheets outside.

"Why would anyone come so far to put metal on the ground in a cave?" Hunter asked.

"We're testing young Asher, you see," said a voice from deeper in the cave. "To check if he's all he should be."

"Show yourself!" Hunter yelled, reaching for his blade.

Asher broke into a smile as the figure came into the light. "Lattice! How did you get here?"

Lattice stepped into the golden light from the setting sun that crept into the cave, a backpack snuggly strapped against his shoulders. "When we met, I thought at the start. You had a quick wit and a noble heart. Born for secrets, long hidden, rarely shown. You've earned the right to see what we own," Lattice said. "Our most sacred treasure will set you apart."

Hunter stepped forward, hand clutching the hilt of his stowed blade. "You speak in riddles! Speak plainly to your prince. The Apex Blade is mine to claim!"

Asher put his hand on Hunter's chest to hold him back. He could feel the prince's heart racing and his chest lunging as he breathed. "He's my friend, Hunter. Don't hurt him."

Lattice held his hands by his chest, and his fat fingers spread wide. "My prince, the blade is yours to claim. There is more to this quest. For Asher, his gift is the best. There is no need to complain."

Asher felt Hunter's muscles relax, and the prince stood silently for a moment. "So, where is my sword?" he asked.

"My role is not to deliver," Lattice said. "To the right lies the forgotten river. Drink from its flow and rest your feet. There you will find the prize you seek."

"I don't understand," Asher said, kneeling to meet Lattice's eyes. Lattice smiled and leaped behind him into the darkness.

His scurried footfalls carried in the distance until the cave fell into silence.

Hunter paced back to one of the two stones at the mouth of the cave and leaned against it, rubbing his eyes. "Do you know *every* woodland creature? What gift of the gnomes have they bequeathed to you? A left shoe and a dinted stein?"

Asher laughed and leaned against the opposing stone. "I have no idea. Probably nothing even that valuable. One man's trash is always a gnome's treasure, it seems."

Hunter began to laugh, and Asher laughed even more at the situation's absurdity. "Asher, my friend," Hunter said, gasping for air and wiping a tear from his eye, "for leading me here, you are hereby entitled to whatever the great gnome kingdom has deemed their prize."

Asher's cheeks flushed at the thought of earning his first noble title. *Friend*, he thought to himself, silently repeating the word until he could understand its meaning. It was a sword with two edges, each more deadly than the Apex Blade. He feared that by accepting it, he could inadvertently cut his hand. Asher grappled with the thought, torn between the sweet poison of hope that the prince was who he longed for and the bitter reality that one word was no proof. Nonetheless, the title beckoned him closer, even as part of him yearned to flee from Hunter's shadow and the labyrinth of his own selfish desires. One night held in the prince's arms felt as powerful an enchantment as the charm that smoldered like a dying fire on his chest. Both were killing him, and he didn't have the strength to part with either.

"Let's get to that river," Hunter said, pushing himself off the stone.

Together, they made their way deeper into the cave, following Lattice's path. As the light began to dim, the sound of rushing water welcomed them. With hands on the walls to guide their path through the darkness, they shuffled toward the sound. Ahead, glints of light began to appear. Asher thought it was a peculiar light—a blue hue that was neither like the day nor dusk. Basking in its growing intensity, Asher took his hands from the wall and found confidence in his pace. They turned a bend in the cave, and it opened into a splendid cathedral of blue-lit stalagmites plunging toward a gushing river that echoed around them.

They lunged for the water, crashing on their knees and cupping sips into their mouths. Asher bent down farther and dipped his mouth into the stream, sucking the water through his pursed lips. He stopped and looked up when he heard Hunter coughing.

"We need to slow down—it's bad if we drink too much too quickly," Hunter said between gagging coughs.

With his thirst's fever quenched, Asher began to survey the cavern. He estimated his entire house could fit within the cave and never touch the ceiling. He squinted and found the source of the mysterious light. He counted four pillars around the cavern, each with a torch burning blue. He glared into the searing light but saw no smoke.

"What is that? A door?" Hunter asked.

Asher looked in the direction Hunter was pointing, and he waited for the black splotches in his eyes to subside as he adjusted to the light. A dull, lead-colored door sat just on the other side of the river.

"A door into the wall of the mountain?" Asher asked as they waded through the knee-deep river to the other side.

Hunter traced his finger along the door's seams. Asher greeted the metal's cool touch with his palm, searching without success for a knob, lever, or lock.

"Here," Hunter said, pointing to an indentation in the metal. "This plate. It's in the shape of a handprint."

"Maybe it opens if your hand is the right size," Asher reasoned.

Shrugging, Hunter slowly placed his hand in the outline. With the roar of the river behind them, they stood in silence. Nothing. Hunter pulled his hand away from the plate and crossed his arms. Asher leaned closer to the plate and saw etchings of letters that still spelled words.

"Look," Asher said, pointing. "It says Manual Access Panel. The first letter in each word is underlined. You said I was your map, right? What if I'm literally the M.A.P.?"

Hunter scratched his head. "I am the rightful heir to the blade. It should open for me," he said with a fatigue that dampened the indignation Asher anticipated. "Try it, I guess."

Irritated by the prince dismissing his suggestion, Asher nonetheless extended his hand toward the panel. The metal began to vibrate. It started at his fingers, crept up his arm, and buzzed through his body. Clicking and latching. Whirls and grinding. The door began to move, first with a jolt and then with a steady glide, receding into the mountain's side and revealing a darkened hall.

Slack-jawed, they glared at each other. "You first," Hunter said, extending his hand.

Asher couldn't decide whether the invitation was because it was his reward to claim or due to the prince's reluctance to step alone into another pitch-black void. Ignoring the question, Asher took a few steps forward, keeping within the carpet of blue light that cascaded inside. After a few more paces, torches ignited and illuminated the hall, starting at the door and proceeding down the hall. The lights were like the ones in the cave, giving no smoke. Instead of a vibrant blue, the lights were bright, like a day under a cloudless sky.

"What is this magic?" Hunter whispered, taking tentative steps inside the hall.

"Let's hope it's lighting the way to your sword," Asher said, holding the lead as they walked down the hall. Asher jumped at the sound of the door whirring back to life and closing behind them.

"We're trapped!" Hunter yelled, running back to the door, his fist hitting the metal. The prince pounded in vain against the door, breathing in panicked gasps.

Asher turned away from the prince to look toward the unknown path ahead. "We haven't been able to turn back since we began," he said, finding a new strength in his voice. "We can't stay here and tarry in the shadows of fear. There's only ever the way forward. Stagnation is not our destiny."

Hunter held his head higher, his eyes ablaze. "You're right," he said. "For the kingdom."

"For the kingdom," Asher said.

Together, they moved down the hall. The lights buzzed like thousands of captured hornets in their nests. The air carried an acrid stench, like death's warning to the living. Asher thought it might be sulfur, as if the labyrinth had led to the depths of the earth under the mountain. They came upon a sharp turn in the hall. Asher pressed himself against the wall and warily stretched his neck to glimpse around the corner. The hall opened into a round room with walls that curved in long arches. Small lights, like candles behind glass, blinked and glimmered in swarms on tables and cabinets. A stage for no more than a single actor stood in the middle of the room, emblazoned in soft blue light from a twisted web of snakes hanging above it like a chandelier.

"Is it safe?" Hunter asked.

"Dead snakes. They don't appear alive, anyway," Asher whispered behind him.

Seeing no movement, Asher took tentative steps into the grand oval. He heard Hunter's footsteps close behind him. The blue light draping over the stage began to pulse and then flash as they drew near. Its cadence grew more frantic until the flashes appeared as a steady glow. An apparition began to take form in the light. A man's form. Deep wrinkles betrayed his age. Asher almost confused the form for his own grandfather, but the apparition was different. His eyes didn't carry the light of a smile, only the sorrow of burden.

"Who are you, witch?" Hunter asked, reaching for his blade.

"Very bad. Yes, very bad," the apparition lamented. "After

centuries of time for technological marvels, they still peg me as a witch! Good heavens, it seems my last visitor left quite an underwhelming legacy of enlightenment, didn't they?"

CHAPTER 16

THE ILLUMINOUS DR. PRIM

"What are you?" Asher whispered as the image of a man shimmered on the stage lit with a powder-blue glow.

"Certainly not a ghost or a witch," the apparition said, crossing his arms and looking away in disdain. "I am a hologram representing a man once known as Dr. Cornelius Prim. He and his colleagues created this bunker and designed the artificial intelligence that runs his program."

"What's a hollow gram?" Hunter asked.

"Does that mean it's weightless?" Asher asked.

Dr. Prim chuckled. "Yes, yes. Quite clever. Very weightless. It means I am an image that can move about on this stage, but I'm only made of light."

"But you're a person," Hunter observed.

"Why thank you, young man," he said, beaming with a smile.

"In my day, that was a controversial conclusion, but at least times have become somewhat more progressive than I first assumed."

"Where is my sword?" Hunter asked in a commanding voice.

"Yes, yes—the young man wants to play war. Only the weapon. Nothing more," Dr. Prim said as a dour expression took form. "Your sword is here. Other pressing matters. Not much time."

Asher surveyed the room with its rounded corners and bright lights. His stomach knotted, and he worried that his knees were no longer reliable enough to trust with his weight. "What is this place?" he asked.

"I so hoped you would already know," Dr. Prim said, looking quizzically at Asher. "You made it inside, didn't you?"

"I put my hand on the plate, and it opened," Asher said.

Dr. Prim rubbed his chin. "Let's consider it a fool's luck, then."

Asher's face flushed.

"I mean no offense," Dr. Prim said. "Judging by your attire, I'd assume we're still stuck in feudal times. Agriculture, but some industry. Not much. No, not nearly as much as I had hoped." Dr. Prim sighed. "Think of this as a library. Very old. Yes, yes. Older than your kingdom. Built during a great war to help any who might have survived. My job was to teach humanity how to rebuild. It isn't going well. Not much hope. Not much time."

"The war?" Hunter asked. "The fables are true? A great war that made the fields beyond so sick that men still die on them?"

"Myth and legend have no part in this," Dr. Prim said. "It's your history."

"How could I open the door? Where are the books?" Asher asked with a spark of intrigue suppressing his fear.

"Right! You are the one with a lucky palm," Dr. Prim said, punctuating his observation with a finger toward the air. "You have—Oh, how shall I explain it?—tiny machines in your blood. We call them nanobots. You got them from your mother. She got them from hers. So forth and so on. A thousand years of daughters came before you—a son. Lots of people had them in the old times. Now, very few. You might be the last. Very bad. Hard to say. You'll understand it all in a moment."

"Machines?" Asher asked.

"The kingdom forbids machines," Hunter interrupted, collecting the strength in his voice.

Dr. Prim stared with his mouth half open for a moment. "Most unfortunate. Explains quite a lot. Come, come. Boy with the hand. Place it there," Dr. Prim said, pointing to another plate like the one on the door.

"Why?" Asher asked as he took tentative steps to the plate.

"In olden times, I would have taken more time and been a patient teacher. Learn enough for today but not more," Dr. Prim said. "I wasn't meant to operate for so long. Over a thousand years now. Power is going to die. By the looks of it, you may need another thousand years to make a new battery."

"A battery?" Asher asked. "You eat bats for power?"

"Touch the plate. It won't hurt," Dr. Prim said, ignoring the question. "You have unprogrammed machines in your blood. They can do many things, but only one thing at a time. Always need programming. I will program your machines with all the knowledge here. Never tried downloading that much information in one brain before. Some data are corrupted. Very sorry. Very old. Things break. Should be enough. Yes, yes. You'll figure out the rest."

Asher turned and looked back at Hunter with his hand close to the plate.

"Wait," Hunter cautioned. "My father. He... he warned me that knowledge of some things is forbidden. Dangerous. The apparition even said it was corrupted!"

"Young man?" Dr. Prim asked, beckoning to Hunter. "Do you want your toy sword? If he consents, you must let him touch the plate. Otherwise, no sword."

Hunter pushed his chest out. "I am Prince Hunter Bracken, son of the king! You are within his realm, and you will do as I command!"

"Your sword is quite sharp. Very nice. You came all this way for it. Shame to never see it," Dr. Prim said. "Don't take too long to make up your mind. My power is draining quite quickly."

The aura of light around Dr. Prim buzzed and flashed with sparks of light as his image flickered. Asher looked pleadingly at the prince. "Hunter... all I ever wanted was knowledge. Knowledge could help us avert this war. I want to see. That's all! You told me I could have whatever gift the gnomes had for me. Please!"

Hunter glanced at the flickering image and then met Asher's eyes. "We tell no one. Just do it. Quickly!"

Asher felt another pang in his stomach, and he clutched the charm under his shirt. Dr. Prim's image flickered again, and the air smelled like an open field after a thunderstorm. Asher took one last glance at the image of the man whose fate was seemingly intertwined with his own, Prim with his battery and Asher with his charm. Before giving himself time to change his mind, Asher slapped his palm on the imprint.

In a moment that seemed to cleave him from time, a blinding radiance enveloped Asher, plunging the chamber into darkness as profound as a moonless eve in the ancient Thicketwood. Silence reigned but for a hiss that whispered secrets into his soul. Visions cascaded through his mind like a waterfall of shooting stars—numbers and words intertwining with half-forgotten tales, awakening memories buried deep within the crypts of his mind. Dreams of unknown faces, men and women whose stories melded with his own, and nightmares, more real than the darkest stories that would steal him from sleep, all began to flood through him.

Unblinking visions of steam and whirling turbines, great metal birds—no, airplanes—soared through the sky, and lights danced without flame or smoke. The magic of electricity. Images of strange devices—computers, rockets, and nanobots floated before him. Knowledge of the stars, of life itself—astronomy and biology—unfurled in his mind like an ancient, mystical scroll. In this maelstrom of knowledge, Dr. Prim, the master of forgotten lore, seemed to be expending his last vestiges of power to hasten Asher's enlightenment. It was as though the doctor himself was a conduit for the wisdom of the ages, channeling it into Asher with a force that threatened to unmoor his very being.

Caught in the liminal realm between consciousness and

dreams, Asher was assaulted with visions of apocalyptic destruction. Bombs, wrought from the very essence of stars, rained from the heavens, followed by a cataclysmic blaze and the silent, deadly descent of radioactive dust. Unable to blink or turn his head to spare himself from anguish, he saw the world wracked by famine and death, yet from these ashes rose the embers of hope. Survivors, their spirits indomitable, carved out a new path amidst the devastation. Mutations birthed strange new flora and resilient men and women, uncommonly short in stature, who thrived in the reborn wilderness. Gnomes. They were once humans.

As the cacophony of revelations ebbed, the hissing in his ears faded into silence. Asher's vision, once blurred by the torrent of insight, began to clear, returning him to the reality he had almost forgotten. Dizzily, he pulled his hand from the plate and immediately fell to his knees. He looked wearily at the shimmering hologram as Dr. Prim watched over him.

"Yes, yes. Still alive. No vomit. Very nice," Dr. Prim said. "Your mind will clear once the memories are all sorted. Won't be long."

"Asher?" Hunter asked, jogging over to steady him.

The prince's firm hand cupped over his shoulder. Asher welcomed it like a hand pulling him away from a cliff. "Yes... I'm fine. Just. It's just a lot."

"Quickly now," Dr. Prim said. "I have your toy."

Dr. Prim's image pointed to a cabinet near the wall that began to open. A shelf extended from within, displaying a blade made of onyx with a silver hilt. With one more glance at Asher, Hunter gently let go of his shoulder and paced toward the blade. His smile blazed in the blue-lit haze, and he approached his prize like a father to his newborn, love given only because it was his own.

"The Apex Blade," Hunter whispered, gently reaching toward it. He took the blade from its display and brandished it before him. It pierced the air with a whistle as Hunter nimbly maneuvered it in his hand. "The blade of my ancestors. If you drive it into the ground, the earth will shake. If you point it at an army, a bolt of light will cut them down!"

Dr. Prim cleared his throat. "Oh no. None of that. Just a sword."

Hunter stopped flailing the sword in the middle of what Asher thought was an imaginary battle and turned his head. "What do you mean? The blade can heal the wounded and inspire fear in the bravest of men."

"No, no," Dr. Prim said. "Just a sword. It's a special metal alloy, though. It can cut diamonds. Shouldn't break. And... it has a button!"

"A button?" Hunter asked, snarling.

"Yes—on the hilt. There it is. Press it."

Hunter steadied himself and pointed the sword toward the wall. After one more look back at Dr. Prim, he winced his eyes shut and pressed the button. The blade, charred black as night, began to glow a haunting red.

The prince studied the blade as its light filled the room, and the sword softly hummed.

"Lovely, isn't it?" Dr. Prim asked. "Very nice, very nice. No more tripping in the dark."

"That's it?" Hunter asked, his voice breaking. "The sword just glows? No powers?"

"Lovely to meet both of you," Dr. Prim said. "Door is open. Won't be able to close it. Come back any time. Many treasures are below. Last of the power now. Best of luck with humanity."

Before Asher could ask another question, the hum in the room clicked to silence, and the lights on the stage vanished. What Asher now understood to be computers began to blink off, their lights and controls falling dark. Only a few emergency lights weakly glowed, leaving them alone in a room forgotten by time.

Hunter sat beside Asher on the floor in the darkened oval room, letting the sword clank to the ground before him, its sound echoing despair. He held his head low. "Please tell me you're okay," he said, his voice barely more than a whisper.

Asher crumpled to the ground and struggled to find the right answer amid the swirling tempest in his head. His mind began to clear, the intensity of the experience giving way to memory. His bones ached, and his chest burned. He clutched the charm under his shirt to bear down against the labored convulsion in his gut. He caught Hunter's worried look.

"You keep grabbing your chest," he said. "Today and yesterday. What are you holding onto?"

The vise in his stomach began to loosen, but Hunter's words clung tighter. He lost his resolve to find a lie. "The witch gave this to me. A charm. It was supposed to keep me safe," Asher explained. "I was only supposed to use it for a day, but it helped me so much that I've kept using it."

"Helped you? What do you mean?"

Asher sighed and looked into Hunter's eyes. "It keeps me from danger. It helped me climb the cliff with the rope. I gave you the last of my water for the tea. I wouldn't have made it here alive if I didn't have it."

"Asher, let me see this charm."

With a trembling hand, Asher reached under his shirt and lifted the charm. Hunter leaned close enough that Asher felt his breath brush against his cheek as the prince twisted the charm in his fingers.

"Asher," Hunter whispered, "this is no mere charm. This is a powerful amulet that's forbidden. I've been told of such things. It robs from the soul. I can't... I won't let this claim your life."

"How do you know that?"

Hunter pursed his lips and looked away. "There are books. Forbidden books. My mother would let me read them. Father never knew. I remember reading about this charm. I saw the picture— etched in my memory only because Mother told me I'd have to run from it if I ever saw it. Too dangerous."

"I had to," Asher said. "I had to help you."

Hunter slid closer and draped his arm around Asher's shoulder, pulling him closer like a shield against the growing darkness. "You're too good, Asher," he said, choking back a sob. "You're too important for me to lose to a cause that was never yours to bear. A worthless sword and an impending war. I can't let you be another victim claimed by my selfishness."

Asher turned to face him. Hunter's eyes glistened as he held the back of Asher's neck. "I condemned you to forbidden knowledge after forcing you to join me. By all rights, you could have let me die in the sand pit or left my wounds untreated. I was so obsessed with finding this blade that I couldn't see the first person who sincerely cared for me when he didn't have to. I don't deserve you."

"No, you don't," Asher managed to say. "Friendship is a gift. Love... is a gift," he said, wheezing as he felt the amulet press like a weight on his chest. "If it was ever deserved or entitled, it wouldn't be real."

Asher gasped as another convulsion gripped his stomach. His lungs seized, and his throat tightened. Hunter wrapped his fist around the amulet and pulled hard, breaking it from its chain. Asher's world spun, his heart racing in a frantic, painful crescendo.

"Hold on, Asher," Hunter said, squeezing him in an embrace. "If I can't save you, I am unworthy of any title, sword, or throne."

"The pain comes in waves," Asher managed to say as he feebly returned the embrace, his body searing from the amulet's absence like a broken bone. "A moment and I can walk. We need to get back—back to the village."

But Hunter's hold only tightened, a desperate embrace so complete that Asher couldn't feel where his body ended and Hunter's began. As they seemed to meld from two into one, a solitary tear fell upon Asher's brow.

"In a way, I wear my own amulet." Hunter's voice broke. "A guise of strength, a mask of duty. It's a burden I bear to be what my father needs, to do what must be done. But it's not my truth, Asher, and it consumes me, hollows me out from the inside. No one... no one should endure this curse."

"You don't have to hide from me," Asher said, blinking out a tear but not certain it was his own. "I can't say my dad is much better—always wanting me to be his version of a man, wanting to boast to the other men about me when they brag about their sons' victories in sport or love."

"How do you do it? How do you manage to be yourself and avoid the curse of your father's expectations?"

Asher forced a smile. "Protecting his ego isn't my priority. I just see through him. He's scared of his own reputation among men, not mine."

"In my case, an entire kingdom depends on my reputation," Hunter said, looking away.

"How so?"

Hunter sat in silence. Asher thought he longed to speak, but a lifetime spent behind his mask held him prisoner. "The witch," Hunter said at last. "She told me that only one of us would return from here." His arms shook as if straining to hold back the tide of fate, and his voice became the graveled roll of a distant thunder. "I will prove her wrong, yielding to my own death before I will consent to see you suffer."

"Hunter," Asher said, attempting to quell the tempest within. As the final breath carrying the name left his lips, the room spun around him, and his muscles grew numb. Darkness enveloped him as he closed his eyes, his head cradled in the prince's arms.

CHAPTER 17

SPREADING FIRES

"Bishop's archers have amassed here, here, and on the western wall," Rosen said, his finger tracing ink-smudged lines on a weathered map spread across an oaken table in the diplomatic wing. "Arrows tipped with fire from the forbidden longbow have set homes alight in the outer boroughs."

"Have our archers reached the battlements in the towers?" the king asked, pulling the corner of the map closer to him.

"Yes, Your Highness. Their knights are still a distance out. Villagers are carrying hot tar to the men in the towers to run the murder holes. But our trebuchets are inoperable, I fear," Rosen said.

"Inoperable!" the king roared.

Rosen held his hands in front of him. "Aside from the gnomes, this kingdom hasn't faced war in over a generation."

The king heaved himself away from the table and moved through the crowded room of guards and diplomats. Queen Verity sat at the other end of the long table. Needing no map to see her kingdom, she considered the situation.

"Rosen," she said, "the western wall is the highest and best reinforced. Battlements at the gate are the priority."

King Bracken rubbed his chin. "We could empty all the ore meant for shipment to Bishop Falls at the gate—make a mountain for them to push through."

"My king," Verity said, "we would risk the rains washing away the only leverage we have for negotiation."

King Bracken pounded his fist on the table. "They do not seek negotiation! They seek our destruction!"

"Your Highness," Rosen said, looking away from the map, "they know the harvest has been poor and famine is soon upon us. I don't believe they would be likely to breach our walls when a short siege could be more deadly with less risk to their men."

The king glanced down at the map. "Indeed. No need to waste the ore on a wall they won't soon seek to breach. What of the tunnels?"

"We have no intelligence to suggest that they've been discovered. Knights could man them, but it risks revealing the locations to spies," Rosen said.

"Our knights are held in reserve," the queen said. "Could we use them to help quell the fires in the village?"

"We have the resources, my king," Rosen said.

King Bracken stalked the room like a caged beast. "No... We let the village burn," he said with a voice that prickled the hair on the queen's arms. "Seeing the smoke, the enemy may be emboldened to overplay their hand and attempt a breach. If not, then the kingdom can withstand the siege longer with fewer mouths to feed."

A hush fell on the assembled men and their queen. Conversations stopped in their places, and Verity took notice of the sound of fire lapping within the torches on the walls. "Your Highness," she began before she knew what to say next. "The flames that consume the village today could ignite a fire of dissent in the hearts of our people tomorrow."

The king reached for his ale. "My queen would have us host the entire population behind the castle walls. Dress them in fine silks and let them feast at our table. We must not conflate pity with pragmatism."

Rosen took a seat by the king's side. "My king," he whispered with urgency yet barely loud enough for Verity to hear, "the fires will spread. Thatched roofs in the boroughs will send the fire to the main square, likely even the upper houses—we're talking about thousands of lives."

"I take your counsel, and I do not question your loyalty," the king said, swirling the ale in his stein. "Better that they perish in fire's embrace than suffer the slow agony of famine. We fool ourselves into thinking there are any other options."

Rosen opened his mouth to protest, but the king cut him off with a wave of his hand. "You have given your counsel, and I have made my decision. We are at war. Time does not favor deliberation, and your station does not permit debate."

Queen Verity, recognizing the futility of further argument, shifted her approach. "What of our son?"

The king's face burned red, a tempest of rage growing in his eyes. "What son? The selfish child who abandoned his duties and kingdom for folly? The one who claims my name and betrays its honor? Let him meet the enemy on the fields. Perhaps in his last breath, he can discover honor by depriving the enemy of a single arrow. That would offer more service to Crown than he ever gave in life."

"Reginald!" Verity yelled, her chair tipping over and crashing on the stone as she leaped to her feet.

The king stood and braced his arms on the table as he leaned across it. "Let it be known. I renounce my son. Any person who gives him aid or comfort will be sent to the dungeons below!"

Fearful of the stranger in front of her, the queen gasped for air and stood frozen, unable to tame his raging fire.

"For hundreds of years," the king said, raising his voice, "this kingdom found peace in the Apex Blade. A weapon that inspired nightmares with its legend of bringing certain death to anyone who opposed its rule. Strength and fear kept the peace, my dear Verity! In its absence, wars will beget wars. Such is the folly of man."

"You confuse peace with fear," Verity said, regretting her words only after they were spoken.

King Bracken glared at her, but she did not recognize the man. "The queen's counsel is no longer desired. She will excuse herself. Otherwise, she can find a more receptive ear among the walls in the dungeons," he said.

The queen clenched her jaw and recovered her stature. In silence, she made her way out of the room and felt cooler air on her face as she walked down the hall. Reginald was not himself, she thought to herself. How could this be the man she met those years ago? Her mind reached into memory. The man she first met was heir to a throne, a fact she didn't learn until their second date.

She met him at the royal court, barely older than their son was now. She led the planning committee for a harvest festival, and Reginald came to volunteer, eager to help. He was dressed as unpretentiously as he spoke, giving no indication of the stoic rigidity that gave away any other highborn. They spent the afternoon planning seating arrangements for the highborn, delicately employing the most recent gossip to give a subtle touch to promote favorable diplomacy.

His eyes told her before he found the words. She knew he trusted her—looked to her for guidance and nuance. As they strolled along the castle walls in the waning evening air between summer and autumn, he casually mentioned that his father was the king. She glanced at his loose-fitting shirt and mud-stained shorts, balancing his lofty claim against his unassuming appearance, and thought he must be joking. But his invitation to his royal suite later that night confirmed the truth, and it came with his promise of honor and restraint. He proved himself to her as a man of his word on both accounts.

As queen, she presided over the court of equity—fashioning justice for the aggrieved when no royal decree would otherwise resolve the matter. *The burden of leadership is too heavy for one person alone,* she would tell him. There was a time when he listened.

Despite the queen's efforts over the years, she wondered whether the burden was too great for even two people. Resigned, she entered the royal chambers and did not sit by the fire with her selection of books. Instead, she departed from custom and headed into her own chambers. She peered out of a south-facing window. From this angle, she could not see the smoke from the village nor hear orders being bellowed out by her troops. But when she closed her eyes, the terror played out before her, nonetheless.

After her bath of lavender and rose, evening matured into night. She opened her door to her handmaid's familiar knock, soft as a bird's fluttering wings. The handmaid handed the queen a sealed envelope. Her eyes told the queen what her lips would not say. Verity nodded her silent thanks and took the letter to her reading table. Under the flickering light of a candle, she gently peeled open the envelope, breaking Rosen's wax seal. Her fingers delicately tugged out a note.

My queen, the note read, *there are many in the court who look to your wisdom even while bowing to the king's will. You have many friends here. I will go to the villages and help as I can. If your son should return, I will pledge myself to his safety.*

Verity held on to the letter for a moment and read it again before tossing it into the fire beside her. She watched it burn until that last ember of its hope charred to ash. She protected Lily's secret. While she accepted that the first act of dissent was her own, she would not relent to sleep that night as she considered that the next act could be beyond her control.

CHAPTER 18

A Secret You Must Always Keep

Asher blinked his eyes open. His limbs were too weak to move. No, he realized as he began to wake, the prince's embrace bound his arms. Hunter's chest pressed against his back, the prince's breathing steady and peaceful. In the dim emergency lights surrounding them, he saw the prince's shirt and jacket rolled under him, making the soft pillow that cradled his head.

A slight twitch of Asher's wrist was all it took. Hunter's breathing changed from soft and rhythmic to quick and choppy. "Asher?" he asked. "Are you awake?"

As the prince pulled himself up from the ground, a chill took the place of his arms. "Yes," Asher said, his head throbbing in painful stabs as he labored to sit beside the prince.

"Careful," Hunter whispered. "Not too fast. I refilled our water at the stream. We have plenty of food. You should eat a little— if you can."

"Thank you," Asher said, taking a sip from the canteen beside him, situated next to an assortment of fruits and dried meats from their rations. Asher couldn't help smiling, imagining Hunter laying out the offering like his servants might. Unevenly cut slices of cheese took a roughly spiral pattern on a plate. A smattering of crackers was piled nearby but without the same artistic flourish.

"We have a long journey today," Hunter said. "I found some more rope downstairs."

"Downstairs?" Asher asked, glancing at the prince as he reclaimed his shirt and pulled it over his chest.

"Not only rope. Medicine and spoiled rations," Hunter said. "It seemed like there were many floors beneath us, but I didn't want to be away from you for too long."

Asher rubbed his eyes and took a chance on a bite of the cheese. "Where are we going?"

"Back to the Canopy of the Elders," Hunter said, collecting more of his things.

Asher glanced at the Apex Blade, which the prince had dropped the night before. "We need to get back to the village..."

"It can wait," Hunter said, flashing an expression that Asher dared not challenge. "Let us hope that the Canopy can draw out the last of the amulet's poison. The village will need to wait while the Elders do their work." Hunter glared at the Apex Blade near his feet. "It's not as if I can do anything to help the village. At least I can help you."

"There's always hope," Asher said.

"I know you mean well," Hunter said, not turning from the sword.

Asher's fingers traced circles on his temples, reminding him of a tavern patron burdened by the remnants of the prior night's excesses. Thoughts clashed in a tumultuous melee, each vying for supremacy like drunken brawlers.

"What did it do to you? The corrupted knowledge?" Hunter asked.

It hurt when Asher tried to laugh. "Dr. Prim didn't mean it that way. For him, it meant some chunks of the data—the knowledge—were missing. It wasn't a moral judgment."

"And what was this *knowledge*?"

Asher thought about the question and searched for an answer like he was looking for a single strand in a spider's web. "The past," he finally said. "Technology. Machines. More than that, though." Asher struggled as his memories began to resolve. "History. How we got here, I think. A war. It's hard to explain. I can't sort them all in order. Once I focus on a memory, it's like opening a box to discover others within."

"Listen, Asher," Hunter said, holding Asher's shoulders. "No matter what, we must never tell anyone what happened here. The kingdom has no tolerance for such things."

Asher looked down at the crumpled coat serving as his pillow and the well-intentioned plate of food the prince had prepared. "No... I understand."

Hunter picked up the Apex Blade. "We just have this. The

fabled blade in all its glory," he said, limply pressing the button on the hilt to briefly illuminate it.

"What if the legend is still more powerful than the blade?" Asher asked.

Hunter snorted. "A glowing blade that can pierce a few knights is hardly enough to rain down fire from the skies and inspire waking nightmares."

Asher's head jolted, and a spasm twitched through his arms. "What if it could?" he asked, almost to himself.

Hunter lowered the blade and studied him. "It would solve the problem, but how do you propose we do that?"

"Gunpowder," Asher said, smiling.

"What is that?"

Asher pulled himself up. "It's an explosive. A powder meets a flame or spark, and then blows up into a fireball. You point the sword at it. Then we make it explode."

"And Bishop Falls would think the sword caused it," Hunter mused.

"It could work, right?"

Hunter rubbed his temples. "And where do we find this gunpowder?"

"We don't," Asher said. "We need to invent it again."

"And how do we do that?" Hunter asked, his shoulders sinking.

Asher looked at the floor and pinched his chin. "Potassium nitrate... Let's see. People once called it saltpeter. Best guess— we'd need manure from the stables. Charcoal from a low-burning fire—that would be the tavern. This cave has sulfur. I could smell it. Pulverize it all at the mill..."

"Please tell me that you have a plan to put all that together," Hunter said.

"I think I do," Asher said. "We need to sneak back into the village. The gunpowder will take some time to dry. We don't have much of that to waste."

Asher packed away the food and hoisted his bag over his shoulder. A sharp pain stabbed his back, and his left knee gave out, forcing him to fall into the prince's arms.

"We're not going anywhere fast," Hunter reminded him. "First, the Canopy. Then we talk about your plan."

The prince slung his travel bag over one shoulder before hoisting Asher's bag over the other. Together, they went down the corridor and back toward the hidden river. The ancient metal door remained open behind them. Asher took a deep breath. Now certain it was sulfur in the humid air, he considered where he might find its source.

"Lattice!" Asher yelled, his voice echoing into the cave. He and Hunter stood together, eyes searching through the shadows.

After a moment, Asher turned toward the sound of scurried footfalls. Lattice stepped into the light near the two stones at the cave's mouth. "You've found your way in and out, I had no doubt! And what about? Now the choices you make, oh, what is at stake! What path will you take?"

Asher kneeled. "Dear Lattice. You and your people know these mountains well. Have you seen steam rising from the ground? Perhaps by a pool of hot water?"

Lattice tugged at his evergreen vest. "In these mountains, we play and dwell. I know them well. Less than a day's journey to the vents and back, the directions I can tell."

"The kingdom is at war, Lattice," Asher said. "We have a plan, but I need your help. You will find bright yellow crystals by those vents and pools. I need as much of it as you and your kin can collect. We're headed back into the village. You can drop them off at the mill."

Lattice waddled over to the prince and tapped Hunter's shin with his walking stick, his expression carved from stone. "I won't do this for free, you see. A small request, in return, from me. Let my kind harvest in your realm with glee. And then, my help, you shall have plenty!"

Hunter scowled and glared at Asher. "If a kingdom is left after this war, I pledge to petition my father to permit your request personally."

"Works for me," Lattice said, heading back into the shadows deeper within the cave. They stood among the shadows until silence found them again.

"Asher," the prince said with a sigh, "if we survive this war, you're setting us up for another."

Lost in thought, Asher cast his gaze at the horizon. Like dominos in reverse, he considered the problem. Agriculture. Shortage. Improve yields. He thought of a machine. *What was it called?* A tractor. Combustion engine. *Won't work yet.* Refined gasoline. *Too* much carbon. Fine machinery. Factories. *Why not steam? Need to work out metallurgy before there's any hope of building a centrifugal governor.* First steps. Earlier than that.

Asher smiled as a sensible solution came to mind. "Our problem isn't the gnomes. It's shortage. I know how we can grow more crops. Improve the harvest. New ways will settle old problems."

"New ways might bring new problems," Hunter muttered.

"They did before," Asher said dreamily. "This time, we can see those consequences and adapt. Forethought. We can skip steps. No need to let ideas languish. In the past, lifetimes could pass before an idea found its use."

Hunter cocked his head and stared at Asher as he spoke. In his gaze, Asher glimpsed a reflection of his father's expression, a familiar countenance that often greeted the tales Asher recited from the books he and his mother cherished. It was a look steeped in layers, complex and enigmatic—like struggling to taste the nuanced notes of fruits and berries in a tea. He longed for a more discerning pallet. Was it the visage of a man entrenched in his ways, obstinate against the winds of change? Or did it betray a deeper shame, a veiled acknowledgment of one's own ignorance? His father's literacy went no further than the few words he recognized.

Perhaps the expression was a facade skillfully crafted to conceal simmering envy, a covetous longing for the words and wisdom contained in those pages. Could such a mask, so flawlessly worn, also serve to shield the vulnerabilities of doubt and fear? Asher recalled his father, a figure of stoicism, lingering near as he narrated stories during meals. Any interest was implied only by his complicit silence, yet he offered no hint of approval or enjoyment.

Asher wondered where Hunter learned the expression. From his own father? Could it be a silent pact, a wordless agreement where love and acceptance lie buried beneath layers of tradition and expectation? In this dance, Asher found solace and sorrow— solace in the unspoken acceptance and sorrow in the unbridged distance it created.

They elected to follow the same path back rather than risk unknown hardships along the second trail. Even in his condition, Asher was relieved to discover that climbing down the mountain took far less time and effort than climbing it. Asher pulled himself from his thoughts as they approached the cliff.

"We can drop the bags," Hunter said, tying the rope to the metal hook by the side of the cliff. "Do you think you can rappel down after me?"

Asher patted his hand on his chest, groping for the charm that once hung around his neck. "Gravity will get me down one way or the other."

Hunter pursed his lips and dug through his bag, pulling out a spare shirt. He ripped the sleeves off and began to weave each piece of torn fabric around Asher's hands. "Here," he said. "This should help you keep a grip on the rope."

Like a skilled mountaineer, Hunter grabbed the rope in his hands and walked backward off the ledge. The rope snapped taught and groaned under the weight. Nervously, Asher scratched at the knots holding the fabric to his hands. Slowly, the prince walked down the side of the cliff, passing one hand over the other as he made his way down. Asher took tentative steps toward the cliff to keep Hunter in sight. The wind whipped and howled through the prince's hair, and Asher's stomach tightened.

"Your turn!" Hunter yelled up after he leaped off the rope at the bottom.

Asher took the rope, and it gripped the fabric in his hands. Knuckles white, his legs shook as he walked backward as Hunter had, his feet pivoting off the cliff. The rope took more of his weight. He let go of his grip just long enough to match the time of his heart's skipped beat, and he clinched the rope again. He could feel the fabric loosening around his hands. In slow, jerky steps, he made his way down farther. The wind caught him in gusts. Strength came back to his knees as he found his confidence. Boldly, he pushed off the cliff with his legs and listened as the rope slid over his hands. Instinctively, he gripped tight and caught the face of the cliff with his legs as he swung back to meet it. One more jump, smaller this time, and his toes met the ground.

"Well done," Hunter said, helping him off the rope. "Very well done. Where did you learn that?"

Asher tugged the knots loose from his hands, heart racing. "I... I don't know."

Hunter began to say something, but Asher couldn't hear anything over the ringing in his ears. He wiped his nose and saw the blurry sight of blood on his hand. Head pounding, he lowered himself to the ground and strained to fight the darkness from taking him.

"Asher!" he finally heard the prince yelling, like a lifeline cast into the sea to bring him back from the choppy abyss.

"I'm fine," he said, the ringing subsiding. "I just need a moment to rest."

Branches cracked and snapped farther down the winding trail, like a false note in nature's symphony of bird song timed with the metronome of crickets announcing the coming dusk. Hunter drew the Apex Blade and stood in front of Asher.

"Something's coming," Hunter whispered.

CHAPTER 19

ONLY ONE
SHALL RETURN

"Announce yourself!" Hunter yelled into the wind.

Asher's senses sharpened, the taste of metal on his tongue as fear transformed into a rush of adrenaline, invigorating his weary limbs. He rose, leaning over Hunter's shoulder, his eyes piercing the twilight to discern the figure emerging from the shadows of stout pines along the graveled path that crept down the mountain.

"Put the sharp stick down, Your Heinie," came the voice.

"The Witch of the Forest," Asher said, gripping Hunter's shoulder.

"What is your business here?" Hunter asked, his grip unwavering as he pointed the blade toward her heart.

She pushed back the brown hood on her cloak, and her gray eyes glowed in the setting sun's light. "I'm here to visit an old friend," she said. "From the look of the blade in your hand, you two have already met him."

"You know Dr. Prim?" Asher asked as she drew near them.

"We have a history," she said. "I just needed the key to get in."

"You used me to get inside the vault?" Asher asked, balling his fists.

"No, dear. That's just a matter of perspective. Can't two things be true? I recognized your potential to receive a wonderful blessing," she said, bowing slightly. "Given that our prince now wields his treasured sword, I would have expected a bit more gratitude from each of you."

"Gratitude?" Hunter scoffed. "You deceived me about this blade. Worse, my absence could be misinterpreted as a declaration of war!"

The witch laughed. "I merely said it was the fabled sword. It is, after all. I never said it was magic. As for war, why blame me? Surely, you knew the consequences of leaving your post. It wasn't my job to remind you."

"But you did know this would happen. You *wanted* it to happen," Hunter seethed.

"Kingdoms rise and sometimes fall, particularly those that are unwilling to change. Would it be so bad if Bishop Falls prevails? They may be more accommodating to new ways of doing things, no?"

"How did you know I had the nanobots?" Asher asked, holding Hunter back.

Her mouth winced into a smile. "The worthless charm in your

pocket is more useful than I let you believe. Among its other uses, the coin responds to those who have nanobots in their blood. When you held it out to me, the image moved. It's a rare gift, Asher. Very few remain. Lucky indeed."

"How do you know of this sorcery?" Hunter asked, stiffening his arm to sharpen the sword's aim.

She sighed, and her gaze drifted toward the sky. "I haven't lied to either of you. I am immortal, you know. No magic tincture or spell. I have nanobots as well. Asher's have been programmed to give him knowledge. Mine were programmed to give me longevity."

Asher rested a hand on Hunter's arm, urging him to lower the blade. "You lied when you told me you'd grow old if I didn't make a wish."

"It was more of an exaggeration than a lie. I do get older—just slowly. I bent the truth to put you under my spell so I could set you on this path. You can't resist a chance to help someone, Asher. There's only one type of magic in this world, and anyone can practice it once they know what someone else desires."

"Did Dr. Prim let you live forever?" Asher asked.

She laughed. "No, sweet boy. Mine were programmed before the war—over a thousand years ago. Sadly, that prevented me from using them to open the vault. The vault's lock only opens to descendants without specialized nanobot programming—a most unfortunate feature the prince's great-grandfather contrived. It does, however, prevent that sword from killing me. I'd just stitch back together. It wouldn't be the first time."

A pit formed in Asher's stomach. "Why would you ever choose to be immortal?"

"Choose?" she asked. "Not all of us had nanobots—only the wealthiest people. After civilization's fall, necessity had a way of solving ethical dilemmas. Scientists used what tools they had—made some women's nanobots heritable. Other men and women were deemed *essential* and made immortal, like me. I was a doctor before the war. That choice was not given to me."

Hunter stowed the blade in its sheath on his belt. "Your journey is in vain," he said. "Dr. Prim is spent. His image died in front of us. He used his last breath to impart his corrupted knowledge into Asher's mind."

The witch sighed and put her hands on her hips. "Shame. I had hoped to discuss the resurgence of impressionist art with him—just your typical immortal banter. No matter. I'll see him another time."

"I don't understand," Asher said. "His power is gone forever."

"Fascinating," she said, rubbing her chin. "I gather you don't recall anything from after the war?"

Asher hesitated, straining to sort through his memories and the glimpses of knowledge imparted upon him. A blinding flash from a bomb. Scant memories of events after, more like clips of information without any order or connection. His head began to throb, and a sharp pain in his temple overtook him, making him wince as he held his hands over his eyes.

"What have we here?" she asked, moving closer to him. "Dark circles under the eyes. Nosebleeds. Gaunter than the last time I saw you, if I can believe it. What became of the charm I gave you?"

Hunter moved between them. "He wore that charm in secret. He sacrificed his body to serve my cause. You will not harm him again!"

"But the charm shouldn't have lasted so long," she said, ignoring the prince. "Unless... Oh, clever boy. Clever, clever boy. You noticed the mint?"

Asher nodded, his stomach churning at the thought of the charm. He rubbed his eyes to remedy the blur.

"Your prophecies are false," Hunter said. "Only one of us would make it down from the mountain, you said. Yet here we stand."

The witch flipped her hood back over her head and walked past them along the mountain trail. "Look at the boy. You're not off the mountain yet. I have no cure for his ailment. He didn't heed my warning. I only hope the charm hasn't taken too much."

Hunter took a step forward into her path. "Why was the sword in the vault? How did the gnomes get in to hide what they stole?"

The witch folded her arms across her chest, her eyes scrutinizing him as if he were a riddle to solve. "What lies have they told you? Your great-grandfather returned the sword to the vault. He knew better. He asked the gnomes to guard it, keeping people from finding the vault, much less the sword."

"Why would he do that?" Hunter asked.

The witch scoffed. "I suspect you'll need to learn on your own. You're too foolish to take any warning I may give you."

"Where are you going?" Asher asked.

She stopped and hesitated before turning to face him. "Our paths may cross again. You are in no form to fight or follow me.

And you, dear prince, have a raging war waiting for you in the kingdom. You are armed with a sword and a companion who has proven his loyalty to the kingdom and his devotion to you. Use both weapons with respect and care."

"We haven't much time," Hunter whispered. "Let's return to the fields and rest in the Canopy."

Together, they took to the trail as the witch continued toward the cave. Asher focused his thoughts on the present, allowing himself to be neither distracted by the past nor overwhelmed by the prospect of what the next day could bring. Asher's thoughts wandered to a song sung in the tavern by men who stayed until the last keg was dry.

In the heart of the kingdom, 'neath the tavern's dim light,
Songs are sung of brave souls, wandering through night.
O'er the mountains they travel, through the fallow fields they tread,
With the Watchers as their guide and the stars o'er their head.

Through the valleys and forests, with spirits so bold,
Armed with hope, more precious than gold.
They seek the truth, learning why the poisoned winds have blown,
Through the journey they find, a truth of their own.

Drink to the wanderers, in the tales that we sing,
Drink to the heroes and legends, and the hope they bring.
Drink to the kingdom, where the old stories flow,
Drink to these lost souls, bound closer than they know.

Hours passed in silence, their feet beneath them making the only sound. Under the silvery glow of the moon, the path transformed with such little warning that it went unnoticed. The harsh crunch of gravel yielded a tapestry of moist, softened earth and tender patches of starlit grass. Each step was gently muffled as if the ground sought to soothe Asher's weary feet. The night air, potent with the earthy perfume of pine and the damp, green scent of moss, carried its balm on the gentlest of a crisp breeze. In the embrace of the forest, whose towering trees coveted the moonlight, the symphony of the night began to unfold. Crickets serenaded from their hidden nests, each chirp a note in the endless melody of the woods. Fleeting sparks of light, reflections in the ever-watchful eyes of owls, flickered from the dark limbs of trees.

"We made it," Hunter whispered as if not to interrupt the chorus of the night.

Asher saw the Canopy of the Elders, its entrance marked by woeful trees bending their limbs at the mouth of the arched tunnel of translucent green as if their branches were too heavy to carry themselves alone. In this living vault, no branch stood alone; each wove into the next, making it impossible to discern where any limb began or ended. Their unbroken embrace reminded Asher of the prince's arms around him. Asher imagined that if one tree fell, the others would strain to carry their own weight for only so long before they could bear it no more. How did they find one another, he wondered. Was it planned to always be, or did they come to rely upon one another out of necessity?

As they ventured beneath the Canopy's verdant shelter, a surge of cool, invigorating air swept through Asher, filling his lungs with crisp vitality. It was as if a morning mist had been lifted from the landscape of his mind, bringing with it a clarity that washed away the fog of uncertainty. The knotted cords of tension in his neck unfurled. Asher pondered in silent wonder—had the mystical powers of the Canopy intensified, or was it his own need for its ancient blessings that had grown more desperate?

"We can make camp here," Hunter said when they reached the midpoint in the tunnel.

Asher sifted through his bag and began to roll out a blanket on spongy moss littered with fallen leaves and dirt. He did his best to brush away the debris and flatten the blanket's corners, forging a semblance of order amidst nature's uncertain whims.

"You should sleep in my tent again tonight," Hunter said, matter-of-fact, as he assembled the poles and tugged at the tarp.

"It's not cold in here. I promise I'm not going to die in my sleep," Asher said, trying to soften the prince's somber tone.

Hunter let out a slow breath, a hint of gravity in his demeanor that drew him down to the moss. He sat cross-legged and looked up at Asher as if to brace him for what was to come. An unspoken invitation hung in the air between them, drawing Asher in like an invisible rope pulling a heavy burden. Asher moved to sit across from him, accepting his summons.

"I envy you, Asher," he said. "Your eyes can linger on the men in the village. Mine are not so permitted. Were they, I would have hoped by some miracle to have let them search the crowds in the village to find you even a day sooner."

"What are you trying to say?" Asher asked, suspecting the answer.

Hunter dragged his hand over his glassy eyes, wet with unshed tears. "I give you my word to never look down upon you again. I beg you to never look up to me again. We stand as equals, as one—or not at all."

Moved by his sadness, Asher slid closer to put his hand on Hunter's leg. "I'll do my best."

"I want to hold you in my arms," Hunter said, his lips quivering unabashedly. "Tonight. Every night. It's selfish. I don't want to burden you with my disgrace—make you complicit in my shame."

"Shame? You're ashamed that you're gay?" Asher softly asked, seeking to cut through the layers of Hunter's heart, each more fortified than the kingdom's walls.

Tears fell with abandon, leaving trails down his cheek. The prince nodded and sniffled his confession.

"When I first met you, I thought you *hated* me," Asher said. "You were cruel."

"I know," Hunter said. "I tried to convince myself that I could never care for you. I've lived this lie for so long that I began to believe it. No other deception has been more convincing than the one I set upon myself. I needed to hate you so that I wouldn't hate myself. You were right about Gertrude. I was too narrow in my view to even see my own truth. From this day forward, I will aspire to match a measure of her bravery. I'm sorry, Asher. I'm so, so sorry."

Asher couldn't bear to look into Hunter's eyes. "I've kept something from you. About the witch."

Hunter rubbed his nose on his sleeve and cocked his head. Asher took a deep breath. "I knew about the impending war. The witch told me I could wish for anything if it was a wish just for me. I couldn't wish the war not to happen, but I thought that if I wished for you to... to love me... then I could avert the war."

"*That's* what you wished for?" Hunter asked as his eyes smiled through the last of his tears.

Asher returned the smile but only for a moment. "I'm worried that her enchantment makes you feel something you don't—like The Madness."

"Asher," Hunter began, taking time before he spoke. "She didn't give me a tincture nor cast any spell. She didn't even touch me with her cursed hands. She offered me a way to get what I've always wanted," he explained, examining the hilt on the sword."I just didn't know any better than her that you would be the only treasure worth finding."

Asher wrapped his arm around the prince's shoulder, and Hunter nestled his head into Asher's chest as if he were purging his self-inflicted poison out with his tears. "I forgive you, Hunter. I forgive you." As Hunter's sobs began to ebb, Asher gently lifted the prince's chin, offering a small, wry smile. "Well, there's one good thing about all this," Asher said. "If we're sharing the tent, you can use that sword to keep me safe from the spiders. I *really* hate spiders."

Hunter laughed and wiped his eyes. It was a genuine laugh, unburdened and young. It rang clear like a bell's first chime. Asher chuckled and squeezed Hunter's shoulder. "To be clear," Asher asked, "are you asking me to be your boyfriend?"

Hunter smiled and rocked up to rest on a knee, taking Asher's hand. "If you would be willing to have me, then I will let my father's castle burn to the ground if they will not accept us."

"Don't we have to save it from burning to the ground?"

"Well, yes," Hunter said. "But if they don't accept us, then we'll burn it again on our own."

His chest warm and heart racing, Asher urged Hunter to sit once more. "They won't make me wear any silly robes, right?"

"Never," Hunter said, smiling.

"Then, with an open heart, I accept your offer," Asher said, eyes locking with Hunter's. As if pulled by instinct or destiny, they leaned closer to one another. Asher closed his eyes and met tender lips against his own, the scent of cedar, the taste of wild berries.

An exuberance swelled within him, and he pulled Hunter into a warm embrace. No charm or amulet ever made him feel as safe or as fortunate. If one moment could last a lifetime, he wished it were this. Of all the memories that flooded his mind, both from his past and those he never knew, this was the only one he was determined to cherish.

"I guess this means that the witch was right," Asher whispered in Hunter's ear. "We started the journey as two but returned as one." If ever the first sparks of love were worthy of a song remembered well into legend, Asher already heard its melody in the sound of their hearts beating as one.

CHAPTER 20

BENEATH THE
SHADOWED KINGDOM

Asher opened his eyes as dawn's first light crept through the seams in the tent, casting its soft, golden glow on the blankets. His mind struggled to discern dreams from reality, his own memories from those imparted to him. Safe in Hunter's arms, he smiled with the assurance that his sweetest dream was no dream at all.

"You're awake?" Hunter whispered lazily.

Asher squeezed Hunter's arms closer to his chest. "Yeah—not sure I want to move quite yet."

"Do you still feel the amulet's absence?" Hunter asked.

"No, not that," Asher said, smiling. "I just like being held in your arms."

"Good, because I never want to let go," he said.

Asher's smile broadened, but he couldn't say why. He laced his fingers around Hunter's and drew his hand to his lips, softly kissing it. "That said, we should have taken the opportunity to bathe in the river when we had the chance."

Hunter laughed. "I'm glad you're doing your part to keep me humble."

"We have a kingdom to save," Asher said, yawning and gently separating himself from Hunter's embrace.

Asher unbuttoned the tent's drapes and winced in the morning light. He climbed out and stood under the trees. Where once the Canopy had thrived with its vibrant green leaves, now stood a solemn tribute of withered brown leaves covering the moss and bare branches above. He felt a profound gratitude for the sacrifice mingling with a sense of loss. Brittle and lifeless branches swayed in the breeze above him, reminding him how unworthy he was to take all their riches.

Would they ever bloom again, or had mankind once again stolen nature's treasures to pay for their indulgences? Was it a gift of mercy, freely given by the Elders, or did his very presence force nature to bend toward his will? Thoughts of past plunder, oil, timber, choking smoke, and rising seas flooded his memory.

"Don't worry," Hunter said, standing beside him. "Hope remains. Life is as determined as it is resilient. We call them the Elders because they're wise. They give no more than they can. We will let them rest now. One day, they will return."

His assurance was of little remedy as Asher mourned their sacrifice. "I feel like I took too much from them."

Hunter wrapped his arm around Asher's waist and followed

his gaze across the Canopy. "I can't measure how much of their grace was given to you and how much was given to me. I've never told a soul before you. I carried that burden for so long that I grew accustomed to the weight. I thought the secret kept me safe, too distracted to notice it robbing my soul as it exacted its payment."

Asher smiled and gave him a gentle kiss. "I can't imagine how hard that was to endure. Just think how much stronger you've become because of it."

With newfound strength, Asher helped pack their bags. Together, they tied strips of cloth around their faces, preparing to endure The Madness just beyond the Canopy. Silently and quick-footed, they passed through the tall grass and bogs. Strange fears and dark thoughts still crept into Asher's mind. Anticipating the enemy, he acknowledged the thoughts and let them pass without letting them take root. Understanding their source was a remedy to avoid their traps and snares. Like a fire deprived of air, the thoughts subsided, leaving their path through The Madness clear.

They took a respite under the midday sun with a picnic of dried meat and cheese. Face red with laughter and his hand held in Hunter's gentle fingers, Asher was brimming with a warmth that made up for the tepid touch of an autumn sun.

Hunter stretched out on the grass, looking toward the sky. "After this war, you'll be feasted at the castle. One dish will follow the other until you forget what it was ever like to be hungry."

"As long as there's no frog," Asher said as he stretched out and observed the same sky.

"Frog? Never," Hunter said, laughing. "Too gamey. Disgusting."

"Good," Asher said with a grin. "One more bite of it, and I'd probably croak before the frog did."

"Then we will ribbit from the menu," Hunter promised as Asher groaned.

As they packed up for the last bit of their journey, a foreboding anxiety began to grow. *Have we languished too long in service of our own desires at the expense of the kingdom's needs?* A weight returned to his shoulders, heavy as the great walls of the kingdom itself. Glancing at Hunter, Asher found the same expression burdening his boyfriend's face. The unasked question lingered between them as they hiked on in silence.

Gradually, the open plains on the outskirts of the kingdom began to roll into familiar hills, the last of which would give them a sweeping view of the towered walls and ancient castle in the distance beyond. His pace slowed as they approached it, uncertain whether he wanted to see.

"Just a bit more," Hunter said, taking long strides up the hill. Asher followed behind.

On their hands and knees, they breached the top of the hill and looked over the horizon under what remained of the day's fleeting light. Black smoke billowed from within the walls. A line of trebuchets formed to the right of the kingdom's walls. Beyond them, ranks of Bishop's archers. Horses strained to position other enemy trebuchets along the distant horizon, drawing ever closer to the walls. Far enough away to be spared the harrowing cries of war, Asher watched as arrows glided silently through the air and over the great walls into the village. Suddenly, a trebuchet snapped forward and launched a flaming mass over the wall and deep into the unseen village within. Seconds later, the springing thud from the launch echoed to them on the hill.

"It could be worse," Hunter finally said, voice steady.

"Worse?" Asher asked, unable to mask the anxiety in his voice. "The village is on fire! There are hundreds of archers. Where are the kingdom's knights? Why aren't we fighting back?"

"You just have to know what to look for," Hunter said, not taking his eyes from the horizon. "The main gate hasn't been breached. The enemy is holding back their own knights. There is no belfry. No battering ram. No ladders. It's what you don't see that's important."

Asher's mind unlocked new knowledge of military tactics, and the battlefield took on a new meaning. "They mean to hold the kingdom under siege. No means to get in or out. No trade. No food. They wait for us to die, and then they will breach the walls."

"Exactly," Hunter said, turning away from the battle to gaze toward the other end of the walled city.

"How can we sneak past them and get into the village? I don't think our odds of just walking through the main gate will be so good."

"Good news. It appears that they don't know about our secret tunnels. Look over there," Hunter said, pointing toward the closest of the walls. "See the small hill about a quarter mile from the wall?"

"Yes," Asher said, squinting through the setting sunlight.

"We go there. Earth and grass cover a hidden door. Once night falls, we climb down there. It takes us through a narrow tunnel, opening in the tavern's basement."

"There was a secret tunnel in the tavern all this time?" Asher asked, dumbfounded.

"It wouldn't be a very good secret tunnel if you knew about it," Hunter said, flashing a casual smile.

Asher thought about it for a moment. "It's perfect. We need to get to the tavern anyway. We'll have a long night ahead of us."

"Does this have to do with the crystals you sent that gnome for?"

"Absolutely," Asher said. "His name is Lattice. If we prevail, you will have him to thank. Gnomes are proud people. They respond better to respect than threats and belittlement."

"In that case, I will do well to remember his name," Hunter whispered.

"We still need a lot of ingredients, and we'll have to improvise with whatever tools we find," Asher whispered.

The ever-fleeting days gifted them a short wait before the castle's long shadows blended into darkness. They made their way down from the hill and ran toward the mouth of the tunnel, crouched as they moved to take cover from any scouts. Hunter slowed as they approached. He gripped the hilt of the Apex Blade in its sheath and stealthily crept around the hill, his head cocked to the side to catch the slightest sound.

Asher watched, hearing only the distant commands being shouted to archers. Glimpses of flames caught his eye as burning arrows dipped behind the towering walls. Wood smoke and hot tar tainted the air.

"It's safe," Hunter said as he ran his fingers over the side of the mound. Finding a latch, he wedged open a hidden door, its hinges protesting. Ducking his head and placing one foot into the tunnel, he motioned for Asher to follow. Once inside, Hunter lowered the door, taking care to make as little noise as he could, and latched it closed. Darkness overtook them.

"Maybe use the button," Asher whispered.

He heard Hunter give a resigned sigh, and the tunnel flickered in red light as he held the glowing blade in front of him. Unable to fully stand, they stayed hunched down and moved through the tunnel, their feet splashing in puddles of water that filled divots on the ground, the sound reverberating down the narrow passage. Wooden beams angled and braced the earth above them every few feet, and long, distorted shadows danced beside them as they moved. Asher could taste the stale, earthen air that lingered wet on his skin and coated his throat with each labored breath. Driven by fear that the tunnel would collapse with the slightest budge against the jolting wood slabs, he quickened his pace. The wood creaked as he ran by neglected, rotted slates. A clump of earth fell on his face. He brushed it off with his sleeve, leaving an oily streak on his cheek.

Abruptly, the tunnel narrowed, forcing them to move in a single file with Hunter in the lead. The walls, slick with moist earth, closed around them, scraping their arms. The air seemed to compress, and Asher took deep gulps of it as he shimmied on his side farther down the passage. Too narrow to move more than one careful step at a time, the earth tightened its grip around them.

Hunter paused, his blade casting a red glow on a rusted hatch embedded in the ceiling above them, its edges encrusted with dirt and age. Asher's heart skipped a beat at the sight. With trembling hands, Hunter set down the blade and reached for the hatch, his fingers struggling to find a latch on the slate. Asher held his breath as Hunter pushed his fingers in the narrow crack around the hatch and pulled with all his might.

"Won't budge," Hunter said, still straining to open it. "Meant to open from the inside. It's for people to escape the village, not invade it."

Asher squeezed closer, his body pressing against Hunter. He took the sword and pressed its button, examining the hatch in the light. "I see the hinges on this side," Asher said. "That means the latch is on the opposite side. Prim said this sword is made from an alloy strong and sharp enough to cut through diamond."

"You're right," Hunter said, accepting the sword. Carefully, he slid the blade into the crack where the latch should be. He urged the blade up. It moved easily, and the crisp sound of metal snapping echoed around them. Hunter pulled once more on the hatch, and the rusted hinges creaked as the door opened, flooding the chamber with light from above.

"At least the fires haven't spread this far toward the center of town," Hunter said, pulling Asher through the hatch and onto the cellar floor.

"Shh," Asher mouthed, pointing to a glimmer of light creeping through gaps in the floor planks above them. "We're not alone."

CHAPTER 21

THE TRAP

Taking deliberate steps to avoid a creaking plank on the cellar floor that could betray them, they moved toward the stairwell leading up to the storeroom. Asher remembered the layout as clearly as he knew his own home. He climbed to the top of the stairs and pushed gently on the door. Hazy moonlight cast its glow from a window in the barren storeroom, and muffled voices filtered in from a distance.

"It's coming from the back room," Asher whispered. "Let's get closer."

"Closer? Can't we just take what we need and leave?"

Asher dismissed the question and snuck into the main hall in the tavern after assuring himself the voices were coming from elsewhere. Some chairs were stacked on tables, while others lay broken on the floor. Dying embers cast their glow from the fireplace, and the main door was plastered with planks of wood nailed into the frame.

"Whoever's here must have barricaded themselves in," Asher whispered, pointing toward the door to the back room. "That's where the voices are coming from."

"I should go in first," Hunter said. "One quick stab before they even see me."

Asher held up his hand. "Wait, I know those voices. They can help."

"Careful," Hunter said, grabbing his arm. "War confuses friend and foe."

"All the more reason to talk," Asher said. "If we confuse our neighbor for our enemy, then the war is already lost, and we have nothing to fight for."

Light streamed out from under the door to the back room. Asher placed his ear to the door but couldn't make out the hushed conversation. Swallowing, he placed his hand on the knob and slowly pushed the door open.

"Asher!" came a voice.

"Shafer! Rosen!" Asher said as he walked into the candlelit room.

"If anyone were to come here when I have no food to serve nor coin to pay, I should have suspected it would be you," Shafer said. "You were always my most dedicated employee."

"Where have you been?" Rosen asked. "The Crown believes that the foolhardy prince abducted you, squandering the king's legacy and..."

"Look no further," Hunter interrupted as he entered the room.

"Your Highness," Rosen said, falling to a knee and bowing

his head. Shafer clumsily rose from this chair, using the table for support. Despite his notoriously troublesome knees, he managed to kneel.

Hunter smiled. "Please rise. Are you friends of Asher?"

"Yes, Your Highness," they said in near unison.

"Then you are friends of the Crown," Hunter said.

"Your Highness," Rosen began, head still bowed, "I apologize for my tongue. War is upon us. I've had little food and less sleep."

"I would never condemn you for speaking the truth," Hunter said. "I only take issue with your facts." Hunter drew the Apex Blade from his scabbard and held it above his head. "Our mission was to reclaim the sword of my ancestors. The weapon to end all wars."

"The Apex Blade," Rosen gasped.

"Behold!" Hunter said, pressing the button on the hilt. The sword began to glow, setting the room ablaze with its ruby light.

Asher rolled his eyes as Rosen and Shafer stood in awe. "Anyway," Asher said, "we need more than the sword of his ancestors to stop the war. That's why we're here."

Shafer stood at attention, wearing the same expression he'd adopted right before he reached across the table to take all of Asher's gambling chips. "If either you or our noble prince should need anything I may offer, it is yours... for a modest 'post-war' fee, of course."

"Thank you, Shafer," Asher said as Hunter returned his blade to his side. "I need to clean the hearth and take manure from the stables."

"By the Watchers!" Shafer said. "You're telling me that the kingdom's salvation rests in you doing your chores at the tavern?"

"What possible advantage can be had with ash and manure that the Apex Blade cannot already offer?" Rosen asked.

"Right now," Asher said, "they're two of the most important things in the world. Sometimes all you need is a shovel and a strong stomach."

"Your Highness," Rosen said, "I will not question the Crown's wisdom in these affairs, and so I do need to warn you. Our king is enraged by your disappearance at such a sensitive time. Whether by anger or official proclamation, he has disowned you, calling for your arrest if you should ever be found."

Hunter unflinchingly stared at Rosen. "Once the sword lays waste to the enemy, my father will beg for my forgiveness just as those who stand against will me beg for my mercy. Tell no one that we are here."

"Yes, Your Highness," Rosen said, bowing slightly.

Shafer cleared his throat. "In service to the Crown, I will offer you the apartment upstairs if you need a place to rest and prepare. No charge. None at all," he said, eyes fixed on the sheathed blade on Hunter's belt. "The boy can sleep in the stables, naturally."

"Asher will be by my side, always," Hunter said. "You will afford him the same loyalties you bestow on me."

"Thank you, Shafer," Asher said. "We have a lot of work to do."

Asher returned to the main dining room with Hunter following behind. He knelt beside the giant hearth, deep and wide enough for ten men to stand within, took an iron by the hearth, and gently prodded the unkempt ash within.

"What are we looking for?" Hunter asked.

"Here," Asher said. "See these dark pieces of burnt wood under the ash?"

"I do."

"The hearth's fire always burns so slowly because Shafer never has people clean out all the ash. It deprives the wood of oxygen. That causes a chemical reaction that makes this into charcoal. We need to collect as much of it as we can."

"You mean to tell me that we could silence more of the archers' bows if only the good innkeeper had set more potatoes to boil?"

Asher gave him a dismissive glare before lunging deeper into the hearth.

"What's charcoal?" Hunter asked, pulling a few chunks of it out.

"It's everything," Asher said. "It burns hotter and longer than wood. We can use it in medicines. It purifies water. Mix it with soil, and the ground holds water longer. One day, we can use it to make steel."

"The kingdom forbids that alchemy," Hunter whispered. "Steel production was outlawed generations ago."

"It's a tool, Hunter. It's not a curse. We can teach them. Imagine gleaming cities with soaring buildings. Imagine strong metals that can tear through the earth and do the work of twenty farmers with only one. Food for all our people. If you want to ban something, criminalize the ignorance that forbade it."

"Who can convince my father?" Hunter asked.

"Me. I can. I have all the answers locked inside my head," Asher said as he angrily harvested charcoal from the pit.

Irate, Asher stopped himself from elaborating. His hands moved swiftly, shoveling ash onto the floor with a frenetic energy that gave him an outlet for his mounting frustration. Beside him, Hunter worked in contrast, his movements deliberate and measured. Each scoop of ash seemed to underscore a quiet disapproval, a wordless critique. The prince's silence hung like a palpable presence that spoke louder than any words could. It could have been a merciful gift, a chance for Asher to temper his rising ire. Yet, beneath Hunter's calm surface, Asher sensed an undercurrent of caution, a subtle admonishment that perhaps he was overreaching, demanding more than what might be wise or possible—to succeed where others had failed.

"What's next?" Hunter asked, his voice listless.

"Great job," Asher said, trying to barter praise in exchange for his apology. "We can bag this up later. Let's get started in the stables. We'll need two empty barrels from the cellar."

Before leaving for the night, Shafer unlocked the rear entrance to the tavern and left Asher with the key. Together, he and Hunter rolled wooden barrels that once held the season's wine to the stables behind the tavern. As he set a lantern near a stall in the stables, Asher was overwhelmed by the putrid stench of manure. Still, in the early hours of the night, he took comfort in being among the horses. Their slick coats and graceful eyes fixed upon them.

"This is repulsive," Hunter said. "Who would ever suffer the indignity of cleaning up after these beasts?"

"Me, for one," Asher said as he worked to cut small holes in the bottom of each barrel. "I did this for a few months when the stable boy was hurt. I needed the extra coin. Fortunately, it doesn't look like the stable boy was quite as diligent as I was."

"You had to do this? How many jobs did you have?"

"As many as it took to help my family," Asher said, handing the prince a shovel and taking one himself. "We're similar in that way. From what you've told me, I think your sacrifices for your family were no less unpleasant."

Hunter looked at the manure for a moment. "Honestly, this may be preferable. What do we need to do?"

"We'll get rid of the top layer from the manure pile. What remains has been stacked here with straw for at least a year. Probably longer," Asher said as Hunter heaved his shovel into the mound. "That's good. We want as much organic decomposition as we can. We'll shovel the manure mixture into each of the barrels and then pour water into each one. Water will filter through the mixture and then drain into the trough."

"What's that good for?" Hunter asked as he scrunched his nose and plunged his shovel into the mound.

"The decomposition creates salts that the water flushes out and collects. Some of those salts are called potassium nitrate. That's what we want."

"How do we get the salt out of the water, then?" Hunter asked.

"Boil it. The water goes away, and the salt remains. We can add some ash to it while it's still hot to help purify it. Or at least I hope it will," Asher said. "We might need to do it a few times to purify it. Let it cool each time."

"How long will this take?" Hunter asked.

"I'm not entirely sure. A night. Maybe two. We can see how fast it drains. Can't add too much water all at once. We can take breaks. Work in shifts. One of us can add water to the barrels while the other collects wood for the fire so we can boil it afterward."

"What does this salt do?" Hunter asked.

Asher's mind became a hive buzzing with thoughts and ideas. "We can use it to make better fertilizer. Spread it on crops to improve yields. Imagine celebrating the war's end with fireworks— colored explosions in the sky. Different shapes and patterns."

Asher went on to explain all the uses he could recall or imagine. Hunter looked on with passing expressions of bemusement and apprehension. Silence eventually found them as they focused on the task at hand.

When the barrels were nearly half full, Hunter took a break, leaning on his shovel. "You know, Asher, I'm here to support you. You hold all the world's knowledge, but what of its wisdom?" he asked. "Think of the Elders. They only give what they can. Otherwise, they would be spent and never bloom again. I worry that you're taking too much of this responsibility on yourself without counting the cost—like what you did with the amulet."

Asher gave a weary smile. "I know, Hunter. It's hard. I may be the last person to ever hold all this knowledge. I'm not immortal like the witch. I only have so much time to teach everything I've learned."

"I can help," Hunter said. "This requires nuance. Even if my father can be persuaded, our people won't so easily leave the old ways."

"I appreciate your offer. I know I'll need it. I just can't ignore the weight upon me. I always wanted to learn about the world. I thought it would free me. Now I fear this knowledge was a lure to a snare I can't escape. I may walk alone for some parts, even when you're still by my side."

"Just promise me you won't get yourself lost in this," Hunter said, eyes solemn.

"I promise," Asher whispered in his ear as he gently hugged him.

CHAPTER 22

OF BRAVERY AND SURRENDER

A bitter wind whipped the queen as she tugged at the flowing fur jacket around her chest. The royal gardens had begun to wither, even before the first snow. She mourned for the lilac and canary florals whose colored vines so recently clung to arches. Plump green bushes faded to hues of white and rusted orange. *Have hope*, she thought. *Do not surrender too soon.* How cruel that a season of time should demand such a sacrifice. She brushed her fingers over withered and lifeless vines that crept over the garden's gate. She offered a forlorn smile as her tribute, confident that no winter would be too harsh to bear. Spring flowers would bloom as if in defiance. *I have suffered, but I have not succumbed.*

Rosen sat alone in the neglected garden, his face blanched of color. Fine lines tracing a lifetime of smiles marked the passage of time on his face. The queen saw them as gradual harbingers of age, but Rosen's face seemed stricken with a burden that outpaced his time.

"Thank you for meeting me here, my queen," Rosen said, kneeling.

The wind gusted again, scratching dead leaves over the stone as the queen walked nearer. "The gardens are the emptiest this time of year, when there is no need to tend them. They have already surrendered to what is to come."

"There is hope, my queen," Rosen said as the queen sat on the bench beside him. "I dare not bring this news to our king without first seeking your consultation."

"Go on," she said, leaning in.

"Your son has returned with the village boy. He now bears the Apex Blade."

The queen's eyes widened. "You saw this yourself?"

"Yes, my queen. I do fear that madness has taken them both—clouded their judgment," Rosen said, lowering his voice to a whisper barely louder than the breeze. "Our prince could end the war on this very day. He could slay the armies and instill a fear that would be passed down for generations, yet he does not."

"Why?" the queen asked.

"The village boy has him convinced that victory demands that they collect burnt wood and manure from the stables. Our prince was always of sound mind. Now, this? They even share a bed at the tavern in the village."

"Is that so?" the queen asked, her gaze drifting.

Rosen leaned in. "We could send our knights to surround the

tavern and take the sword in the night. Our most trusted men. They could keep the prince safe until the war ends and our king's temper settles. Our king could wield the sword of his forbearers and do what your son's poisoned mind cannot."

Queen Verity smiled and turned back to look into Rosen's eyes—eyes that seemed to yield before the battle had begun. "My dear Rosen... *love* is no poison. My son is wise not to share his plan, but that does not mean he doesn't have one. It takes a keen eye to see what is unsaid. A mother's eye always does. It always has."

"Scores of villagers are without their homes, camped just beyond the castle walls. Our stores have not been opened to them. They will panic. Riot. We have less time than I fear we need. I beseech you—let me have the sword reclaimed!"

"Absolutely not, Rosen," she said. "That sword was entrusted to the prince for a reason. What was his to claim is not ours to steal. Not a word to the king. His wrath would be beyond any knight's best defense."

"But, my queen..."

"Enough, Rosen," she gently said. "My husband's temperament has driven him to madness I can only hope to cure with time. You know as well as I that his quick vengeance and anger will not bring peace, even if it brings victory."

"Are we to do nothing?" Rosen asked, his cheeks flushing.

"Quite the opposite. Tell no one. Keep an eye on them. Help them if you can, but do not interfere."

"And when the king learns of this deception?"

Queen Verity narrowed her eyes. "I will blunt his rage, and

then he will endure my own. A mother will defend her son with a ferocity that would make battalions of our bravest knights quake in the shadows, where death becomes their best hope. Only woe betides anyone—bearing spear, sword, or crown—who comes between me and his safety. *Trust him*, Rosen."

"But..."

Verity stood and wrenched her fist around her long coat, pulling its tail from the bench. With long strides, she took the marble stone path back to the greenhouse by the gardens. She pushed the glass door with her hand, keeping her pace, and it sprung open, banging as it met its end against the wall.

Without speaking to any of the passersby in the long halls or the grand stairwell, Verity made her way up to the residence wing. Her pace slowed as she arrived in the rotunda at the top of the stairs and proceeded toward the guest wing. Gently, she opened the heavy oak wood door to the library and found Asher's mother exactly where she expected her to be.

"My Queen," Lily said, dropping the book in her lap to the floor by the fireplace as she stood.

"Oh, Lily, there's no need for those theatrics. You're a guest in my home. Please just call me Verity."

She flushed red. "Of course. So sorry."

"What are you reading?" Verity asked.

"*The Hymn of the Poisoned Fields*," Lily said, reciting the title like a stanza in a poem. "It's about brave men in the past who set out to explore the world beyond and fell to the Poisoned Fields beyond the kingdom. The Crown was wise to forbid such things."

"Yes," Verity said, sitting next to her on a velvet green sofa, "the line between brave and foolish is often drawn based on whether a person survives the quest."

"Have you any news about our boys?" Lily asked.

Verity considered the question. "I may. In fact, I think they are quite brave."

Lily covered her lips with her hands as she gasped.

Verity gently touched Lily's knee. "Their safety demands a mother's resolve. We must not tell anyone—not even Simon or the king."

"Of course," Lily said, nodding as a joyful tear slid down her cheek to reach her smile.

"I need to impose a few questions upon you to help keep them both safe," Verity explained. "Tales often pass through the generations. Lore. Does your family have any such legends?"

Lily stiffened, but her eyes quivered. She pursed her lips and shook her head. "No, my queen."

Verity leaned back on the couch. "There was a time—many years ago. Families who were thought special. Peculiar or... unique. The Crown hunted them. Legends say they were imprisoned in this very castle. Some were banished. Worse, even. Have you heard those stories, Lily?"

"I have," Lily said, her composure faltering.

"It was all true," Verity whispered. "Those times have passed, but the danger remains. The Crown believed there were no such individuals left. I believe we both know that isn't so."

Lily turned to glare into the fire as it crackled nearby. "My mother. She's not actually... my mother."

Verity leaned in.

"She is a very, very great aunt of mine," Lily explained. "My real mother passed when I was quite young, so she raised me. She was so disappointed when Asher was born, and I could not give birth to another. Daughters are needed to keep our line, she'd say."

"Did she explain why?" Verity asked.

"Only in riddles," Lily said, turning back to face the queen. "The Watchers wanted her to live such a long life to help bring light back to the world when the time came. When Asher was born and I could not get pregnant again to birth a girl, she said the time must be soon."

"You have trusted me, so I will trust you," Verity said. "Our king must not know, but I've learned that our sons look upon one another with an uncommon affection."

Lily laughed. "You mean they're gay? Yes, I know Asher is. Simon would prefer him not to be, but he cares more about a man's work than the company he keeps. I just want him to be happy."

Verity smiled as the tension left her shoulders. "I should want the same for Hunter. My husband would forbid it. Just as your line may end with Asher, ours could end with Hunter. But in our case, it could end a government based on hereditary rule. This knowledge could be dangerous—for both of them."

"I will never say a word," Lily said. "Still, truth has a way of coming out. If this affection is love... love makes one foolish."

Verity clenched her jaw and sat straighter. "All the more reason for us to be on guard—to help keep this knowledge a secret. Your son's life may depend on it as much as my own."

CHAPTER 23

THE WEIGHT OF A TITLE

"How has your skin not fallen off yet?" Hunter asked, examining a rash on his own forearm.

Asher laughed. "It's not that bad. Soap is expensive. People just make it strong enough to last."

"If our knights use this to bathe, their skin will grow thicker than armor. Do you have a better soap recipe in your head?" Hunter asked.

"Too much lye, I bet. But perfecting your bath routine is a bit lower on our priorities," he said with a smirk.

"Speak for yourself, babe," Hunter said as he carefully slid his arms into the shirt that had been drying by the fire while he bathed.

Asher smiled at his growing list of royal titles. *Asher, the Friend to the Crown, Boyfriend of the Prince, and Babe of the Kingdom.* He raked his fingers through the barrel of crystals, the product of two nights spent boiling water, cooling it, filtering, drying, and repeating the process.

"This should be enough," Asher said.

"I'm glad. We can make this faster than the horses can supply the materials."

"You're catching on," Asher said, hugging Hunter's shoulder.

Just then, the back door creaked open. Instinctively, Asher held his breath before hearing the *clump, clump* of Rosen's distinctive walk. "Just in time," he told Hunter as he headed for the back room.

"You two look better rested today," Rosen said, removing his coat and draping it over a table.

"We got a lot done," Asher said. "But I will need a favor."

Rosen sighed. "Naturally. How may I assist the prince's... well, what is the nature of your relationship with our prince?"

Hunter walked into the room, buttoning his shirt. "He's the prince's boyfriend. I thank you in advance for your service, Rosen," he said dismissively.

Rosen opened his mouth but hesitated. "Your Highness," he said, bowing his head.

Asher unrolled a map of the kingdom on a table. "Given the Crown's disfavor and the fires in the lower village, we need safe passage to Grayson's mill. We must take what we collected here in a wagon carried by one of the horses in the stables. We can hide in the wagon if you can manage the reins."

"You want me to help you deliver horse manure and burnt wood?" Rosen asked.

"It's not manure," Hunter said. "We cleaned it. It's necessary for the war."

"Your Highness, archers surround the kingdom with knights on their way. Their siege will starve the village. Respectfully, how can manure, however clean you should make it, ever rebut the tips of their arrows and swords?"

"It's not merely burnt wood and manure. Asher brokered an alliance with the great gnome kingdom. They're bringing pink crystals," Hunter said.

"An alliance? With the *gnomes*?" Rosen said. "Shouldn't the king be informed?"

"I will prove my honor with deeds, not words," Hunter said. "You will not share this with anyone."

"I understand," Rosen said, resigned. "I will prepare a cart and saddle a horse."

Asher and Hunter nailed a lid on the barrel of crystals and filled two potato sacks with charcoal. Gently, they rolled them to the stables. Rosen, after some protest, helped them hoist the barrel into the back of the wagon. With barely enough room for the two of them, Asher and Hunter squeezed themselves around the cargo and pulled a burlap tarp over themselves. Within a few moments, the horse began to move, and the wagon jolted forward, bouncing unforgivingly over stones and branches.

With a final bump, the wagon found smoother terrain and picked up speed. They must have reached the same well-trodden road Asher would walk when he left the tavern for the mill or the other way around. It was as worn with footsteps and the regular cadence of horseshoes as it was with his memories. He didn't need to peek from the tarp to know when they passed by the road to the lower village, toward his home. The sloping hills with trees bearing their fall leaves appeared in his mind—burnt orange, fire-scorched red, and lemon yellow. In the summer, the ancient tree at the fork in the road would bear its red berries.

Trees were not always so, he thought. There were no such berries in the times forgotten. No trees with healing wisdom. There were no gnomes. What survived the war only did so by adapting to a new world. Change presented a stark choice—adapt or die. He considered whether his own war against the old ways would demand such a sacrifice from the people. *Could accommodation be given to those who took solace in walking familiar roads? Or would the foolhardy and brave rob them of their choice?* His mind answered his question with another. *Should anyone be given the choice to walk through muddy roads just to come home to an empty pot where life is only promised to be so short and cruel?*

With his argument unsettled, the wagon drew toward a slow stop. The horse shook its head and jangled the reins. Asher leaned against the cart's side and lifted the tarp just enough to see the mill, still fixed and unmoving.

"Whoa there!" came a familiar voice. "The mill is closed. No grain."

"I am here on the Crown's business," Rosen called out.

Asher whipped the tarp off and lunged over the crate. "Mr. Grayson!"

Mr. Grayson smiled and put his hands on his hips. "I should have known."

"It's a lot to explain, sir," Asher said. "I... er... the Crown will require the use of your mill. Not for grain. Minerals. It's for the war effort. We won't break anything. Only need it for the day."

"I don't suspect you'd be willing to give me any more information," Mr. Grayson said, peering up from the official diplomatic license Rosen offered him for inspection.

"I can't. I just need you to trust me," Asher said.

Mr. Grayson looked up at the stilled arms of the mill. "I'm not using it anyway. I'll be up at the house if you should need anything."

Asher thanked him and waited as the mill owner climbed back up the path to his home. Deciding that he was far enough away, Asher tugged the tarp off the cart, and Hunter scurried inside the mill. Rosen and Asher followed behind with the barrel and bags of charcoal.

"I've never seen a mill before. Just drawings," Hunter said, marveling at the structure built beside a brook.

"This is the future of civilization," Asher said, spreading his arms and beaming like a child witnessing his first snowfall. "The wheel outside catches the water as it flows. The water forces the wheel to spin, and that spins this horizontal shaft. The rotational movement of the shaft is converted with these gears to make another shaft spin vertically. That shaft turns the millstones in this box, which mills grain down to flour!"

"It smells damp," Hunter said, grazing the wall with his hand.

"I share our prince's enthusiasm, Asher. Why have you brought us here?" Rosen asked.

Asher barely heard the question. He followed the long, horizontal shaft with his hand and saw visions of what it could be. "This same concept will kick off an industrial revolution. Wire. Magnets. We could even make electricity."

"What is he talking about?" Rosen asked.

Hunter shot a warning glare at Asher. "You know these people from the lower village—they have their own vocabulary for things. I don't understand half of it either," the prince said.

Asher thought for a moment and smiled. "Lattice?" he asked softly. "Are you here?"

The familiar sound of the gnome's wooden shoes clacking against the floor crept into the room.

With his eyes fixed on Rosen, Lattice stepped into the light. "I've come as I said before, your request I did procure. I was unaware that another from the Crown would stand at the door."

"Thank you, dear Lattice," the prince said, squatting before him. "You have done a service to your prince and the kingdom. I have not forgotten my pledge. In fact, I mean to prove my honor." Hunter drew the Apex Blade, and Asher flinched as the blade pointed toward the gnome. "War claims too many before they can fulfill their promises," Hunter said. "If my fortunes will not permit me to bestow this honor later, I will do it now. I, with the Apex Blade of my forefathers, hereby knight thee, Sir Lattice."

Hunter took great care to gently tap the side of his blade on each of Lattice's shoulders. The gnome stood still for a moment before resting himself on one knee.

"Dealings with the Crown always end in dismay. What slurs offered as titles for my kind in the past, I do not wish to say. A hearty meal, our only plea. Yet with this honor, I will kneel at its decree," Lattice said.

Rosen grabbed Asher's arm and pulled him aside. "You bring

the prince here to grind manure, and he stains the Apex Blade by giving title to a gnome? What sickness has overcome your minds?" he hissed in Asher's ear.

Asher jerked his arm free. "There are things you don't know—things you can't yet see! If you don't trust my words, then you can witness my deeds. By the end of the day, you'll know *exactly* what I mean. If you want that sword to spill blood so much, then touch me again!"

Rosen held up his hands and backed away. Asher's heart began racing, his mind spinning. He fought against the instinct to move, to kick the back of Rosen's knee and use the momentum to land more blows in quick succession to a certain end. Asher looked at his fists, having never used them to fight. Yet, he knew he could if called upon. The idea sent a cold chill over his arms.

"Asher?" Hunter asked for possibly the third time.

"Uh... yeah?"

"Now what?" the prince asked.

"Right. Now we open that box—the one that houses the mill-stones. We grind each ingredient separately. Let's start with the charcoal."

Methodically, they set about their tasks as the day stretched into the early evening. Rosen helped without needing to be asked. Lattice cupped handfuls of the ground dust from the mill back into the burlap bag, each scoop no more than a teacup. Asher was relieved that no one questioned him when he explained how dangerous it was for the ground ingredients to mix too quickly. Lattice found a long rope and soaked it with Rosen's help in a vat of water mixed with the powder. The paste clung to the rope as they stretched it out to dry.

Asher took a small grain bag from the back of the mill and gently scooped two handfuls of the blended powder inside. He tied it closed and placed it gently on a worktable by a window, watching it in reverent silence.

"So, this is what we've been working toward?" Rosen asked as he wiped the sweat from his brow.

"I believe so," Asher said, carefully lifting the bag to judge its weight.

"Great. What's next?" Hunter asked.

"Has the fire pit been lit?" Asher asked.

"It's ready," Rosen said.

Asher cupped the bag in his hands and drew it to his chest, closing his eyes for a moment. "Fine, then. Now we must test it. Rosen—tie the horse and its carriage to the other side of the mill. Tie it as tight as you can!" he instructed. "Lattice, please stay inside. Watch from the window upstairs. You two should join him."

With everyone in place, Asher opened the door and stepped into the crisp night air. There was no breeze, as if the wind was holding its breath. Twenty paces out stood a fire with flames gently lapping the air. Asher took the bag in his hand, and it felt heavier than a moment before. He took a deep breath and tossed the bag into the fire. As it arched toward the flames, he bolted back into the mill, slammed the door, and spun around to the window by his side.

A second passed. Then another. Without warning, the night erupted with a deafening bang that tore through the stillness, as if one world had ended and another had begun. A wave of heat overcame him, unabated by any protection from the rattling glass in the window. The once-tamed fire became like the tongue of a fabled dragon as it bellowed into the air. Too frightened to breathe, Asher fought to shield his eyes from memory—a memory of another flame that ended history and reduced the world to ash and death.

Asher looked up the stairs, his ears ringing and his heart pounding. Rosen turned from the window, mouth agape. "Asher, what evil have you birthed into this world?"

CHAPTER 24

SMOKE AND EMBERS

Tears welled in Asher's eyes, but he didn't understand why. They crept outside and inspected where the fire once burned. In its place, charred earth stained the ground, and bits of wood like shrapnel lay scattered around them. The horse whinnied wildly in the distance. Thin wisps of smoke took the place where flames once burned.

"I'm sorry—I'm so, so sorry," Asher wept in Hunter's arms.

"Shh, it's okay. We're all fine," Hunter whispered in his ear.

Hunter's arms gripped him tighter, holding him back from despair that sought to consume him in his memory of the flames. The fire kept burning over and over. His memories mingled with those that were not his own. Bellowing flames, reaching into the clouds and raining down poisoned ash, burned so bright in his mind that he squeezed his eyes shut and pressed his knuckles against them.

"What *was* that?" Rosen asked as he squatted by the pit and combed through the ash with his fingers.

"It was a weapon," Hunter said with a steady voice. "A weapon to end a war and to still the hands of others to ever wage another."

Asher tried to find words, but he was overcome by feelings he could not explain. Shame, fear, and futility mixed like the components of his bomb, erupting inside him, leaving him too devastated to take solace in anything beyond Hunter's embrace.

"That was barely two cups," Rosen said, eyes wide and wild. "You have almost a full barrel still inside."

"Asher! Asher!" Mr. Grayson bellowed out into the night as he stumbled down the hill toward the mill.

Asher wiped his eyes and put on a brave face. "It's okay, Mr. Grayson," he called out. "We're all fine!"

The mill owner strained against his own momentum as he approached the fire. "What was that sound?"

Hunter hastily stepped forward and drew the Apex Blade from his sheath. "Good sir, do not long fear the war. I have returned with the blade of my forefathers."

"Your Highness," Mr. Grayson gasped, dropping to a knee.

"You've heard of the Apex Blade?" Hunter asked.

Mr. Grayson stood. "Yes, my lord. Only tales. It can command nature herself—rain lightning from the heavens and shake mountains from their mooring."

"That's right," Hunter said. "We needed to come to your mill—to test it. Learn how it works. Harness its power. What happened here is a preface to the justice it will deliver to our enemies."

"It is my honor to host you, my lord," Mr. Grayson said, bowing again.

"We need to get this back to the tavern before it grows too late," Hunter said. "We have a war to end tomorrow."

The air carried a burnt scent that fields had long forgotten. Asher looked out over what remained of the fire as the others retrieved the barrel. He didn't need to impress upon them how essential it was to carefully move the deadly barrel into the wagon. Lattice and Rosen cautiously wound the dried rope into a spool and settled it beside the barrel. With darkness as their cover, they abandoned the tarp.

Lattice climbed into Asher's lap. "In one hand, a tool; in the other, a blade. To think it controlled is a dangerous charade. What's harmless to one, to another brings pain. To wield even with care is to court disdain."

"I know," Asher whispered. "We can be safe. Then we'll never need to use it again."

"It's folly at best, a naive undertaking. For the ripple effects are far beyond your making."

Asher pursed his lips and looked toward the stars. Silently, they steadied the barrel as the horse began returning to the road. In less time than Asher expected, the horse came to the fork in the road—the last choice to go one way or another.

"Knights are riding ahead," Rosen called back to them. "We will take the longer way, down toward the lower village."

The wagon lurched as the horse took a sharp turn at the fork. Asher held his breath as he caught the barrel before it rammed against the side of the cart. As they steadied back into a manageable rhythm, Asher looked to the road ahead, expecting the dip that would reveal his favorite view of the village. From the top of the hill, the houses below would be lit in the golden glow of a setting sun, casting long shadows that climbed the kingdom's distant walls.

He poked his head a bit higher, hoping to catch the twinkling candles in homes being set for dinner. Instead, darkness cast its unbroken shadow into an abyss. With only the light of stars, Asher could see wisps of smoke rising from where thatched roofed homes with well-tended fences once stood. He thought of his parents in the house that leaned on its neighbors as much as they leaned upon it.

As they rode closer to roads ever more familiar, he craned his neck, hoping to catch a glimpse. He didn't need a sign to tell him when he reached his own street. Asher rose to rest on his knees and peered around the horse, his breath quickening. The winding street had only burnt frames of homes to line it.

"Mom!" Asher yelled, bolting out of the cart and running toward a thicket of smoldering fires and skeletons of wood holding up what little remained. Counting the houses, he came to the one he called home. Its red door hung from the hinges.

"Mom? Dad!" Asher yelled, wading through ash and broken beams, the acrid scent of smoke lingering in the air.

"Asher!" Hunter called from behind him.

"Mom!" Asher yelled into the kitchen. Tears found their way to his cheeks once more, and he fell on his knees beside a pair of boots, untouched by flame.

"Asher!" Hunter said, running to him.

Asher took the boots in his arms and held them to his chest.

"Surely they got out first," Hunter said, draping his arm around him.

"No," Asher sobbed. "These are my father's boots. He'd never leave without them. If there was one thing he'd take, it'd be these."

"Why?" Hunter asked, holding tighter.

"No boots, no work. He had to work. He always had to work," Asher said, his words trailing off into sobs.

Hunter stroked the frayed leather on the boot. "Then bring them with us because he'll need them when we find him," he said.

"I have to find them," Asher said, rubbing his nose. "It's my responsibility to keep them safe! If I never left, they'd be safe. It's my fault, Hunter—it's all my fault."

"You didn't send lit arrows into innocent families' homes, Asher. We both know who did," he said. "Why must you see the world as a mirror and not a window? You're not responsible for fixing everything any more than you're liable for causing every terrible thing that happens."

"My grandmother. We need to find her. She's not far," Asher said, pulling himself up.

Hunter folded his hands around Asher's neck and gently pulled him close. "We must not linger here. We shouldn't have this salt so close to smoldering embers. When we get back to the tavern, I will dispatch Rosen to search every street, every house. We will find your family and make sure they're safe."

With legs as unsteady as the burnt frames around him, Asher followed Hunter back to the street. Asher's path was a penance, each step a weighty testament to a sorrow that seemed to bleed into the earth. He took one last look behind him, lingering over the remnants of his past, the sum of his choices smoldering behind him. Hunter''s words resonated like a bard's tragic refrain: We both know who did this. The mantra summoned a swelling rage. This inferno of grief and fury sought retribution and a reckoning, a storm of righteous indignation that yearned to sweep over the kingdom's walls and consume the heartless, craven enemy just beyond.

Once back at the tavern, Asher and Hunter stored the gunpowder in the stable. Rosen borrowed a horse and rode hard back to the lower village in search of Asher's family. Lattice took to his knightly duties and insisted on staying near to contribute what he could in the battle to come.

Asher climbed the stairs at the back of the tavern and made his way to the roof. He looked out over the edge toward the village below. Distant shouting in the streets echoed up to him. Burning arrows sailed over the walls in the distance. Their cadence was slower than two nights prior. He thought of it as a drizzle—unsure whether they foretold a coming storm or whether they were the last drops of one spent and passing.

"Here to survey the field before the war?" Hunter asked, sitting beside him.

"Not so much," Asher said, looking toward the stars. "More interested in seeing how peace can come from such ruin."

"My father would say that peace is kept by fear. You would say that is no peace at all."

"What do you think?"

Hunter sighed and matched Asher's gaze toward the heavens. "I think it's like nature. Peace and war pass like seasons. A summer's day is lovely, but do we not wait for the heat to break? And when it does, do we not complain about the snow? If every day were temperate, would we not miss the palette of fall's splendor?"

"We complain about the weather, but at least we usually survive it," Asher said. "Do we not owe people our best effort to avoid our past mistakes?"

"We do," Hunter said. "You're a map. You can lead us to a peaceful future where we adopt new ways to feed more people and improve lives. Let that knowledge blunt the severity of our seasons but not the certainty of their coming."

Asher smiled and rested his head against Hunter's shoulder. "I finally know what they are—the Watchers," Asher said, pointing to the sky. "They called them satellites. Micro-fusion reactors power them. They can spin around the planet almost forever."

"What do they do?" Hunter asked.

"They used to send information down from the skies and receive it from the ground. They could make paintings of the earth from a point higher than the Blue Mountains—see us from a different perspective."

"What do they do now? Silently call out to people who cannot listen?"

"I suppose so," Asher said. "I fear that our journey will be no different."

Hunter smiled. "For a time. One day, we will learn to ask them what they know. Seems odd that they glimpse us so fast, passing only a few times each night. Such a waste."

"It is odd," Asher said, drawing himself away from Hunter's embrace. "Some satellites would stay fixed in one spot. Others would travel the globe like these, unseen by day. Hunter, we may not be the only survivors."

Hunter shook his head. "Nothing lives beyond the Poisoned Fields."

"Those fields may have been poisoned once. Now? Too much time has passed. Just like your sword, the stories may not be so."

"Then hope remains for Gertrude and Ruth," Hunter said. "Let tomorrow be the last of this war. Then we can send explorers to discover what may reside beyond the edges of our maps. Hopefully, they can rescue them both before they consign themselves to an unnecessary fate."

Asher found Hunter's hand as he shifted his gaze back to the stars. The warmth and firmness of his grip brought Asher a comfort he hadn't felt before. Solace enveloped him, drawing from the prince's unwavering confidence amidst his own uncertainty and borrowing strength in his moments of weakness. He pondered if this was what Hunter meant—a partnership where rage met compassion, courage rebutted fear. Nestled under the cold embrace of a cloudless night, teetering on the edge of war and peace, a wave of gratitude washed over Asher. Though he faced a profound abyss of uncertainty, the darkness was no longer an endless journey he traversed alone.

CHAPTER 25

A Hero Worthy of His Title

Rosen returned to the tavern before sunrise. His slumped shoulders and weary eyes spoke of his failure before his words confirmed it. Asher was relieved to know his grandmother's house still stood, even though there was no trace of her inside.

"What's the plan?" Rosen asked.

Hunter gripped the sword in its sheath. "We worked it out last night. Your part is simple. Bring us to the kingdom's gate. After passing through the gate, draw the horse and cart to the first oak by the hill to the right, near the entrance to the mines. It should be far enough. Asher and Lattice will be covered with the barrel in the cart."

"Once you get there, unhitch the horse from the carriage and ride as far away as you can," Asher said. "Hunter will try to negotiate with Bishop Falls. If that doesn't work, a spark from a flint stone will light the fuse, and the rest you can imagine from what you've already seen."

"Prudent plan," Rosen said. "Our archers report from the towers that the enemy is marshaling away from the gate today, likely to reposition their arrows to find more homes to burn. They would never expect us to open the gate."

"We must ride with haste. There is no time to waste," Lattice said as he scampered past them and hoisted himself into the cart.

"Well said, Sir Lattice," Rosen said. "I do fear for leaving you so exposed. Won't they see you beyond the gate?"

Hunter smiled. "I'm counting on it. You heard our esteemed knight," he said, climbing in the cart.

Rosen took the reins, and he and the horse brought them over familiar roads, down to the lower village and toward the city's main gate. The cobbled streets were deserted, save a few villagers walking aimlessly through the ruins at day's first light. Asher sat in silence as the cart drew nearer to the gate.

They approached the gate's grand doors, which climbed higher than the tallest house in the village. The imposing doors were sealed shut. Massive timbers lay securely in their latches, holding the doors closed. This was the first time he had ever seen them shut.

"This will do," Hunter said, calling to Rosen.

The horse came to a halt, and Hunter gave Asher a quick kiss before leaping over the side of the cart. He strode casually toward the guards at the gate as if inspecting the knights in formation as

Asher had seen him do in a parade. As the guards took notice, he stopped and slowly pulled the Apex Blade from his belt. The onyx blade, dark as a starless night, stood in stark contrast to dawn's golden light.

"Guards of Barbshire, loyal and brave!" he yelled. "I am Prince Hunter Bracken, son of the king and bearer of the Apex Blade! It has been recovered to end this war and the suffering it has brought our kingdom," he said as some guards whispered among themselves and others prostrated themselves before him. "Open the gates of Barbshire, and I will set my blade upon the enemy's throats!"

"Your Grace?" one of the guards called out.

Hunter took another deep breath to carry his words. "The Apex Blade of my forefathers is the bringer of death, author of nightmares. I command you to open the gates, and I will set myself upon our enemy!" he yelled, pressing the button on the hilt.

The guards gasped at the glowing blade, and those still standing in confusion's grip met the ground with their knees. The lead guard started to shout his orders to the men. Horses were hitched to ropes that pulled the timbers off their latches. The beasts neighed and whinnied, strained and pulled. Slowly, the timbers began to lurch from their latches, and the splintered crack of wood announced the great doors' parting. Light from the rising sun flowed in through the widening passage.

Hunter leaped back into the cart. "Ride!" he commanded in a voice that rang so clear Asher thought the horse took its order from the prince rather than its rider.

Asher and Lattice gripped the barrel with all their strength as the horse galloped at full stride into the open fields beyond the gate, littered with spent arrows and abandoned encampments. Rosen stopped the cart at Hunter's command. The prince sprang out and slapped the cart, signaling Rosen to ride on to his designated stop by the caves.

Asher angled around the barrel to see the prince, his hair dancing in the wind and his sword drawn at an angle to the earth. With a steady pace, Hunter strode toward the assembling archers. Bishop Falls' knights had joined the fray at night, their city's flag adorning their horses and armor. With only the shield of confidence, Hunter continued his approach.

The horse came to a sudden stop, jolting Asher to take his eyes off Hunter. With practiced hands, Rosen unhitched the horse from the cart. Bidding Asher good fortune, he followed his orders to ride toward the horizon, far from the cart and its weapon.

"Take this end and run toward the cave on the other side of the hill," Asher said, handing Lattice one end of the gunpowder-coated rope. Asher tied the other end of the fuse to the barrel and threaded it through a hole carved into the lid. A few inches of the fuse were not completely dry, but it would have to do. He gave the fuse two tugs to ensure it was secure and then bolted over the hill.

Joining Lattice behind a boulder, he took the end of the fuse and held it with the flint stones in his trembling hands. From his position, he could still see Hunter in the distance but not the cart. One man, accompanied by two of the enemy's knights, began his approach toward Hunter. The scene played out as Hunter had assured him—seeing the prince, Bishop Falls would be obligated by duty and honor to send a negotiator before casting out their arrows.

Lattice grabbed Asher's elbow. "A chance of mishap, I can't dismiss. There are gnome holes in the hill, amidst. I'll guard the fuse, to this task I submit, and seek refuge before the blast is lit."

"You will not," Asher whispered, listening for the start of Hunter's speech. "Too dangerous. Go deeper into the cave!" he said, pushing the gnome back harder than he should have. "I know what I'm doing!"

Hunter stopped walking fifty paces before meeting the Bishop Falls delegation. "I, Prince Hunter Bracken, son of the king of Barbshire, command your armies to surrender!" he yelled, his bellowing voice clear for Asher to hear.

The man leading the delegation stepped forward and took off his helmet. "I am Governor Wicker of Bishop Falls!" he yelled. "I demand that you release my daughter from captivity."

Hunter shouted back. "Your daughter is no prisoner of Barbshire. She left the realm on her own accord, with her hand-maid Ruth. I encountered her in the Blue Mountains, where I reclaimed the Apex Blade, the terrible weapon of my forefathers and the blade I will use to lay ruin to your treasonous army!"

"What harm did you bring to my daughter with this blade?"

"Harm?" Hunter scoffed. "She chose to wager her fate crossing the Poisoned Fields rather than condemn herself to marriage when she loves another. She has nothing to fear from me, only you—a man who would sacrifice her will for the sake of power."

"You speak of power, but I doubt your blade's strength. Myth and legend will not save you from my archers' arrows," the governor yelled.

"Behold, the Apex Blade," Hunter said, lifting the sword above his head.

Asher knew that was his cue. He tapped the flint rocks together. Errant sparks flew away from the fuse. Hands sweaty, he dropped one of the rocks and scrambled to pick it up again. He hit the stones again. Heart racing, he tried again, chipping the rock at its corner against the fuse. The rope hissed and smoked. Asher shuffled backward on his hands and knees, watching the fuse burn down its length, counting down the seconds in his head.

"Anyone wise enough to recall legends of old will dare not come farther! This blade will bring lightning from the sky. It will decimate armies and make widows of your wives!" Hunter yelled out.

Asher heard a rumbling in the distance. Growing closer. He glanced outside the cave and saw another rank of Bishop's knights charging from their reserves toward the hill. "Too close, too close!" Asher yelled, glancing in vain at the burning fuse and knowing he could not stop what he had begun. Asher continued his mental countdown, an estimation intended to time the blast with the end of Hunter's planned speech to the delegation.

"I will remind a new generation of the blade's terror so that none need perish a certain death!" Hunter yelled, glancing back toward the cart and its payload by the distant hill. "Let... let this serve as a warning. Let this serve as a promise! Let this show the kingdom's unwavering resolve."

Asher's chest tightened, fearful that Hunter may have lost track of his mental countdown. Unable to do anything but watch and hope, Asher crouched down and plugged his ears with his fingers. Galloping horses drew closer, their hooves shaking the ground, growing ever louder.

"Witness the wrath of the Apex Blade!" Hunter shouted, pointing the sword toward the hill.

Asher's mental countdown was only a second behind. He winced his eyes shut, anticipating a blast that did not come. Panicked, he unplugged his ears, listening for the fuse's hiss. *Too far away to hear it.*

As Asher looked afar, he saw the Bishop Falls governor speaking with his knights; their rigidly attentive formation began to break into confusion.

"Behold!" Hunter yelled again, this time pressing the button on the hilt as he stabbed the air with his glowing blade toward the hill.

Asher was caught off guard by the cataclysmic blast that followed. In the relative safety of the cave and behind the hill, he was overcome with searing heat. Toppling on his back, he curled his knees toward his chest and pressed his hands over his ears. Unlike before, the blast resonated out, ferocious enough to surely be heard throughout the kingdom, reaching every corner of the only world he ever knew.

As the sound trailed into a memory he would never forget, Asher's ears hissed, and he crawled out of the cave to find smoke rising from the other side of the hill. He paced up the hill and surveyed the plains behind him. Horses lay strewn about the grasses, their riders motionless beside them. Others ran with flames consuming the flags adorned over their armor on their chests, howling in pain as they struggled to take off their helmets. Chaos ensued in the lower field. Hunter still stood, not budging from his station, sword held high. Forgetting their formations, enemy troops bolted in all directions, tripping and stumbling over one another in a frantic retreat.

His stomach tightened in anguish, Asher ran back to the cave and tripped, falling to his hands and knees. "Lattice!" he yelled, searching for the gnome. He was only met with the echo of his voice from the cave. He raked the ground with his hands, searching for the flint stones.

Oh no, please, no. Asher scrambled to his feet and ran around the hill, screams of pain surrounding him from the fallen. A crater had replaced the cart, the ground seared and blackened with the pungent smell of smoke and burnt flesh and hair. There lay a crumpled body, adorned in a green vest corrupted by the blast, the esteemed, brave knight—Sir Lattice, the victim of Asher's folly, the consequence of all his conceits. A thread of fuse littered the ground, burned at both ends, marking the points at which Asher's wet fuse extinguished and where Lattice relit it. Two flint rocks rested at Lattice's side as tombstones, commemorating his sacrifice.

He faintly heard the prince calling his name. His voice grew nearer, but Asher felt himself falling farther away. "I should have listened to him," Asher sobbed. "The knights came out of nowhere—they shouldn't have been there. I killed them. I killed all of them!"

Hunter fell to his knees beside him and sat silently before

resting a hand on Lattice's body. "It was an accident, Asher. Neither of us meant for this to happen. War is neither fair nor kind. It demands more than it should."

"It's my fault! I should have stopped it," Asher said as his voice trailed off, weak and defeated. He could hear his mother's words: *You can't save everyone.* He squeezed his eyes shut tighter, not wanting the memory to absolve him.

Hunter rested a gentle arm around his neck. "He chose to help. He put his life at risk to end this war without even more falling. Let us not allow the veil of our sorrows to blind us from seeing the heroism of his sacrifice nor diminish the nobility of his final act," he said, his voice shaking. "I have never known a knight of this realm so deserving of his title."

CHAPTER 26

THE KING'S DILEMMA

"It wasn't a wall, Your Highness," the palace guard reported. "Watchers at the castle tower confirmed no breach."

King Bracken flung his fork across the table and took the turkey leg from his plate in his hand, biting down on the meat. Verity observed that the king was seemingly unaware of the juices that squished out onto his fox fur–lined cape. He took a long gulp of the ale by his side as the queen looked away.

"Let us hope that was the sound of a wall falling and not what I fear," the king said after swallowing. "Search the walls again."

Verity's heart still raced. It was an awful sound unlike anything she could ever recall. Not a tree falling, but an entire forest of them. All at once. If the great city walls still stood, her mind struggled to find a cause for the menacing sound.

Just then, a squire crashed through the dining room's doors, forgetting any notion of propriety. "Master guardsman!" he yelled to the king's personal knight. "The prince has returned! He carries the Apex Blade!"

The king choked on the flesh and hit his chest. "Bring the squire closer to the table!" he yelled before a cough overcame him. "Speak the truth, not wild tales nor rumors!"

"Men by the door," the squire said, heaving his breaths too quickly to speak.

"Calm down, young squire. Come, sit here," Verity said, pushing out a chair beside her and turning to the nearest servant. "Bring him a glass of water."

Fear flooded the squire's eyes. Verity motioned again to the chair beside her. The squire resolved his hesitation and took the seat. With both hands, he grabbed the stein the servant placed in front of him and gulped down its contents. Verity glanced at the king as he rolled his eyes and tore more meat from the bone.

"What's your name, squire?" she asked.

"Pip, Your Grace," he said.

"It is a pleasure to have you join us at our table, Pip," Verity said, taking a graceful sip from her tea. "Let's start slow. From the beginning. You said men by the gate saw the prince?"

"Yes, Your Majesty. He came from the village, drawn in a carriage by horse. He held the Apex Blade, metal black as a moonless night. It glowed as fire as he commanded its power. Demanded that we open the great doors so that he may meet the enemy in battle."

The king dropped his food on his plate and leaned forward. Verity placed her hand upon Pip's, steadying him. "Then what?" Verity asked, forcing her voice to show disinterest. "The very next thing that happened."

Pip took a deep breath. "I was in the tower with our archers.

Bringing water and taking their waste pots. I saw everything. The horse brought him into the field beyond the gate. Then he demanded his audience with Bishop Falls," he said, his tongue sticking dryly against the roof of his mouth.

"More water for Pip, please." The queen said.

The squire swallowed another long drink from his refilled stein. "His voice thundered over the hills and up to the tower. I heard every word. Our prince held the blade and demonstrated its power."

"Its *power*?" the king asked.

"Yes, Your Highness. The blade burned red again. As Bishop's knights rode hard toward him, he pointed the blade afar. Fire erupted from the earth with a sound that made the tower sway. Knights were felled. Some burned, and others were thrown from their horses. The rest of their army fled. They left their weapons where they stood," Pip explained. "Didn't even return for their dead."

Queen Verity took a long breath and read the king's face. His expression was new to her. Were it anyone else, she would name it fear. After a moment, his brow became familiar. It creased as his eyes became slits.

"Your Highness!" yelled the captain of the knight guard as he entered the hall, dressed in his finest armored regalia. "Our prince has slain the enemy! Villagers are assembling in the streets to welcome him home! The enemy is in retreat!"

"We know," the king said, his voice no more than a wolf's growl.

"Shall we pursue them in retreat?" the captain asked.

"Tell me," the king said, turning to the squire. "You said a rider took my son into the battle. Who was that rider?"

"Lord Rosen, Your Grace. A young man was also with him."

King Bracken took in a rumbling breath and closed his eyes. "Bring Rosen to me. Immediately."

"Yes, Your Highness," the captain said.

"And," the king said, catching the knight before he left, "send your guards to arrest my son and his companion. Bring them to me."

The queen jerked her head to face her husband, seeing no compassion in his eyes. "Arrested? Reginald!"

"My king," the captain said, voice hesitant. "He wields the Apex Blade. Do you mean to send my men to their deaths? I will volunteer to be the first to die if it is your command, but we may yet need the lives of my knights."

"Reginald!" Verity hissed. "The entire capital will welcome him as a hero. Savior of our kingdom. Bearer of the Apex Blade. There is still peace to be won. Do our subjects not deserve to feel joy in his victory? After all they have suffered."

"There is no *joy* in his victory," the king said, barely loud enough for the queen to hear him. "Our queen is right," he said, raising his voice with a cunning smile. "Open wide the doors to the castle as they approach. Welcome them in honor. Bring them to me so I may recognize them for their deeds."

Verity leaned across the table and whispered, "Reginald, our son took on an entire army and ended a war, saving our people. Saving our kingdom. What vengeance are you planning?"

The king leaned in and whispered, "Bishop Falls was plotting this war. I see now that the marriage proposal was a pretext. A distraction. I am glad the war with Bishop Falls is over, but I take issue with our son's means."

"He recovered the sword," Verity said.

"I don't care about the sword!" he shouted, pounding the table. The servants flinched. "Long has been the time since the last purge. Time may soon tell whether we are overdue."

Verity steadied herself, clenching her jaw. "Yes, my king. I fear you may be right," she said as she stood and smoothed her coat. "I will prepare and meet you at the throne."

The king returned to his plate, and Verity calmly strode across the hall toward the door. Her handmaid followed behind. Once she reached the hall, she hoisted her silk dress and broke into a jog. "Beverly," she called to the handmaid, "come quickly!"

She took to the grand stairwell and skipped every other step as she raced to the residence wing. Her palms, now slick with sweat, fumbled at the library doorknob. It slipped from her grasp once, twice, before she finally managed to turn it. The door sprung open. Lily was absorbed in a book, seemingly oblivious to the chaos brewing outside, while Simon dozed peacefully by the fire.

"Lily!" Verity said. "We need to get both of you out of the castle. Immediately."

"Why?" Lily said, starting to stand.

"Your son is back. Safe. The war is over," the queen said. "Do you remember when I said that the kingdom used to hunt down people like the woman who raised you—people who were special?"

"Yes..."

"You and your son are special," the queen said, taking the book from Lily's lap. "That means you're all in danger. Beverly knows where to take you—away from here."

"What about my son?" Lily asked as Simon startled awake, looking bewildered.

"Quickly now!" Verity said, grabbing Lily's elbow. "I will do my best to keep your son safe," she said, stopping to look into the fellow mother's eyes. "My son has found favor in yours. I will treat him as my own."

"The streets will be crowded with people celebrating," Beverly said. "We can escape through the servants' hall and take the hidden path to the safe house."

"When you arrive, have Rosemary try to contact the Eastlands on the Watchers," the queen instructed.

"Those tools haven't been used in... I don't know how long," Beverly said.

Verity huffed. "Rosemary built it. She'll know how to fix it."

The Statue Garden

In the wake of the Bishop Falls retreat, the rolling hills beyond the city's gate fell silent. Panicked screams and futile orders shouted by the troops' commanders drew ever farther away until they fell silent, muted by distance and the wind. Asher walked with Hunter toward the gate, their procession silent and mournful. The smell of spent gunpowder wafted over the field like a silent companion to their funeral march.

Ahead, timid villagers peeked their heads outside the main gate. One apprehensive step after another, a growing number walked beyond the threshold. Asher could almost feel them wrestling with the tentative hope that the kingdom's walls were not to be their tomb. After having surrendered to hopelessness and despair, it was hard to trust in hope again.

"Now we play the part," Hunter said, his words strained by exhaustion. The prince flashed a broad smile as they approached the assembling crowd, drawing the Apex Blade from its scabbard.

Cheers erupted from the crowd, startling Asher. Unbridled

exuberance. Children sat hoisted on their fathers' shoulders. Women fell to their knees, weeping joyous tears. Men applauded and called out their thanks and well wishes. Asher smiled back at the crowds and waved by Hunter's side. His frozen grin was contrived, and his body moved like a marionette where the crowd held the strings.

"Brave subjects of Barbshire! Your prince has returned from war, having reclaimed the Apex Blade. Our kingdom is safe; the enemy vanquished!" Hunter yelled to the growing crowd around them. Asher was starstruck as the prince drew energy from the exuberant cries. The prince raised his voice and held the sword higher. "To the valiant hearts who fell and those who still stand, I swear my fidelity to this kingdom, its people, and our enduring recovery! This blade, a symbol of our resilience, has carved a path to peace. To Barbshire!"

The masses shouted back the refrain: "To Barbshire!"

Hunter thrust the blade again into the air, and the people shouted back. "To Barbshire!" The prince yelled along with them.

Villagers parted in the road to make room for them as they returned to the castle. *Thank the Watchers! Long live our prince!* Strangers dared not touch the prince, but Asher received handshakes and hugs as he walked by Hunter's side. Buoyed by joy, Asher began to recognize his smile once more.

"My prince, Your Highness," a young woman cried out as she stepped from the crowd with a toddler in her arms. "My son is sick. He coughs blood. His skin burns. Please bless him with your blade so that its mercy may heal him."

Hunter looked at Asher with pleading eyes. Asher stepped toward the toddler, whose head rested weakly on his mother's shoulder. His mind flooded with insights. Medicine. Symptoms. Diagnosis. Treatment.

"Hunter, the boy likely suffers from tuberculosis. He needs medicines we don't have—at least rest and clean water with a moist cloth to bring down the fever," Asher said.

Hunter's smile broke, and he looked uncertain. The crowd chanted his name. The woman's eyes quivered as her welling tears begged for help. Clenching his jaw and recovering his stature, Hunter drew his sword again, and the crowd cheered louder than ever.

"Let the Apex Blade sap this illness from your son," Hunter called out loud enough for everyone around him to hear. He gently rested the side of the blade against the child's back to the crowd's roaring approval. The child's mother wept and offered her emphatic and inconsolable praise, repeating *thank you* as if they were the only words she knew.

Hunter put his arm around Asher and leaned toward his ear. "I know it won't heal him. Sometimes the people need hope more than medicine."

"And when the child dies?" Asher asked. "What of the next child? Their mother and father? False hope will just lead to resentment."

"I know," Hunter said. "That's why we need to walk faster."

As they hastened ahead, the rumble of hooves greeted them. Knights came over the hill, and the villagers cheered them on as they approached. The knights brandished their swords in celebration. The crowd began to circle them. Asher searched among the crowd for faces he may recognize—his mother, father, grandmother. His heart began to sink. The entire capital seemed to be swelling into the streets. Above, people held the kingdom's flag from the windows. Alleys leading to the main road were jammed with people, shoulder to shoulder, leading back as far as he could see.

"Sir knight," Hunter said. "My companion and I will need your horse. Your men can escort us back to the castle."

Companion? Asher frowned at his least illustrious royal title. Without hesitation, the knight dismounted his horse, and Hunter took the reins.

"Hop on," Hunter said, holding a hand down to Asher after he climbed up.

Asher slipped his foot in the stirrup and took the prince's hand. The crowd cheered with new vigor as he mounted the horse and held on to Hunter's waist.

The prince raised the sword again and led the horse to turn a half circle. "I will return to the castle and share the news with our king!" he shouted. "May your memory never forget this day—the day we celebrate the end of a war—the day we celebrate the end of all wars!" he said as the crowd cheered, their voices growing rasp. "I ride with Asher Snow, my companion. My friend... my partner. As much as we owe our victory to this blade, we owe equal devotion to Asher!"

Asher's face burned scarlet as the crowd chanted his name.

Hunter waited for the crowd to settle. "We also honor the fallen—the brave and loyal. Let it be known and forever remembered that I, Prince Hunter Bracken, knighted Sir Lattice of the gnome realm. He gave the fullest measure of his devotion and his very life to our cause."

Asher counted confused faces passing among the crowd. Some stood in bewildered silence as others, overcome with exuberance, continued to cheer. Two of the other knights drew near to one another, speaking quietly between themselves.

"It needed to be said," Hunter whispered. "Just in case I can't say it later."

"Why wouldn't you?" Asher asked.

Hunter looked away. "I don't know what will happen when we return to the castle. Just know that no matter what, I will be at your side. Always."

Asher squeezed Hunter's hip as the horse began to pace ahead. As the crowd made way, Hunter squeezed his legs against the horse, and it began to run faster. With two knights trailing behind them and an open road ahead, Hunter urged the horse into a gallop toward the castle rising over the next hill.

The drawbridge began to lower as they approached. A new delegation of villagers stood near the sculpture garden leading to the castle. Asher recognized statutes of heroes from past wars, their fortitude cast forever in stone. Their carved faces showed no doubt or regret, only the steadfast resolve that made their lives into legend. Asher wondered whether a statue would ever be commissioned for Hunter. Would they have one for Lattice?

Hunter dismounted the horse and helped Asher down. Handing the reins to a guard, he turned and looked again back toward the assembled masses behind him. He drew the Apex Blade, its dark gleam catching the sun's light. The people shouted their excited praise back to him, their voices reverberating off the castle's walls. As the shouts faded and Asher's eyes adjusted to the candlelight in the great foyer, he thought of Hunter's warning. He wondered darkly whether the people's support would prove as fleeting as the echo of their cheers.

With an honor guard numbering eight knights, each dressed in their finest ceremonial regalia of silvery metal, Hunter walked toward the grand stairwell with Asher by his side. Asher could smell the lilac-scented wax burning from the candles that marked their path to the throne room. He felt filthy as he walked over pristine rugs with ornate handwoven patterns dyed in royal blues, untarnished yellows, regal greens, and bold hues of red.

Guards on opposing sides of the hall moved in unison to open the throne room doors—each carved from mahogany, heavy and thick. Inside, the ceiling soared above him. A red carpet led a path from the doors to the base of a throne adorned in gold and silver. Asher almost stumbled as he looked toward the ceiling, painted with images depicting the masses stretching their pleading hands toward a regal figure dressed in jewels, holding a blade stained black.

"Guards and members of the royal court," the king bellowed. "The queen and I will have an audience with the prince and this boy. Leave us."

Hunter stopped some twenty paces from the base of the throne. Asher stood beside him as the others filed out of the room. The heavy doors boomed shut behind them.

As the room fell silent, the king leaned forward. "What have you done to me?"

"Father," Hunter said, his voice cracking. "I went on a quest and recovered the sword of our ancestors. The Apex Blade," he said, drawing the sword and holding it before him. "Asher and I repelled Bishop Falls, ending this war and saving your kingdom."

"You did much more than that," the king sneered. "This boy. Asher. What role have you played in recovering this blade?"

Asher tried to speak, but his throat seized shut. He swallowed and looked up toward the king. "Your son found me. I accompanied him on his quest, and we found the sword. It brought down lightning from the sky, drawing fire from the earth and scattering the enemy."

The king cast a sidelong glance at his queen before carefully removing his weighty golden crown, placing it beside him. "No, boy. That was not magic. From the accounts given, I reason that it was gunpowder. That secret chemistry, and all its kind, has long been forbidden, forgotten by history. Its secret rests in the forbidden library. Where did you find it?"

"We didn't find it," Asher said. "We made it."

King Bracken rubbed his chin. "How did you know how to do this?" Hunter tried to interrupt, but the king held up his hand, urging Asher to answer for himself. "Speak truthfully, Asher."

Wearily, Asher took a deep breath. "We came upon a vault

within a mountain. My hand opened a door. There, we found an instrument that transferred knowledge of gunpowder—knowledge of a great many things forgotten by time—to me, all of which can benefit our kingdom. Agriculture to feed the entire kingdom. Medicines to cure the sick."

As Asher recounted a litany of possibilities, his voice growing stronger as he envisioned a future blossoming with potential, he noticed the king's face contort with growing frustration. The king's hands clenched into fists. Tension filled the room, and it tightened like a vise around Asher's chest.

The king surged to his feet. "Enough!" he roared like a cracking whip. His chest heaved, and his eyes burned like a furnace. "You must also know our history—how that technology begot technology that begot billions of deaths. You know what must not be known."

"I do know that history," Asher said, his voice cracking with emotion. "I can't stop seeing blinding flashes from bombs. I can smell the stench of death. I fear what we once became. So much of that technology was inspired by war. A computer was invented to break codes in war. The internet was invented under the shadow of nuclear war to decentralize information. Both technologies revolutionized society in peaceful times. Now we can have the technology without paying for it with blood and suffering."

"And your first use for this grand technology was a weapon of war!" the king bellowed back. "How many people have made that drunkard's promise? 'It was necessary.' 'Just this last time.' There is no end!" He swatted at his crown in fury and sent it clanking against the cold stone floor. "Once the door is opened, humanity will walk through it, for better or worse. Embark on this journey, and you consign us to the doom that haunts your waking nightmares."

Asher's shoulders sagged, a heavy silence enveloping him. The king's words lingered like a shroud, stifling and unyielding. His gaze drifted downward, memories flooding his mind, unbidden and relentless. He saw Lattice's lifeless form amidst the wreckage, a poignant testament to the brutal cost of their quest. Lattice, who had been both a beacon of hope and a casualty of their ambitions, lay etched in his memory as both hero and victim.

The king broke the silence. "Your history teaches you that the agricultural revolution was a stable time. Countless generations have lived much as we do today," he said. "I applaud your intentions, but be mindful. We maintain a delicate balance. With a heavy heart, I must do what my forebearers have done. For the kingdom's good, we must lance the wound to stop the infection from spreading."

"You will not harm him!" Hunter yelled, standing before Asher with his sword held toward the king.

King Bracken smiled and took lumbering steps down from the throne, walking toward Hunter and the point of his blade. "What will you do?" he asked. "Strike your father down with your blade?"

"Come no closer," Hunter said, the blade shaking in his trembling hand.

The king stopped at the tip of the blade. "You will mind your place and do well to remember your fealty. His death will be quick and joyless."

"I... I will die first," Hunter said as his eyes filled with tears.

The king smiled and reached for his son's hand, holding it for a moment before wrapping his fingers around the sword's hilt and pulling it out of the prince's loose grip. "The sword has been returned, and the village will see you as their hero," he said, admiring the blade as he twisted it in his hand. "You will not leave the castle grounds save for royal functions."

Verity stood. "I invoke the queen's mercy," she said. "The boy is naïve but unworthy of death. In the past, some of those with the blood were banished in the purges. Others were merely imprisoned. That is the just decision. At least for now. There may be others involved. He may still have worth to us."

One strenuous step at a time, the king carried his weight with considerable effort as he climbed the stairs back to the throne, sword held at his side. His face typified consternation. "Our queen is more merciful than wise," he finally said. "He shall meet his justice at the parade. My duty to the kingdom transcends the bonds of fatherhood and the vows of marriage. Forgive the bitter taste of justice; its sour grapes are preferred to the poison of moderation. Guards!"

Two royal knights barged through the door. The king commanded them to take Asher to the dungeon below. Each knight grabbed one of Asher's arms. He called out to Hunter as they began to drag him away. Hunter stood motionless, like a statue in the garden, eyes cast down—a figure not of lionized triumph but of a haunting, lifeless resignation.

At that moment, Asher grasped the true potency of the

figurative amulet Hunter described wearing all those years—how it siphoned away his valor, rendering him subservient to his father's dictates. It was as though the prince was ensnared in bonds far more burdensome than any Asher would encounter in the darkest depths of the dungeons. Without raising his sword, the prince capitulated, succumbing to defeat before engaging his most daunting enemy in battle.

CHAPTER 28

ROSEMARY

One knight led the way down the spiraled stairs into a dungeon, and the other marched a few paces behind Asher. He didn't protest. His arms throbbed in pain from his rough ejection from the throne room. The pain barely registered as a more searing sensation overshadowed it—seeing Hunter break his promise. Fewer lanterns glowed on the walls as they traveled farther down the winding halls of empty cells and rusted chains. Long shadows from iron prison bars were cast into empty cells as they walked, like ghosts of those who perished within.

With a shove to his back, Asher stumbled forward into a cell, the metal lock clanking shut behind him. Bars reached from the stone floor to the ceiling. Standing twice his height was a narrow slit in the wall, spilling a sliver of midday sun into the hall—a cruel reminder that freedom was just beyond his grasp. The bars were cool as Asher grabbed them and peered as far as he could to watch the knights leave, their footfalls growing distant. Asher sat in what was to be his bed—no more than loose straw and a ragged blanket, not much bigger than a potato sack.

He tucked his legs underneath him, saving them from the damp mold that claimed the ground. A drip splashed into a distant puddle as he closed his eyes. After a few moments, another. As he sat, he came to rely on the sound as his only evidence for the passage of time. Each drop refuted his mind's determination to ignore the present and ruminate on the moment Hunter silently betrayed him.

He opened his eyes, taking note of the rust-flaked iron ring in the middle of the cell—likely to hold a prisoner's chains. *What did the queen say?* Others were imprisoned here, people with nanobots like him. He watched as the sliver of light from the window crossed the cell wall with the sun's passing in the sky. Then, something new. Uncertain whether his mind was already drawing him into insanity, he moved from the straw bed and examined the wall. There he found words etched into the stone surface: "There is hope in the Eastlands."

Beneath the inscription read another: "Coin and blood. Share the blessing." Asher was puzzled by the message. He traced the scratched words with his fingers, trying to connect the meaning. Beneath that was a list of names belonging to people he never knew. Compelled to add his name to the wall, leaving some evidence that he lived even if another may never read it, he searched for a stone. He longed to leave a timeless mark on the world, trusting stone to at least endure longer than love or loyalty.

He returned to the scrawled letters on the wall again, taking comfort that he was not truly alone in the company of those who came before—people who may have known more than he did about the affairs of his world. Rather than feeling isolated, he took solace in a swelling warmth that began to grow within him. *I am not the first. I'm not the only one.* The names spoke of a world larger than his troubles—a world where others had faced and overcome challenges. He wasn't a lone soldier in the battle. Unknown till now, he was part of an army.

As the sun swept across the cell and grew dim, Asher stretched out as much as he could on the patch of straw, tugging the blanket close to his chest. The absence of Hunter's arms around him stirred like the hunger growing in his stomach. He yearned for them as badly as he did for water. As darkness fell, he closed his eyes. The night softened his rage. Emboldened by the messages on the wall, hope returned to him. He decided to trust that Hunter shared the same feelings—that he would find a way to honor his promise. He had to.

"Asher! Asher!" came a hissing whisper that drew him awake.

Asher blinked, struggling to parse dreams from reality. "Rosen?" he asked.

"Yes!" Rosen said from behind the bars. "I'm here to rescue you."

Asher pulled himself up. "You can't be here," he whispered just loudly enough for Rosen to hear him. "The queen would put you in a cell next to me."

"Who do you think sent me?"

"What?" Asher asked, gripping the bars on his cell.

Rosen stopped fiddling with the keys in his hand. "You're not alone, Asher. The queen and others have been working in secret for a long time."

"Secret? What for?" Asher asked.

Rosen found the right key and slid it into the lock. "Technology. Progress. The war with Bishop Falls. We're partially to blame. I told Bishop Falls about the iron plow," he said, the words falling out of his mouth with urgency. "That's why their crop yields were so much better than ours. I didn't intend a war—not this way, at least. I just thought we'd force the king's hand to permit the new plow throughout all the cities in Barbshire. Instead, the king didn't give in, Bishop Falls refused to abandon the plow, and then they plotted a war to overthrow the king instead."

"Finding the cave wasn't my fault?" Asher asked, trying to make sense of the puzzle from the pieces he had been given.

"Fault? No, boy. They were waiting for someone to access it. They would have waited longer—until the king's reign ended, if they had to. But you were the last in your line. It had to be either you or your mother. I was told your mother was too worried for your safety to ever take such a risk—either for her or you. The witch and others had their own plans for you."

"And Hunter?" Asher asked as he walked through the open gate, legs shaking.

"He hasn't forsaken you," Rosen said. "A good soldier knows the difference between surrender and a strategic retreat. The queen will work to help him escape."

"Escape to what?"

"One step at a time, boy," Rosen said, ushering him down the hall. "We can talk more once we arrive at the safe house."

With freedom from the cell came a more profound liberation—an understanding that the world's burdens need not rest solely on his shoulders. Beyond a sense of kinship with the names etched in the cell, he discovered a purpose: to carry on their struggle. Finding strength in his legs, Asher jogged to keep up with Rosen, who led Asher down a different path than he'd taken before. Through a door. Up a narrower flight of stairs that wound like a screw.

"Servants' exit," Rosen whispered as they gently opened a door leading into a kitchen with rusted knives on dirty countertops and murky water collected in bowls. They snuck down narrow halls and took refuge through nearly hidden doors. A chill wind met Asher's face as they escaped the castle from a long-neglected door leading to an outdoor atrium. The air had never felt so good on his skin. Sprinting at a full run, they made their way across a courtyard and climbed through a hole in a wall hidden behind a potted plant.

Finding an overgrown path beyond the castle's walls, their pace began to slow. Rosen wheezed to catch his breath. Asher looked toward the road ahead, unfamiliar with this part of the city.

"Are you a part of this secret group?" Asher asked.

Rosen chuckled. "Only the small part I was told about. Didn't know that the sword was just a legend."

"It lights up when you press a button," Asher muttered.

"The truth is, I've never been fully privy to all aspects of the operation. Our knowledge is compartmentalized to minimize risk," he explained.

Amid a soup of fog rolling in from the mountains and nearly hidden behind overgrown weeds, they came upon the pointed tip of a roof atop a small house. Rosen brushed the tall grass aside, making a small walkway. Asher followed, the knotted tops of the weeds whipping his cheek as he made his way ahead.

Smooth river stones lay in a path around the hut. The rocks gave way to a stoop leading to a door. By Asher's judgment, the small cottage was well-maintained. Fresh paint on the door and bricks stacked neatly atop one another—no cracks and each a deep hue of fire red.

Rosen knocked on the door three times in quick succession, then once more. He opened the door and stepped in, waving Asher to follow. "He's safe," Rosen called out to whomever resided within.

Asher took a few tentative steps inside, his eyes adjusting to warm hues of light from a small fire and candles adorning the walls. Lily stood from a chair and clasped her hands over her mouth. "Mom!" he yelled, rushing to her arms. Lily's eyes brimmed with tears, and her cheeks burned bright as she hugged him. The room seemed to embrace him at the same time, warming his arms and face, softening his heart. Wherever he was, it didn't matter—he could almost smell the broth boiling in the copper pot over the open flame in his mother's kitchen and hear the neighbor's hen softly clucking in the distance.

A familiar hand gripped his shoulder. Not letting go of his mother, he wrapped his other arm around his father, pulling them as close as possible. "I'm so sorry," he said with his face against his mother's arm.

"Don't be," Simon said. "Your mother and Rosemary filled me in. I'm still trying to make sense of it all. I'm just glad you're safe."

"Rosemary?" Asher asked.

"Don't tell me you've forgotten your own grandmother," Rosemary said.

Asher pulled himself from his parents and turned toward the familiar voice. Grandma Rose. Rosemary. *Of course.* His grandmother was leaning over a table with a screwdriver in her hand and circuit boards strewn in front of her, wires flailing in every direction. *Circuit boards? It couldn't be. Not here. Not now.*

"You were always so bright," she said, smiling as she placed the screwdriver on the table. "That, and good health—benefits of the nanobots. Even before they're programmed, they're quite useful. I suspect you know that now, though."

Asher's mind spun. The hobbling woman, kind and evasive, who searched for her long-dead cat, stood before him. Clear-spoken and focused, she held her smile as she watched him—almost inviting him to solve a riddle.

"I have the nanobots, so my mother must have them as well. Same as you," Asher said, surprised that he hadn't considered this yet.

"Close enough," she said, offering her soft applause. "Though I'm not exactly your grandmother. Let's settle on great aunt, lest I get insecure about being quite so old. I survived the great war."

"You're immortal?" Asher asked.

She laughed. "Thankfully, not quite. It's a misnomer. Nanobots slow aging down when they're programmed the right way, but we aren't immortal. I'm sure I'll pass on in a century or so, but not today. Yes, yes—I know I play the aloof old woman routine. If you look this old, it helps to play the part and avoid suspicion."

"You were dedicated to your part, placing posters around the village every morning."

"It's a perfect excuse to wander the city, get to this safe house, and meet with the others without drawing suspicion," she said. "I never even had a cat."

"And the circuit boards?" Asher asked.

"Sounds like the knowledge Prim forced into your head is all there," she said, picking up a board and inspecting it under the light. "You got the better deal with your nanobots. I'm just stuck with the knowledge I came with. Before the war, I was an electrical engineer. Set up a communication station after to talk with other survivors over satellite. Haven't used this station in longer than I care to remember."

"Others?" Asher said, accepting the chair his mother carried over to him.

Rosemary looked at him with the same scrutiny she gave to the broken board in her hand. "Don't remember anything after the blast in the last war?"

Asher shook his head. "No. Nothing really. Glimpses of things. It never makes sense."

"Figures," she said. "Surprised the vault even worked at all. So much time has passed. Information after the war was stored on its own server. Must have broken. You didn't get all the information, which could be a blessing. Can you find the soldering iron in that box?" she asked, pointing toward the corner with her screwdriver.

Absentmindedly, Asher walked toward the box and rooted through the tools, barely noticing that he only just remembered what such a tool was for. "What is it that you did? After the war. With the other survivors who had nanobots?"

"Well," she said, drawing the word out like a yawn. "We'd send a descendant every generation or so to the vault. Prim would just give us what we needed for the time. You got the whole database, it seems. Didn't matter much after a few hundred years. Bracken isn't the first king who thinks a light bulb would wreck society. At least we made it this far into whatever make-believe feudal kingdom we find ourselves. Better than being stuck as hunter-gatherers. Had to work undercover and avoid the purges. Occasionally, we would employ a bit of subterfuge to keep moving the ball a few yards down the field. Football. Remember football?"

"I... I don't think so," Asher said. "How would we stop the king? Should we?"

Rosemary looked back toward him after a bright flash from the soldering iron lit the room. "A thousand years of history will take a bit longer to explain than the time for a pot of tea to brew. We can talk about that later. Now we try to see if any of this works. The Eastlands will want to know the news. Assuming there's anyone to pick up the message."

CHAPTER 29

The Fate of the Past

Verity sat on the edge of her son's bed, looking over the despondent lump curled under his blanket. Crickets chirped in the distance from beyond the window in the tower. The night air was brisk, even sitting so close to the flames crackling in the fireplace behind her. The room told the story of her son's life. Whittled carvings of knights on their horses were still proudly displayed on a shelf above Hunter's bed, artifacts that proved to her he wasn't always the young man he so quickly grew to become.

How tragic, she thought. The carvings of noble steeds in mid-gallop with their brave knights astride them. Each figure forever memorialized a type of victory that only existed in childhood fantasies, where every conflict ended in glory and every knight was the paragon of valor and virtue. She lamented that her son never play-acted scenes that would prepare him for an actual war—one where both defeat and victory were often confused, where hardships forced even the most heroic knights to question their purpose.

"Hunter," she said, touching his ankle. He jerked his leg away. "Hunter," she said again, "Asher is fine."

Hunter pulled the blanket off his face and sat in front of her. "Fine? He's in a dungeon... I wasn't able to stop... I couldn't stop my father," he said, lip quivering. "I promised to protect him."

Verity leaned closer. "So did I," she whispered. "I gave the same promise to his mother. He's beyond the castle. Somewhere safe."

Hunter broke into tears and leaned over to hold his mother. "I love him," he said. "I love him so much. I just let him go."

Verity closed her eyes and smiled, holding him tighter. "It's okay," she said, rocking him back and forth. "Sometimes the bravest thing is letting someone go. It's also the hardest."

"I need to be with him," Hunter said, gently pulling away from Verity.

"You will be," she said. "Your father must not know. For all he knows, Asher escaped on his own."

Verity heard footsteps beyond the room. With years of familiarity, she possessed an intimate knowledge of her husband's gait. She could discern his emotions merely by the cadence of his steps. Whatever words he shared with her may be evasive, curt, and leave more unsaid. His feet were his confession.

Each step resonated with an urgency that reverberated through the stone corridors. They were angry stomps, brimming with vehemence as if each footfall was an attempt to crush the very stone beneath. The rhythm was irregular yet insistent. The air grew tense in anticipation, and in the flickering firelight, the shadows danced more wildly as if agitated by the impending arrival.

Verity sighed and closed her eyes. She counted down from three seconds, and the door predictably sprang open. "Hunter!" the king yelled, storming into the room with a jewel in his hand. "What is this? It was in your travel bag."

Hunter met his father's eyes before looking at his mother as if to ask permission. Verity nodded. Hunter clenched his jaw and sat upright in his bed. "It's an amulet of protection. The Witch of the Forest gave it to Asher."

"It's forbidden ancient technology," the king mumbled, holding it closer to his face. "What does it do?"

Hunter glared at his father, their eyes evenly matched in intensity. "Asher wrapped it in a sprig of mint. It charged the jewel and granted him... powers."

"Powers?" the king asked.

Hunter rolled his eyes, and Verity's heart leaped in fear that the king would see it. "It protected him from harm," Hunter said. "He could scale the face of a mountain unharmed. Balance. Endurance. It just... protected him from any physical harm."

"Mint," the king whispered.

"It comes at great cost," Hunter said. "It's addictive. Soon, it was all he wanted. He needed it, even though it made him sick and brought him near death before I rid him of it."

"I am familiar with the stone's legend," Verity interrupted. "If a cutting of mint could do so much, imagine what a vat of it would bring."

Verity caught a glimpse of shock in her son's eyes. She pursed her lips and squinted at him to hold his tongue. She once read him stories of the stone's gifts and its costs, warning him against the same encouragement she now gave to the king.

"If I can hold my ale, I can resist addiction to a rock," the king said, placing the stone in his pocket. "Hunter was right to do what was necessary to remind the people of the sword's legend. They will expect to be reminded again—proof that the legend is real. I intend to give them that proof at the celebration tomorrow."

"I won't touch that stone," Hunter said, eyes narrowing.

The king laughed. "You won't. I will. With the Apex Blade in my hand and the jewel around my neck, I will remind our subjects that loyalty is the price they pay for peace. Without that reminder, the war's end would still bring rumors of rebellions. Desperation gives confidence to fools. The blade's myth will keep a sobering peace, as it did before."

"Asher did nothing wrong," Hunter said, his voice nearly as stern as his father's. "He's not to blame."

"That is not your decision to make."

"What of the people?" Hunter asked. "I told the crowds of his bravery. Won't they expect to see him alive and well? I announced him as my companion... as my partner."

Verity held her breath, watching for any sign as subtle as a tick in the king's face. The king's eyes narrowed to slits, and he studied his son.

"You will be there, doing your part at the celebration," the king said. "People will forget his name. I urge you to do the same."

"I will *never*," Hunter said, drawing himself up from the bed to stand before the king. "Let me rot in the cells with him if you must. Even the bleakest darkness would be a far better life than any I may find without him."

"Reginald," the queen cautioned, reaching for her husband's arm.

The king studied his son. "Do you... regard this young man?"

"I *love* him," Hunter said. "I will renounce my title before I renounce him." Verity watched as her son's hands tightened into fists, his eyes brimming with unspoken rage. Hunter took a deep breath. "If you want to parade me before our people, then you will never, never search for him."

The king opened his mouth to speak, then seemed to change his mind. "Search for him? He's in the dungeon, is he not?"

Hunter's face flushed red, and he paced across the room with his arms folded at his chest. "I mean to say that you should release him and never search for him." Silence gripped the moment, but it seemed to crackle like the flames lapping beside her.

The king folded his arms. "We have let you run through the fields, wild and untamed like a foal—only caring for yourself. You will need to be broken if we are to save you from yourself. Strong-willed, you would surely endure the whip and chew through the bit. Harsher means must be employed. Only then will you submit to carry the burden of your duty."

Verity cast a warning glance at her son before following the king as he stormed out of the room. "Reginald," she said, dashing to catch him, "we must show our son compassion if we ever hope for him to extend it to others."

"The peasant boy is dangerous," the king grumbled as he strode down the hall toward their suite. "Risks upsetting everything I and Hunter's forbearers sacrificed to create."

"Would that be undone by technology? Or would your undoing come from the shame of having a son who loves another boy?" Verity asked as they entered the foyer joining the study and their two rooms.

King Bracken rubbed his eyes, walking toward a portrait of his father hanging above the hearth. "The prince of Barbshire is an asset. Marriage makes foes into allies. Allies keep us strong. It's the way it always was. Change that, and we risk weakness. Things we can't control. It spirals. First, with an iron plow. Then one made of steel. Then one drawn by an engine—polluting the air and perfecting the means for carrying men to war."

"How long can the line truly endure, my dear? Ancient books— the ones we lock away—tell us of entire empires that would rise and one day fall. Are all our best efforts merely delaying that inevitable day? And when that day comes, will we have any control over the choices people make?"

"You ask me to consider two paths, each shrouded in uncertainty," the king said. "The path I've chosen has worked for this long, and if we don't permit any break in the chain, it could last forever. If not forever, then for every generation we hold back the flood of progress, we save one more from the inevitable consequences." The king turned to her, fierceness returning to his eyes. "You speak to me of compassion, but is this goal truly bereft of merit? If compassion for one boy means so much, what of the mercy owed to entire generations? I can sentence one boy to death, but I dare not condemn the future of all humanity to the fate of its past."

"Says the king who would forfeit so many lives if the siege continued," Verity countered.

The king waved a dismissive hand. "A few hundred lives? Small wars will come and pass. We must protect against the deaths of billions. One peasant's life is a fair price to pay."

Verity sank into a velvet chair. "What compels you to take so much responsibility for things beyond your control?"

"History," the king said, collapsing his weight into an opposing chair. "People with power cannot help themselves. Time and time again. History's lesson was the same."

"And you're different? With the Apex Blade?" the queen teased with a coy smile.

The king laughed and returned a gentle smile. "The sword's only power is its lie. We pacify the people with superstition and fear—better than bombs and guns."

"Some may disagree," Verity said, watching as her husband's face began to sour.

"You almost sound like one of the keepers, making an eloquent plea before their purge."

Verity clenched her jaw and forced a smile. "You always told me you liked how I challenged you—keeping you from being your only counsel. Challenging you in the privacy of our study is hardly the same as doing it in public."

"I'm glad you still see the difference," he said, standing and slipping his arms into his royal robes.

Verity felt a chill and tugged at her own robes, looking toward the fire. "Has anyone found Rosen?" she asked.

"I was going to ask you the same. I will speak to the captain knight and have someone bring water to the peasant boy, assuming our son has not already seen to his escape."

The queen kept her focus on the fire. It grew weaker, consuming everything it was given until it inevitably burned to ash. "What will you do with the boy?" she asked, her tone as inconsequential as she could manage.

"It would be a cruel thing for me to say," the king said. Verity felt his eyes upon her, but she did not turn. "Crueler still if the boy has escaped. Either way, I will see that his death will not be by my hand."

As the king took his leave, Verity considered putting another log on the fire. It would keep the flames burning a bit longer. Eventually, her warmth and comfort would demand yet another log. It was the same every night, she thought. The night was still young. Her ritualistic sacrifices would persist until she retreated to bed or ran out of wood. Whether one should occur before the other, she could not estimate. She only knew that the king was wrong. The fire would not last forever.

She closed her eyes and leaned into her chair. Her thoughts turned to the next moves in her game. She estimated that the king would learn that Rosen hadn't returned before the hour lapsed and that Asher had escaped. Knowing no end to her husband's paranoia, she anticipated the king would grow more suspicious of her—easily remedied once she reminded him that Rosen had been helping Asher from the start. The only reasonable explanation, then, would be that Rosen acted alone and rescued him.

Poisoned by lies, his subjects would cheer his unearned victory at his parade. Drunk on their adoration, his temper would fade, she assured herself. With Asher and Rosen safe and the war ended, she allowed herself a sliver of hope. Despite the fire, a chill ran down her spine as she considered her failsafe—a backup plan. An awful one at that. Moved by what love she still held for the man she met so long ago, she closed her eyes and begged the forgotten gods of old that such a plan need not come to pass.

CHAPTER 30

No Path to the Past

Well-rested, Asher enjoyed the morning sun warming his face by the window in the cottage kitchen. A steaming cup of tea rested on its saucer on the kitchen table. His grandmother's notoriously inedible biscuits sat untouched beside it. Asher tried and failed to tear off a piece of a biscuit. He considered taking a bite, only to reconsider. Without the amulet to protect him, he worried that his teeth would break in a battle of wills with the pastry.

He looked over the parchment draped across the kitchen table as he massaged his cramped hand. The ink from his pen covered a substantial portion of it. He had scratched out equations from Faraday and Maxell, capturing electromagnetism fundamentals, along with the photovoltaic effect. Material sciences would be more challenging. Even a basic silicone semiconductor would require more intermediary steps than he could put on paper.

He yearned to plot a path to skip coal and oil and build an infrastructure powered by solar energy, but every journey needed a first step. Glass manufacturing was expensive, but at least it was already a thriving part of his society. Now he just needed to teach them how to turn glass into a lens. For that, he would need schools. Armies clad with knowledge, not armor and shields. He couldn't do it alone.

"Ink is too expensive to waste writing out gibberish," his father said, taking a seat next to him.

"It's not gibberish," Asher said. "It's a six-hundred-year head start into our future."

"Looks like gibberish," his father said, taking a drink of his tea and studying a biscuit. "The queen said I'd get a work voucher for the days I've been away from the mines. They rushed us out before I could get it."

Rosemary took more biscuits from the oven. She used her free arm to push away circuity on the counter to make room for the hot pan. "Feed the body to feed the mind," she said in a sing-song melody.

"We can't just stay here forever," Asher's father said. "When will it be safe to go back to work?"

Rosemary gave a sympathetic smile. "Your house burned in the fires. Asher says mine survived. You can stay with me until it's rebuilt, assuming the Crown makes provision for it. But for the moment, we're all still in danger."

"What about the Witch of the Forest?" Asher asked. "She lives beyond the city's walls."

"You mean Dexter?" Rosemary asked with a chuckle.

"Who?" Asher asked.

"She wasn't always called a witch," she explained. "Dexter survived all of the purges and forced the king to grant her exile."

"A man's name?" Asher asked.

"When you're essentially immortal, you have to wear disguises every lifetime or so. Otherwise, people get suspicious when you don't die. For the last hundred years or so, she's embraced her drag persona from the times before. Do you know about drag?"

"What does she drag?" Asher asked.

Rosemary sighed. "It's when a man, usually a gay man, dresses like a woman."

"Why would someone do that?"

"Sometimes a person needs to adopt a different persona to find a way to be their authentic self," Rosemary said. "It's fine to call her *she* when Dexter wears the wig. Otherwise, you can call him *he*. This isn't to be confused with someone who has a different gender identity from birth, naturally."

Asher scratched his head, and Rosemary took a seat next to him before continuing. "Still, Dexter wanted to meet you—make certain you had nanobots. I arranged for you to run into her at the carnival. She said it was time for you to find the vault. I couldn't share any of this with you—didn't want the information to fall into the wrong hands."

"How did she convince the king to give her exile over execution?" Asher asked.

"Long story," Rosemary said, dunking one of her biscuits in her tea. "The trick is to see a problem from a different perspective. Always know what someone wants the most. Once you know that, you've found their weakness and your leverage. Write that bit down," she said, tapping her finger on his parchment.

"What do you know of the nanobots?" Asher asked.

"More than I wish," she said, biting into her softened biscuit.

"I thought Dr. Prim merely downloaded data into mine," Asher said, struggling to find the right words to explain a sensation just beyond his grasp. "But it's more than that, isn't it? I rappelled down a cliff with a rope. I've never done that before. My body just... knew how."

Rosemary smiled and placed her tea on the table. "It's called muscle memory. It's one thing to understand the mechanics of mountain climbing. It's another to remember how it's done. I'm sure there are a great many things you're able to do now. The mind can only process so much information. Time and necessity may unlock more of those skills."

Rosen hoisted himself off the couch in the living room, blinking the sleep from his eyes. "I'm up," he declared. "The king will speak to everyone who assembles in the main square today, celebrating the war's end. If we are to escape the safe house, that would be a good time—when everyone's distracted. Dangerous to linger too long in one place."

"About time," Asher's father said. "I want to see what remains from the house. The mines will reopen tomorrow. Asher and I can get back to work."

A spark of rage erupted in Asher's mind. He held his tongue as his face flushed. There would be no more work in the mines. He wondered why his father couldn't understand. The world had changed. They would be hunted, jailed—or worse. What life could they have, secret and hidden? Asher imagined himself banished like Dexter, a recluse. Alone and unable to breach the tower's walls to find Hunter. Empowered to bring knowledge to people but destined to share it with no one. He knew he could never return to the mill or tavern—nor the dank mines and inevitable death that would await him there.

Lily walked into the room wearing one of Rosemary's nightgowns. Wordlessly, she trudged into the kitchen and poured a cup of tea. Asher knew his mother would need two cups of tea, leaves steeped until the drink was unbearably bitter, before she'd be prepared for the day. It comforted him to know that not everything was destined to change.

"I'm so sorry," his mother said, sitting beside him. "I never spoke to you about these things—never prepared you. I convinced myself that if I never mentioned it, the day would never come."

"But you did prepare me," Asher said. "You raised me to care about others. Dad raised me never to substitute a duty with an excuse. If I didn't learn those things, this burden would be too great to bear."

She gave him a tender hug. "All the same, a mother will never stop trying to protect her child—even when he's too old to need it."

Asher pulled away, startled by a sound. It started as a low rumble, like thunder echoing through the hills. It grew louder, and Asher grabbed his cup tighter as ripples formed on his tea. "Knights!" Rosen yelled, rushing to the window.

"Quiet!" Rosemary hissed, motioning for them to crouch down. "They will pass."

The stampede came to a halt just outside the cottage. The horses' neighed as one of the knights barked orders. The voices were near the front door, then the window. They were surrounded. A pit formed in Asher's stomach. He had no weapons to fight with nor any places left to run. *Bang. Bang.* Asher turned to the door, the sound of metal splintering wood.

"Under the king's authority, you are commanded to come out!" yelled a knight.

Rosemary ushered Asher toward the bedroom and waved to the others to follow. Collecting herself, she smoothed her dress, picked up a cane, and assumed the posture of a woman much older and more familiar to Asher. She called out in a weary voice, "Coming, dear!"

She unlatched the door's lock, then opened it with a shaking hand. Asher watched from the bedroom door as she looked up to the knight, back hunched, resting her weight on her quivering cane.

"Young man, how can I help you?" she asked.

The knight took off his helmet. "We're here to find escaped prisoners who are quite dangerous," he said. "We did not mean to alarm you."

"Oh my," Rosemary said. "I hope they aren't near. Are your men hungry? I made biscuits."

The knight shifted his weight from one leg to the other. "Have you heard anyone come through?"

"No, I don't believe I've heard anyone named Stew," she said, cocking her ear toward him.

"Has anyone come through?" the knight asked, raising his voice.

"Not in ages, dear."

The knight poked his head past the door. "Those are a lot of biscuits on your counter for someone who lives alone."

"Well, I made one batch and forgot all about it, so I made another," she said. "Would you like some?"

"Is that a gentleman's riding coat on that chair?" the knight asked as he gripped the sword at his belt.

Rosemary made a production as she turned around, taking small steps and ambling her cane with each effort. "Yes, I believe it is," she said. "Must be Huxley's. Fifty years since he passed. I miss him too much ever to move it."

Asher heard the unmistakable sound of metal scraping against metal as the knight drew his sword from the sheath at his waist. The knight took a step forward. "If we search this place and you're lying to me, I will ensure you will join him."

Possessed by a force he could not control, Asher leaped out of the room and charged toward the knight. "Leave her alone!" he yelled.

Time seemed to slow. The knight lunged toward him as he leaned forward. Asher grabbed the man's arm, planted his foot, and pulled the knight's weight toward him, bending his knees and angling the knight over his shoulder. Metal clanked to the ground as the knight flipped in the air, crashing down on the kitchen table, its legs jutting out and collapsing under the weight.

Asher grabbed the knight's fallen sword and thrust hopelessly into the knights assembled beyond the door. Suddenly, an armored elbow struck him hard from the side, sending the sword flying from his grip. He turned his head just in time to catch a flash of silver armor before it slammed into his face. He stumbled before another knight grabbed him from behind, pinning his arms and heaving his body against the front of the house. He heard shouts from inside as knights marched through the door.

"Contraband!" a knight shouted. "Burn everything!"

The rope itched against his skin as it tightened into a knot, binding his arms behind him. Another blow to the neck. His legs went limp, but darkness came before he hit the ground.

Asher woke, dimly aware he was in the back of a carriage with the others. A stranger sat next to him, bound in rope. He overheard a knight call her Beverly. The carriage swayed dangerously to the left as its wheels bounced off an obstruction in the road. Asher braced, waiting for it to tip over. Instead, he bounced hard against the carriage wall as the wheels found their footing.

He passed in and out of consciousness, like a drowsy morning where dreams kept pulling him back from the waking day. Finally, jolted back to life by piercing shouts and a flood of light that cascaded into the carriage as its door opened, Asher struggled against the arms that pulled him outside. He watched as his family, Beverly, and Rosen were led away toward the same door through which he and Rosen escaped.

A burlap rag wound over his mouth muffled Asher's shouts. Its bitter taste made Asher cough, doubling over and wheezing for air.

"Off to the stage with this one," a knight ordered. "Bind him to the pole and wait for the king to deliver justice upon him."

CHAPTER 31

THE QUEEN'S MERCY

An unfamiliar knock sounded at the door to Verity's chambers. She composed herself, adopting a posture that exuded the poise and authority befitting her station. Her hand lingered above the door handle as she took in one more breath before opening it.

"My queen," her husband's manservant said, bowing his head. "His Majesty seeks the honor of your company in the gallery hall by the grand balcony."

"Where is my handmaid, Beverly?" Verity asked, arching her neck to look past the manservant. A knight stood at attention toward the end of the hall.

"She is not to be found, my queen," he said, bowing his head again. "I apologize for this breach of protocol."

Verity hesitated a moment, risking that her face could betray her with a flash of uncertainty. She couldn't recall a time when Beverly didn't attend her post. Further, knights were never welcomed in the residence wing.

"Very well," she said, striding before the manservant as she headed down the hall. "Knight, why are you stationed in the residence?"

The knight bowed his head. "Orders to keep you safe, my queen."

The manservant caught up to the queen. "Apologies, my queen. With the gardens opened today to address your subjects from the grand balcony, your security is the king's paramount concern."

"Fine, then. Come along," she said, snapping her fingers as she walked ahead—as if she were summoning her pets. Even if Verity were walking into a trap, she was determined to lead the way rather than suffer the indignity of being dragged in chains.

The recent end of the war and the day's public address did little to quell her unease. Guards ahead pulled intricately carved doors to the gallery open, closing them after she entered. The lock latched behind her. She forced herself to keep her composure as she strode down the hall.

Verity assumed the gallery would be a hive of attendants, diplomats, and royal speechwriters, all working to prepare and pamper the king before his address. Instead, it was empty, save for the king at the end, near the doors leading to the balcony.

The gallery hall, Verity's cherished sanctuary within the castle, was a marvel of architectural grandeur. With the balcony doors flung wide and the lavish windows soaring from the floor to the vaulted ceiling, it offered a sweeping vista of the realm. Here, perched high above the world, the village below vanished, leaving only the undulating hills rolling like waves toward the Blue Mountains.

"Do you take me for a fool?" the king asked, his back to the queen.

"Reginald," the queen said, her voice calming like soft velvet, "I think we've been married long enough that we both know the answer to that question."

He turned to face her. "Your handmaid was spotted leaving the castle under cover of darkness with the peasant boy's parents," he said. "Can you explain that?"

Verity glared at him. "You protest the queen's guests and then chide her for sending them away?"

"Would it interest you to know that the guards apprehended your handmaid? She disclosed where she took them. Not back to the village, but a cottage not found on our royal census," the king said. "And before you have cause to cast another lie, you should know that our knights came upon the cottage this morning, apprehending the peasant boy, his family, and our *trusted* diplomat, Rosen."

Verity brushed her hair over her ear. "It does interest me. My handmaid was only following my instruction."

"The house had contraband. Forbidden things. Ancient things," the king said, his voice trailing off. "If every bit of the rot isn't removed, it will still spread. If an infection takes the ankle, we amputate at the knee."

Verity gathered what breath she could muster to whisper, "I invoke... the queen's mercy."

"The queen is in need of her own mercy!" King Bracken bellowed. "You must have known of this cottage and the things it contained. Our son intimated that the peasant boy had escaped.

He was sequestered in his room the entire day, watched by our guards. You were the only one to speak with our son. You must have known of the boy's escape and chosen not to share it with me."

Verity looked away, unable to speak—unable to think. The king raised his voice, eyes burning. "After the celebration, Rosen will be made to speak. Let his last words be truthful. He will barter his secrets for his life. I know you played a role in this deception that was more unforgivable than your misplaced compassion. There will be consequences!"

"Compassion is never wasted upon those who suffer," Verity said, facing her husband. "You know that. Or you once did."

"It is a false compassion to condemn them to greater suffering," he said, gripping his chest. "You will see true compassion today, my queen. I will gift our people with a wonder unlike anything they have seen before. This sword. The amulet glowing on a chain under my robes. Let our people dwell in the blissful twilight of ignorance while cradled in the unwavering promise of peace and stability. This, my queen, is the gift of a *true* ruler."

The door at the other end of the gallery hall unlatched, and stewards wheeled carts of food and wine into the hall, followed by the royal tailor and a delegation of others the queen had expected earlier. Like a cavalry of charging knights to her aid, their arrival allowed Verity to breathe once more.

"Let us put this debate aside, my queen," the king said as his mood lightened. "Today, we will celebrate our kingdom's victory and its peace."

"My king," the manservant said, interrupting, "would you and the queen care for wine?"

"No, thank you," the queen said, waving the cup away.

"Please, Verity—I insist," the king said. "It's a reserve from my grandfather's cellar. Appropriate for a day when we celebrate his sword's return."

The king took a glass and tipped it to his lips, finishing it. Grudgingly, the queen took her glass and sipped it. Wishing it had soured to vinegar, she couldn't argue that it was quite good. She took another drink and returned a smile, thinking that perhaps her situation wasn't yet beyond her ability to influence.

Verity watched as her son was escorted into the galley hall, his shoulders slumped and his head bowed. He was dressed in his ceremonial uniform, but the usual pride and confidence were absent, replaced by a vacant expression that tugged at her heart. His pristine white jacket was adorned with insignia and medals recognizing heroism and dedication to the kingdom. No matter how many awards covered his uniform, they would always be too few.

Verity walked closer to the balcony beyond the double glass doors at the end of the gallery hall. Her subjects filled the gardens and stretched farther back than she could see. Flags waved. Horns blew. An orator performed on the stage set at the end of the balcony. His words were hard to hear through the glass, but his cadence sang like music. The speech swelled to its final peroration, and the crowd responded with roaring applause and cheers reverberating into the gallery.

It wouldn't be long before her husband took to the stage. Verity considered what would be safe for her to say as the royal staff peppered her son with finishing touches—trimming an errant string on his jacket and smoothing down wrinkles on his trousers. They swarmed him like mosquitos on a summer evening.

"Whatever happens out there, be brave," Verity said as Hunter turned away. "Just don't confuse bravery with foolishness."

"I'll do my part. I'll say my lines," Hunter said.

"Your father has," she began, pausing to choose her words carefully, "recaptured Asher. Be prepared. The king may see fit to dispense his justice for all to see."

Hunter whipped his head around to her, enraged. His jaw clenched. She knew he was a boiling pot of water with its lid held down by all the force he could muster. She hoped he would be strong enough to do what he must.

Royal horn players blew their instruments from their posts on the sprawling balcony. Startled by the noise, Verity fought to slow her racing heart. Despite the chill in the air, she dabbed her brow with a lace handkerchief. String players began after the horns, strumming the first notes to the kingdom's anthem. Tradition and well-practiced formalities became like an instinct as she took a ready position behind the king, next to her son.

She looked out over the crowds again from the door and felt dizzy. Her mind spun in a whirlwind of her fears and hopes. So violent was her storm that she lost her ability to distinguish between the two.

As the anthem ended and the crowd erupted in cheers, the king took bold steps from the threshold and walked to the balcony's edge, overlooking the assembled masses. Nauseated, she followed behind him, grabbing the deck's railing as she met him by his side.

"Subjects of Barbshire Kingdom," the king bellowed, "we have laid waste to the usurpers who brought fires to our village, those who sought to starve us in the siege. Their governor will be dealt with, but mercy shall be given to those who swear their loyalty to the Crown."

The crowd's roars and cheers rattled the railing, and Verity gave more of her weight to it. Her vision blurred in the midday sun, and unease fell over her. Something was wrong. She was not so unaccustomed to fear as to surrender like the first leaf in autumn. Her face burned, but she forced a smile and waved to the crowd.

"The Apex Blade has been returned to us," the king yelled, holding the sword high above his head to the fervent cheers below. "Its power will quell wars and put fear in the hearts of men who seek them! It can heal the wounded, bring fire from the sky, and make its bearer invincible!"

The crowd began to chant in unison: *sword, sword, sword*. The king waved the sword from one side of the crowd to another. The crowd cheered louder.

The king smiled and then charged toward the grand balcony's ledge, sword pointing ahead toward another balcony a hundred feet away. The queen and crowd below all gasped as the king vaulted from the railing and soared an impossible distance to land on the other balcony, a red hue glowing around his body. His feet hit the ground, and the crowd erupted in ecstasy. The queen watched as some of her subjects fell to their knees, others collapsing into the arms of those behind them.

The king raised his arms as if to lift the crowd's fervor again. To the chorus of their resounding cheers, he bounded from the deck and sailed once more through the air, landing safely back on the grand balcony. King Bracken rejoined Hunter and the queen at its edge, his eyes glistening with swirls of red. Verity stepped back, instinctively bracing her arm against Hunter's chest.

"I do not deserve every measure of your praise," the king said. "Our prince. My son. Prince Hunter Bracken," he yelled to more cheers from the crowd. "He bravely volunteered to retrieve the sword from the treacherous gnomes who stole it so long ago." The king put his hand on Hunter's shoulder and held the sword high in his other hand. "Your prince borrowed my blade to end the war. He had the grace and humility to place the blade at my feet in honor and devotion to his king."

Hunter looked away from the crowd, and Verity thought that his face was the portrait of revulsion. Verity's knees began to buckle. She gripped the railings ever tighter. If it weren't for her fear, she thought she would collapse.

"Alas," the king yelled. "Our prince faced many hardships in his quest. He came upon a traitor from our village. Asher Snow, the peasant boy. He betrayed our son's compassion and sought the blade for himself!" the king bellowed, and the crowd's exuberance became wrath. "Fear not!" the king said, trying to quiet the crowd. "We have apprehended Asher, and the prince will take the Apex Blade and bring justice for all of us to witness!"

The queen's vision began to darken. She heard her pulse beating in her ears. Guards wheeled out a wooden brace with Asher tied around it. Ropes bound his arms, legs, and waist. Verity grabbed her son's arm as the crowd's din gave cover for her voice.

"Hunter," she said, "something is wrong. A sickness is gripping me. Whatever happens, please free Asher. Free yourself. Run and never, never look back."

CHAPTER 32

FELLED BY HIS OWN WEAPON

Asher's heart lifted from its despair when he saw Hunter. He wept tears of joy even as the king handed Hunter the Apex Blade, and the crowds below demanded execution in their macabre chorus of cheers. The king put his hand on Hunter's shoulder and pulled him over to Asher. Suddenly, the queen screamed out in pain, buckling over and holding the railing on the balcony.

"Mother is ill," Hunter yelled to his father.

"No, she's not ill," the king said, digging his fingers into Hunter's shoulder. "She's dying."

"What do you mean?" Hunter asked, trying to pull away from the king's firm grip.

"I had her wine poisoned," the king said with no more urgency than a musing on the day's weather. "Don't worry. I have the antidote. I'll administer it immediately. All you need to do is to plunge the Apex Blade through this peasant's heart—kill him by your own hand. Your rebellion… your insolence. Your false love. Let it die with him. Justice will be satisfied as long as one traitor dies today. You get to choose which one."

"Hunter!" Asher called out.

The king released his grip on his son and strode over to the railing, leaning against it as the queen struggled to stay on her feet. "My subjects!" he yelled. "Our prince will plunge the Apex Blade through the traitor's heart and restore justice to our kingdom!"

The crowds below erupted in a frenzy of bloodthirsty roars, their voices merging into a savage symphony. Asher couldn't believe that the same voices that cheered him in the streets just days before now bayed like animals for his death. Were the minds of men so easily yielding, their loyalty as aimless as a traveler without a map? Asher searched the prince's face, hoping for a glimmer of mercy or understanding. Instead, he was met with wide, terrified eyes that reflected the chaos below, as if his mind was bound by ropes more constricting than those that chafed Asher's wrists.

"I don't know what to do," Hunter pleaded. "I can't hurt you. I'll *never* hurt you."

Asher raised his voice over the deafening crowd. "I couldn't live if I knew you traded my life for your mother's. She helped me escape, helped my parents."

Hunter cupped his hand under Asher's ear and leaned closer. "She told me to save you and run. Leave with you and never look back. She said the bravest thing is to let someone go, but I can't leave either of you. If that's what heroism demands, I'm unworthy of honors pinned to my chest."

"I've gambled with cards, ignored the amulet's warnings, and lost Lattice to my pride. I know what it's like to want something so much that you ignore the risks. Your father wants the crowd to believe in this blade more than anything. That's his weakness," Asher said, his voice cracking. "If it can heal the sick, then let it!"

Asher watched as an idea took form and displaced Hunter's despair. The prince flashed a familiar smile, pushed himself off Asher's bindings, and strode to his father's side, holding the Apex Blade in the air. The crowds responded in kind, cheering once more.

"Before I use this blade, I must thank my father for his grace," Hunter yelled. Taken aback, the king awkwardly smiled, taking praise from his son and drinking adoration from the crowds below. "Before I continue," Hunter said, drawing the crowd's attention again, "I have learned that a traitor has poisoned the queen!"

The crowd gasped in shock as Verity's knees gave out. She caught herself on the railing, her crown tumbling to her side. Asher watched as staff from inside the gallery hall charged onto the deck, fear in their eyes, helpless to intervene.

"Do not fear!" Hunter said. "I hold the Apex Blade. You have witnessed its power—both on the fields of war and even today in my father's hands." Asher gently placed the sword on his mother's shoulder. She looked up to him with weary eyes. "I draw out the poison from the queen's blood with the power of the Apex Blade!"

The crowd cheered again, a rapturous, fever-pitched cry of joy and relief. Hunter gripped the sword and walked past his father toward Asher. Asher watched as the king's face went white as his son's unblemished uniform. The king looked out over the crowd and then toward his anguished queen. He dove to her aid, taking a bottle from his vest and administering its contents to her under the cover of the balcony wall.

Hunter took the sword and flicked the blade against the bindings, cutting Asher free. "He had to save her," Hunter whispered. "Otherwise, the sword would be exposed as a lie."

Asher hugged the prince, weeping tears mixed with Hunter's, uncertain which were his own. The question blurred into insignificance. Each was shed from the same love, a bond too strong for even the sword to cut.

"The queen is restored!" the king yelled, jerking Verity up by her arm. Her eyes already looked brighter and her feet steadier. The crowd erupted again in cries of joy, thanking the sword and praising the Watchers.

"Now!" Hunter yelled, grabbing Asher's arm and bounding with the sword toward the gallery hall. Seeing the sword, the knights standing guard at the doors dropped their weapons and fell to one knee. The tailor and the others assembled within did the same as the pair raced toward the grand stairwell.

The king's voice followed behind them. Asher stole a glance to see the king running from the balcony toward them, his legs carrying him unnaturally fast. Hunter tugged him to the left, and they ran down a hallway with a grand staircase in view. Leaping every other step, they wound their way down flights of stairs.

"He wears the amulet," Hunter yelled as he pulled Asher toward the stairwell.

"Come back here!" the king yelled, his voice growing closer.

Leaping to the marble floor from the last step, Asher ran at Hunter's side toward the main gate. The king bellowed again, and Asher turned to see him leaning over the banisters at the top of the stairs, a red aura pulsing around him.

"Stop them!" the king yelled to the guards below.

The guards hesitated, taking note of the blade in Hunter's hand, candlelight glinting off its sharp edges like the corona around an eclipse. One followed by the other, they each fled from their post by the exit. King Bracken roared in anger. He vaulted over the railings above and hurtled down through the air. Asher watched as a red ball of light took form around the king, growing brighter as he fell as if fueled by his unbridled rage.

Asher recognized the glow—a thing he perceived with the amulet but never saw, like gnomes hidden in a bush. He recalled his first taste of its power when he leapt over sticklebush. It was as though the cursed charm had whispered in his ear, seductively urging him toward greater risks, promising him the world while veiling its cost. Unburdened by its influence, his mind sober, Asher found a new insight into the amulet's true nature. It was a deceptive siren's song, an alluring lie cloaked in the guise of protection, yet at a dire cost. *How had it become so powerful?* So much power would demand a price Asher could have never paid.

King Bracken collided with the marble floor below, and a shockwave of ruby light pulsed from him in all directions, shattering carved busts on their pillars and snapping portraits into splinters. The wave lifted Asher in the air and threw him against the wall.

Broken glass from once towering windows fell like torrential rain. Asher covered his face as he struggled to breathe air into his lungs.

When the glass ceased to fall, Asher peered from behind his arms to see the king bent on one knee amid crumbled marble at his feet, cracks spreading around him like a spider's web. The king groaned and tipped over on his side. Asher ran to him as Verity shouted from above, running down the stairs. Asher reached out and touched the king's neck. His pulse was still strong, yet he lay motionless amid the rubble. His robes were burnt around his chest, revealing a chain with a broken shard of the amulet still hanging upon it. Asher dared not remove it, fearing that whatever grace was left in the amulet may have been all that kept the king alive.

"Reginald!" the queen yelled, diving to his side and cradling his head. She wept and rocked him back and forth. "You will *not* die. You will not leave me!"

Asher steadied himself. "He wore the amulet. I felt its power when the wave hit me—stronger than it should have been. The amulet protected him at the cost of his soul."

Asher turned to look for Hunter amid the rubble. A sliver of light cut through the darkness from unguarded doors leading outside the castle. The blast had broken the lanterns, and the candles were snuffed out. Among the shadows, Asher spotted a glimpse of light reflecting from a white blazer. Hunter was crumpled on the ground, his uniform defiled by more than the plaster and broken wood piled upon him. Asher's throat tightened, a lump forming like a knot of unspoken fears. He approached with a cautious reverence, each step laden with apprehension. Fear held him back, a fear to touch, to call out Hunter's name, lest in doing so, he would be forced to surrender hope and confirm his deepest dread. He yearned to hold on to hope, his only light in the abyss—his faith suddenly more valuable than any truth.

"Hunter?" Asher asked, trying not to startle him.

The prince groaned and rolled to his side, his jacket blemished with a crimson stain. Asher took the Apex Blade and pulled it from Hunter's abdomen. Asher surmised Hunter must have fallen back in the blast and been impaled by the blade. Approximately four inches deep, missing the spleen, possibly cutting the liver. He no longer cared how he knew such things. Internal bleeding with intestinal damage. *Stop the bleeding.* Asher judged he needed surgery and antibiotics, with sterile dressings—none of which could be invented in time to help.

"Let's get your head up," Asher said, resting Hunter's head on Asher's thigh and pressing his hand over Hunter's. "Keep pressure here."

"Hunter?" the queen asked, running toward them.

"He's hurt," Asher said. "Stabbed by the blade. Pretty deep."

"The royal apothecary can be summoned," Verity said, her voice shaking. "He has yarrow herbs."

"It's more serious than that. Internal bleeding. He's beyond the aid of anything you have," Asher said as an idea took form. "I need your fastest knight to bring us to the Canopy of the Elders—it's his only hope."

Verity placed her hand on her son's arm. "You know of this place?"

Asher nodded his head. "I was sickened by the same amulet. Hunter took me there and the Canopy healed me."

Verity's face sank before him. "Will he make it that far?"

"We have to try," Asher said as tears welled. "It's our only hope. The knight must wear a wet cloth around his nose to avoid The Madness. Quickly!"

"Wait here. I'll bring in the captain of our knights and put you on a royal carriage car. Please," Verity said, taking his arm, "take care of my son."

"I will. I love him," Asher said as his lip quivered.

CHAPTER 33

The Unmendable Wound

The knight urged the horse-drawn carriage over the road with the wind's haste. Asher held Hunter's head in his lap on the carriage floor. An ornately carved door sprang open with a hard bump in the road; it swung wildly, slamming closed before flying back open.

"Asher?" Hunter asked, grimacing in pain.

"Hold on," Asher said, putting more pressure on the wound. "You'll be safe."

"The sword?"

"It's here," Asher said, showing him the hilt.

"I'm so sorry," Hunter said, his voice graveled.

Asher combed his hand through Hunter's untamed hair. "You have nothing to be sorry for. You were right. I can't see the world as if everything rests on me. Neither should you. You didn't poison your mother or force your father to wear the amulet."

Asher braced himself against the carriage wall as the knight diverged from the road and charged through a rocky field. His bloodstained handprint marked the wall.

"Will the bards sing of our victory? Will they remember us well? When the kingdom finds peace, don't let their songs remember me without your name," Hunter said, his voice growing weak. "I found love; love led me to hope, and hope keeps me unafraid of death's shadow."

"You fought bravely," Asher said, unable to hold back his tears. "But that fight isn't over. The war has not yet been won!" he yelled. "Hold on. There is no victory without you."

Asher held the prince tighter. The sun began to sink into dusk as the carriage charged ahead. Long shadows reached from the trees as if their snarled branches were clawing toward him. He thought of Lattice, still resting where he fell, deprived of the honors he deserved. Asher closed his eyes and thought of the nanobots that pulsed through his blood, bestowing him with so much knowledge. What good was it to save society if he couldn't save the only person he loved?

Interrupting his thoughts, the horse began to neigh and cry. The carriage swerved, and the knight urged the horse on. "The Madness," Asher whispered. He took a blanket from the carriage bench and draped it over Hunter's nose, feeling the fever burning from his forehead. The carriage jolted again, nearly tipping on its side. He heard the knight shouting as the carriage slowed to a halt. Gently, Asher rested the prince's head within the blanket's folds and stepped outside.

"What's the problem?" Asher asked.

The knight, his mouth covered by a damp cloth, held the horse's mane, looking into its eyes. "The Madness," the knight said, "It's taken the horse."

Asher watched the horse struggle, crying and shaking its head. "Let the horse go," Asher said.

"Sir, it's too far to carry the prince—not in his condition."

"I know, sir knight," Asher said. "But we cannot torment the horse. It doesn't understand. It could topple us."

The knight dropped his helmet. Forlorn, he removed the bindings, and the horse bolted into a gallop, fleeing back along the path it came. Asher walked back to the carriage and retrieved the Apex Blade. The knight took a few steps back in retreat.

"Relax, sir knight. The prince trusts me with his blade. Stand back."

"But sir," the knight pleaded, "if you wield the Apex Blade, why not use it to cure our prince, as it did his mother?"

Asher looked at the sword in his hand. He stopped before explaining the truth, fearing the knight's loyalty may be conditioned on his answer. "Our prince... his wound was caused by the blade. It can't heal its own wound."

The knight's eyes widened, and he nodded as if reminded of a rule he had forgotten. Asher lifted the blade, nimble and light. He swung it into the carriage's corner post, snapping it and causing the roof to slope. Then the other corner. "Sir knight, I'll cut the other posts. When I do, push the roof toward me."

The knight positioned himself in place, and Asher cut the

remaining posts. With the knight pushing and Asher pulling from the other side, the wood snapped and splintered as the roof and walls came off. Hunter lay unharmed on the carriage floor.

"Now the wheels," Asher said. "I'll cut them away. Hold up the side. Don't let it fall. We'll make a stretcher."

"Stretcher?"

Asher sighed. "A platform. We can carry the prince the rest of the way on the platform."

The knight held the carriage as Asher used the blade to cut the axles holding the wheels. Each cut was like a knife through paper. Asher marveled at whatever metamaterial it was made from, its properties unknown to him. Gently, they lowered the platform to the ground. Taking opposing sides, Asher and the knight strained as they lifted it off the ground. Together, they managed a steady pace, one anguishing step at a time, toward a hill Asher recognized. Beyond the hill, he knew the Elders would be waiting.

Asher's arms strained, and his legs burned as they descended the hill. Hunter still held his hand over the wound, groaning in pain. The knight kept turning to look behind him, sweating despite the encroaching chill in the wind.

"A fool's errand, sir," the knight said. "Lingering enemies from Bishop Falls could be in the woods. It could be a trap. I beg you, sir. We should leave now."

"You took your helmet off, along with the towel," Asher said. "We're almost through The Madness—just a bit more. I *know* that fear, that sense of impending doom. Don't fight it. Let the fear come, and don't dwell on it. Just one step. Then the other," Asher said as he struggled to carry more than his share of the weight. "Do not regard those thoughts. Give them no quarter in your mind. If you don't grip them, they can't hold you!"

"I can't let go of this fear," the knight said.

"Plants in this clearing make a hallucinogenic gas. It's nothing more. I promise that it will pass."

The platform began to shake as their arms began to falter. Asher planted a foot atop the hill and groaned as he leveled the platform. He turned to the Elders. Gone were their fecund branches, lush and teeming with life. In their place, brittle branches strung like dead vines, a hollow tunnel where dried leaves danced in the wind. A chill pierced through Asher's shirt, and his eyes stung.

"Hurry," Asher said. "There must be buds of life within, toward the center of the Canopy."

Desperation brought a rush of strength. Asher hoisted the stretcher higher toward his hips and charged ahead, the knight stumbling before regaining his balance. Moonlight in the cloudless sky filtered through the branches above them, lighting a path. Hunter moaned again as they gently laid the stretcher down on the ground within what was left of the Elders' embrace.

"Go now," Asher said, tears blurring his vision. "Let any mercy of the Elders find Hunter without dividing their grace to another."

The knight hesitated, walking backward before turning to run, glancing back one last time. Asher turned back to Hunter after he was assured that they were alone.

"Hunter," Asher whispered, touching the prince's burning cheek. Asher searched the branches around him in vain for any sprout of life. *Could there not be so much as a quick green shoot in the Canopy's limbs?* His anger swelled toward the Elders. *Where is your will to live, your bravery? Do not succumb! Prove your defiance of death!*

"Let him live!" Asher yelled into the barren branches. "If you covet your own lives, then take from my own! I know what you are!" Asher's voice cracked as it filled the Canopy. "They put nanobots inside you, wanting to preserve you for all time and spare you from the poison."

"Asher," Hunter said, his voice tender and pleading.

"I'm here! I'm here," Asher said, returning to his side.

"The Elders only give what they can. It may take them years to bloom again. They can't spend the last ounce of their grace at the expense of their lives. Neither can you," he said.

Asher abandoned any attempt to hold back his emotions as a rising hysteria began to boil. "They would still thrive if it wasn't for me."

"That was my choice, not yours," Hunter said with a labored smile as he laid his head back and closed his eyes.

"No, no, no," Asher said, cradling Hunter's neck. The prince's breathing came in uneven sputters.

He wished his nanobots granted him immortality, for he would cut his hand and give the Elders' grace to Hunter's wounds. He recalled that even the native, untrained nanobots brought their own blessings—fighting illnesses, gifts of intellect, and recovery. Asher took the Apex Blade to his arm and steadied himself to pierce his own skin, determined to share whatever blessing he could. *Share the blessing.* The words sparked a memory, diffuse and elusive. *Coin and Blood. Share the Blessing.* The writing on the wall in the cell.

Asher dug in his pocket and pulled out the worthless charm he was told nonetheless to keep. *What if it were more than a mere coin?* Irrational and frantic, he unwrapped the cloth around the coin and pressed it into Hunter's wound. Closing his eyes, he begged for help. The coin grew warm. Then hot. Asher pulled his hands away, and the coin basked the Canopy in golden light. It melted over Hunter's body like butter kissed by flame.

The golden shimmer began to dissolve away, and Asher marveled as the wound began to close, knitting itself back together, leaving no scar. Hunter blinked and groaned. Asher brushed his hand over the prince's forehead, his fever broken. With tears streaming down his face, he kissed Hunter's cheek.

"What happened?" Hunter asked, trying to sit. Asher slid to his side, helping him gently.

"That coin I had," Asher said in a whisper. "It's a device. Apparently, it's used to transmit nanobots to people who don't have them."

"So, I have all the world's knowledge now? Immortality?" Hunter asked.

"No," Asher said. "I wouldn't burden you with either. Even before they're programmed, they can help repair cells, maintain blood sugar, treat infection—lots of things."

"My blood is sweetened?"

Asher sighed. "Think of it this way—billions of little machines are working inside you, healing your wounds and keeping you healthy. They can be programmed to do other things. Somehow, anyway. For now, they're why you're alive."

Hunter inspected his hands and wiggled his fingers. "I don't credit the machines. I owe you my life, once again."

"I wasn't going to let you go without a fight," Asher said, helping Hunter stand.

Hunter's face flushed. "In that case, I don't plan on making a habit out of putting you in danger of having to."

Asher wrapped his arms around the prince. Blustery winds howled through the Canopy, but Asher felt no chill of night in Hunter's embrace.

"What of my father?" Hunter asked.

"He survived the fall. He didn't look injured—not outwardly, at least," Asher said. "He was unconscious when we left. I don't know what the amulet took from him—or how he may recover."

"Any regard I had for him was lost when he poisoned my mother and sought to have you harmed," Hunter said as his gaze lifted toward the kingdom. "Of my injuries, this wound will not heal."

"He thought he was protecting you—and everyone," Asher said. "He became so certain of his convictions that he stopped listening. We both know how dangerous this knowledge can be, and your father isn't wrong to fear it."

Hunter draped his arm around Asher's shoulder. "Which is why we have you—someone wise enough only to use the knowledge for the betterment of all. Your compassion is incorruptible."

"It'll take more than just one person," Asher said.

"Then it sounds like we have a lot of work to do," Hunter said,

smiling as they retraced their steps back to the knight waiting at
the edge of the Canopy.

CHAPTER 34

THE WAY FORWARD

H unter declined any assistance from the apothecary who met them at the gates. The apothecary assured them that the king's heart still beat and that there were no serious lacerations, yet neither offered assurance of recovery.

"Is he in a coma? Will he wake?" Asher asked.

"His eyes are shrouded in a pearl haze, unlike anything I've seen," the apothecary reported. "His chest rises and falls too rarely to support life, but he nonetheless lingers."

"I need to speak with my mother. Go to the dining hall. Eat something," Hunter said, his voice so somber that Asher couldn't bring himself to protest.

The apothecary escorted Asher, but his thoughts were too preoccupied to recall how he arrived at his destination. His host, the senior butler, apologized that dinner had just ended. Both highborns and royalty recently dined in the great hall, along with esteemed knights and senior servants. A soiled linen drape still adorned the high table. Half-eaten food lay piled on neglected plates. Asher chose a seat at the smallest table, close enough to the fire to warm his damp toes.

Hanging tapestries on the walls were embroidered with unfamiliar seals. The room echoed with the sound of his knife clinking against his plate. Wordlessly, his host, balancing a platter on one hand, paraded over to him with flawless posture, and served it with such formality that Asher had to stifle a laugh. *It's just the two of us.*

Asher spread warm butter and chilled apricot jam on bread. As he took his last bite, the host returned with another plate of roast duck drenched in a sweet-smelling sauce with plum tomatoes. His host made special mention that the vegetables had been grown in the royal greenhouse. Asher nodded approvingly, reflecting on his own humble beginnings. Just like the vegetables, it seemed their origin mattered more to others than to him. Then came a bowl of stew with more meat than broth.

"Sir," Asher said as the host began his latest approach from the kitchen, "the food is wonderful, but it's more than I can eat."

"I'm so sorry, my lord," he said, bowing. "If the stew has spoiled your appetite for sugar cake, I will reprimand our chef."

"No, please don't! I would hate to insult the pastry chef as well. Perhaps no more, though."

"No tea? An ale, then?"

Before Asher could resolve the complexities of dinner diplomacy, Hunter walked into the great hall with a broad smile. "That will be all, thank you."

The host bowed his head, leaving the sugar cake on the table.

Asher dabbed his mouth with a cloth napkin, as he'd seen highborn do at the tavern, and stood. "Just in time. I was in the process of offending the entire kitchen."

"They're just doing their job," Hunter said. "Now we must do the same. Mother would like to meet you."

Asher's throat tightened. "The queen?"

"She's not that bad, I promise. It's quite casual. Our tailor can find a suitable robe for you."

Asher was sure that the prince could read the panic on his face. Hunter laughed. "I'm kidding! I promised no funny robes. Just come as you are."

Asher caught Hunter's bemused expression as he took a quick bite of the sugar cake before wiping his mouth with his sleeve and leaving with the prince. On their way, Hunter explained that Asher's parents and grandmother were getting settled into guest rooms before Lattice's memorial service later in the week.

Hunter escorted him to a study in the residence wing. Asher marveled at shelves filled with more books than he had ever seen, stacked taller than two men. He blushed when Hunter tapped his shoulder and motioned to the queen sitting at a reading table.

"Your Majesty," Asher said, fumbling a slight bow.

The queen offered a bemused expression, strikingly familiar to the one Asher had grown increasingly accustomed to seeing on Hunter's face. "Please. Call me Verity. Both of you, take a seat."

Hunter took Asher's hand. "I told you he was wonderful."

The queen smiled for a moment before her expression became

somber. "I wanted to personally thank you for everything you've done—for Hunter and the realm."

"I was just trying to help."

"I know," she said. "I also believe you're entitled to an explanation." Verity sighed and looked toward the books on the shelves. "The room you're in contains what we call the forbidden texts—books that teach many of the things you've already learned in the vault. Some were written before the war. Others, just after."

"You knew about all of this?" Asher asked.

"When I married Hunter's father, he shared these books with me. I've read a few, most of which are beyond my ability to decipher. It's like having only a handful of pieces to a puzzle. But you," Verity said as she shifted her weight in her chair, "you can understand the context. And... it frightens me."

"Frighten?" Asher asked. "I'd never do anything that would hurt people."

Verity studied him. "Do you know why people die when they travel into the Poisoned Fields?"

Asher thought about it for a moment. "Areas of the world were bombed with weapons that left a radioactive wasteland behind—where the air would poison any living thing."

"Quite right," Verity said. "But the most harmful radioactivity decayed centuries ago. Why do they still die?"

Asher was at a loss. He shook his head and shrugged. "Governor Wicker's daughter... Gertrude. We met her in the mountains. She escaped to the Poisoned Fields with Ruth, the person she loves."

"I will send word to search for her and ensure her safe return.

Our king has a secret regiment of knights. When brave or foolhardy people set out hoping to find new lands, the brigade ensures the fields are as deadly as the legend promises. They were recently recalled to prepare for battle with Bishop Falls."

"They what?" Hunter asked. "Father never told me that."

Verity gently laid her hand atop her son's. "There's much he hasn't told you. I learned the awful truth years ago. It motivated me to seek out the Guardians—people like Asher's grandmother and the Witch of the Forest. In secret, I learned about their goals. I helped when I could."

"Who are the Guardians?" Hunter asked.

"The Guardians are the remaining immortals from before the war. They call me a Keeper. We support the Guardians. There was a time when Guardians would work together, gradually reintroducing technology—throughout vast kingdoms beyond Barbshire and the Eastlands. The ruling class felt the Guardians had too much power. They were forced into hiding. Our king and those before him all favored stagnation and stability, seeing progress like weeds to be purged from a garden."

Asher's stomach soured as the queen continued her history lesson. The basic philosophy was simple enough: In the past, humanity would always thrive in the brief interludes between wars that some called peace. Those periods of prosperity would coincide with labor-saving innovations, gifting people with surplus time. Time away from labor's toils purchased education. New inventions fueled a cycle that was either vicious or virtuous, depending on one's perspective.

She explained that generations of kings kept taxes high, leaving people with barely enough to fill a plate but rarely to fill their stomachs. Jobs demanding intense labor left the populace with scarce moments for rest, let alone time for indulging in intellectual or artistic pursuits. Relegating the population to a life of exhaustive toil was intended as a mercy to protect them from repeating history's gravest sins.

Asher leaned forward in his chair. "So, you support our goals?"

"Tentatively," she said. "But what if someone learned how you made gunpowder and shared the knowledge with the other cities? I trust Rosen, but he was the one who took matters into his own hands when he shared the iron plow with Bishop Falls, which led them to insurrection. Yet I don't blame him. We can't hold back progress. Still, we must not be imprudent."

Asher winced and looked away as the image of Lattice's sacrifice seared his memory more painfully than any admonishment ever could.

"You may have more knowledge than any human who ever walked the Earth, but I fear you're too young to exercise judgment. Don't misunderstand," she said, punctuating herself with her finger, "I have no doubt that your heart is pure and your intentions are noble."

"Do you mean to stop us?" Hunter asked.

Verity closed her eyes and shook her head. "No," she whispered. "I mean to *help* you. I hope my husband recovers, and if he does, we will need to keep you safe."

Asher rubbed his temples and mustered the courage to say what he was afraid to admit to himself. "What if the king was right?"

"He wasn't," Hunter interrupted. "Knowledge is neither good nor bad. It's what we choose to do with it that matters."

Verity smiled and squeezed her son's hand. "Asher, how did you know about the coin that saved my son's life?"

Asher shrugged. "There were writings on the walls in the dungeon. The coins must have been made after the war—a way to continue distributing nanobots to people."

"And I thought they were merely useful tools to reveal those who had them," Verity said. "What of the charm our king abused? Do you know anything about its magic?"

Asher's mind swirled, and he gripped the arm of his chair to steady himself from vertigo. "It's not magic," he whispered as he clawed his focus back to the moment. "Before the war, people made tools based on quantum physics. I think the charm uses quantum wavefunction manipulation—a way to bend reality toward an improbable outcome."

"Huh?" Hunter asked, squinting his eyes.

Asher ignored him and collected his thoughts. "My best guess is that the charm manipulated the wavefunctions in the king's atoms in relation to gravity. This effectively reduced gravity's pull, slowing his fall as if he were traveling through something denser than air, like water. It could make a person fall like a feather."

"What of my husband's prospects for recovery?"

"It could have manipulated his body too much," Asher said. "It's only a guess. The Elders healed me, but I wasn't as sick. Now they can't help anyone. We may need to wait and see if he recovers."

Verity took a sip of her tea. "I assumed as such."

"You knew when you suggested the mint?" Hunter asked his mother, leaning over the table.

Verity looked away and closed her eyes. "A mother would forsake the world to protect her son. Knowledge, no matter its consequences, is neither good nor bad. There are those among us who are capable of unspeakable evil. Some use tools for compassion and love," Verity said. "You might condemn my actions as the former, but I promise you it was only a last resort to save you both."

"Good and evil are not always as easy to discern as the stories you read me when I was young," Hunter said. "Humanity thirsts for knowledge as often as it does for power and blood. We're naïve to deny either."

"It's just like our journey for the sword," Asher said, looking at the prince. "There's only ever the way forward."

With a final nod from Verity and an encouraging pat on the back from Hunter, Asher stepped out of the study, his mind teeming with thoughts of the future, the balance of progress and caution, and the role he was destined to play in shaping a new era. His shoulders slumped as he walked, burdened with the shame of being feared by the queen and the lingering sense that her beliefs were warranted.

Hunter had promised a castle tour and asked Asher to meet him in his room. The prince had given him vague directions through intersecting hallways. Each hall led to an uncertain end, much like the questions in his mind. Asher kept moving forward, allowing himself to make wrong turns as he found his way. Were the other choices before him so inconsequential? A wrong turn could lead to a war. Entering the wrong room could bring rebellion. He decided that both journeys had one thing in common. He had to keep trying.

CHAPTER 35

BURDENS OF LEADERSHIP

Three days later, Asher's father tugged at the formal blazer, studying his image in a mirror. He twisted at the waist and lifted his arms. "It's still too tight."

Lily stepped behind him and brushed her hands down his sleeves. "The tailor made it just for you. I won't let you bother him with a third alteration."

"It looks fine, Dad," Asher said, not taking his eyes off the stack of pages beside him. He had been writing frantically for the last two days—equations, notes, and instructions—plans too bold for him to accomplish alone.

His parents' guest room was practically nicer than the prince's—with the library across the hall and a comfortable study by the fire. He considered asking Hunter to switch rooms with them. The idea was fleeting. He did appreciate Hunter's room, or rather, their room, as Hunter often corrected him. The miniature carvings of brave knights and their horses, each arranged with care, made Asher smile. Hunter blushed when he pointed them out.

"I'm sure that if Sir Lattice could give his last measure for the kingdom, then you can suffer through this suit to honor his memory," Lily said.

Asher thought about going down the hall to check on his grandmother, but there were still a few hours before the ceremony, and she needed her rest from the night before. They had worked in the library until the candles burned down, all for the sake of their plan to replace them with electric bulbs. As Asher plotted his ideas on paper, he began to appreciate her engineering acumen—a way to bridge Asher's theories and concepts with workable implementations.

Deciding that Hunter would be up, he left his parents and returned to their room. Valets and servants in the hall would bow their heads, addressing him as *my lord*. Having no formal title other than the one bestowed upon him by the prince, their use of the title felt both underserved and inadequate, unable to encapsulate his love.

"Any news on your father?" Asher asked, entering the room and falling backward on the bed.

"Same as yesterday," Hunter said as he pulled on his stockings. "He still just glares at the wall all day. He takes food and drink but never speaks."

"I'm sorry, Hunter," Asher said.

"Mother worries, but I'd think it the golden age of his rule."

Asher rolled his eyes. "Are you ready for the ceremony?"

"Nearly. I welcomed the delegation from the gnome kingdom while you were adding chapters to your pages of squiggles."

"They're called equations."

Hunter smiled. "I know. Princes are still educated. I tease," he said, giving Asher a playful poke in the side. "I can follow the algebra, but I get lost with calculus, and Fourier transforms, as you call them."

"Impressive," Asher said. "With the nanobots helping boost your brainpower a bit, I'd be happy to teach you about it, along with the other squiggles."

"Don't dare," Hunter said, laughing. "I swear I'll try to wake the king myself."

Asher unfolded his formal attire for the ceremony, smoothing out the blazer and shirt on the bed. Hunter helped him mate the cufflinks on his sleeves. He took a last look in the mirror. His unkempt brown hair was neatly combed. Despite countless days laboring at the farm and leaving the tavern at the end of long nights, skin slick with grease from the pans, he could still recognize his boyish face in the reflection. A faint stubble suggested a beard he may one day need to shave. But not today.

Still, the man in the mirror was not quite the same. The untrustworthy reflection concealed an awful truth. He feared the man he could become and understood that the queen saw him in the same light. Asher settled upon seeing himself as someone striving to do his best, acknowledging that not every problem was his to shoulder, nor every solution his to find.

After breakfast on the veranda with Hunter, they proceeded to the castle's courtyard. Asher greeted Lattice's family and the gnome governess, Wintery. Asher did his best to conceal a smile when Wintery called Hunter "Asher's royal companion." The queen offered a diplomatic gift of preserved jams from berries grown in the royal gardens. Asher accepted a wind flute on behalf of the kingdom. Wintery explained that it was an heirloom Lattice treasured but had no heir to bequeath to.

Hunter placed an urn under a granite tile by the Tree of Heroes, the kingdom's final resting place for its bravest knights. He looked back to those assembled around him. "Let us take a moment to observe the silence we all feel in our hearts, knowing that our brave knight no longer walks among us." He bowed his head.

Asher could hear the wind gusting, and the barren Tree of Heroes waved in the breeze. Hunter invited him to speak on behalf of the Crown. Asher dragged his sleeve over his eyes and stooped down to touch the stone that covered the gnome's remains.

"Lattice was a friend," Asher said, unsure where to begin. "In times long past, our kind—gnomes and humans—were not so different. While small in stature, Lattice reminds us that his people's hearts have only grown in kindness. He saw me as worthy to wield a great power. I will not question his wisdom, though I feel unworthy of his trust. Instead, I will honor his memory by striving to be the person he believed I would become."

Songs were sung, and stories were shared until the winter sun began to set in the west. Asher's heart echoed the sky's sentiment; the day, much like the time granted to his dear friend, was achingly brief. He yearned for the sun's lingering embrace, wishing to bask in its warmth for a few more precious moments. Yet, the sun was not destined to toil in earthly labors. It was neither a miner nor a miller but a distant companion. It was a silent friend whose radiant presence alone was sufficient to light the path ahead and warm the hearts of those who walked beneath its fading glow.

Over the next three days, Asher diligently annotated his growing stacks of notes, linking them with corresponding pages from the forbidden books in the royal library. Instead of merely writing for his own benefit, Asher structured his notes as an organized set of steps others could follow. This way, others could easily reference the collection's details, allowing him to share the burden of teaching how and when to reintroduce lost technologies.

After offering a mild protest, he relented and agreed to attend another celebration in honor of the sword's return. As they approached the grand doors to the throne room for the reception, Asher felt a tightness in his chest—an echo of a memory from the first such celebration. The music of a waltz came from the doors as they opened. The royal quartet played their strings as the kingdom's highborn greeted one another with formalized rituals Asher thought better suited for mockery than mimicry. Bunched together at a high table in the far corner, his parents and grandmother sat speaking to no one, appearing less adept at disguising their discomfort among highborn than Asher was learning to be.

"We're early. Why is everyone here?" Asher asked.

"We're nearly late—I didn't want to pull you away from your writing," Hunter explained, making one last adjustment to a ribbon on his dress uniform.

Hunter led Asher to a red carpet with golden edges in the

center of the throne room. Before them sat the queen, dressed in a flowing gown of deep green velvet with a canary-yellow cape around her neck. She smiled as her eyes met Asher's.

"Ladies and lords, guests and friends," she said, standing as the room fell to silence. "Earlier this week, we celebrated a fallen knight whose deeds exemplify a legend's rising. Another equally important duty falls upon me."

Verity stepped down from her throne as her handmaid lifted the edge of her dress. The knight captain handed her his sword, bowing. Verity took the blade and stood before them. "Asher Snow," she said, "you have risked your life helping my son find the blade of his forbearers. In so doing, you have helped bring peace to our kingdom in ways it will never fully know. My son owes you his life, and he gifts you his love."

Blushing, Asher turned to Hunter. His warm eyes and smile were enough to tame Asher's racing heart. Hunter took his hand and gently squeezed it.

Verity continued, her voice imbued with pride and solemnity. "There will come a time when your contributions to our kingdom will number in multitudes. My son would knight you for your service, but he believes himself unworthy to grant a title to his equal." Verity smiled and held the sword in front of her. "This pleasure shall then fall upon me. I, Queen Verity Bracken, sovereign of Barbshire, hereby confer upon Asher Snow the titles of both lord and knight."

Asher bent to one knee, accepting the blade's touch on each of his shoulders. "Thank you, Your Majesty," he said, his voice barely rising above the swell of applause and jubilant cheers that filled the hall.

The queen held up a hand, and the crowd fell silent again. "The title of lord grants you and your family land within the royal estates, though your home is with my son," she said, catching her lip as it quivered. "Furthermore, our tradition would have otherwise forbidden a prince from wedding one not of a noble title."

"Asher," Hunter said, taking both of Asher's hands within his own, "you showed me a compassion that I did not deserve. You set an example for bravery, sound judgment, and kindness that no bard's refrain will ever do justice and no kingdom could thrive without. Lord Sir Asher Snow, will you consider yet another title and pledge yourself to me in marriage?"

Asher tried to speak, but the words were caught in his throat. He tried once more. "We've known one another barely more than two weeks. Shouldn't we wait?"

"We could," Hunter said. "But I was about to marry a woman I had never met. This is already a longer courtship than any in my family's last three generations. As is custom, we have a year to plan a wedding."

"What if I snore in my sleep?"

Hunter smiled. "You don't."

"I don't know your middle name, and your favorite food surely can't be the rationed meats we packed."

"It's Peter. And I'd say it's a tie between frumenty with venison or perhaps shepherd's pie."

Exasperated, Asher ran his hand through his neatly combed

hair, tousling it back to normal. "I mean to say, how can you love me? What have I done to earn it?"

"Earn it?" Hunter asked as if the words were foreign. "You said yourself that love couldn't be earned. Love is a gift—it's not a reward that's earned. If it came by merit or some enchantment, it wouldn't be love."

"I will. I'll marry you," Asher said, the words tumbling out of his mouth so unfamiliar yet truer than any he ever spoke. Tears in his eyes, he held Hunter in an inseparable embrace as the assembled crowd roared in celebration. Yet to Asher, they sounded distant. He was barely aware of the queen or her knights, his family, or those assembled. The world shrank to a place where he and Hunter were alone. He saw a wonder in Hunter's eyes, untamed and unburdened, where open fields stretched forever, and no distance was too far for their love to carry them.

The quartet took up their instruments once again. Wine flowed to the accompaniment of raucous music and a chorus of laughter. Asher shook hands with strangers offering their congratulations. His mother tried to speak but only bit her lip and gave him a warm embrace, crying joyful tears. His father gave him a firm handshake, admonishing him not to forget the value of hard work for an honest wage. After a few glasses of wine, his father added to his comments, suggesting he ask the cook for another plate of steamed frog legs.

Asher rolled his eyes and joined his grandmother at a seat beside a table.

"Planning the restoration of technology over the next hundred years will be hard," his grandmother said. "Planning a wedding will be another challenge entirely."

"I think my father would actually be happy," Hunter said, joining the conversation. "He thinks weddings are strategic tools. Given the gnomes' regard for you, the prospect of a lasting peace with their kind seems more likely than ever."

"We need to make good on that promise," Asher said, drawing him away from the crowd. "The first task will be agriculture. Better fertilizer, the iron plow, crop rotations. We need to train the farmers. By next harvest, we'll have enough surplus to fill every stomach."

"I agree," Hunter said. "Then there's the matter of the sword."

"I told the captain knight it couldn't heal you because its blade was the cause of the injury," Asher said.

"And I used it to 'heal' my mother. I'm not sure what became of the child in the village."

"The longer we let the lie linger, the more enraged people will be when they learn the truth," Asher said.

"Naturally. Perhaps there's a middle ground. We wait to improve relations with Bishop Falls and the other outlying cities. Once we solve the root cause of the conflict, perhaps we can address it then," Hunter said.

"It's pragmatic," Asher said, rubbing his chin. "It still feels wrong though."

"Such is the burden of leadership," Hunter said, placing his hand on Asher's back.

"Did you really just propose to me?" Asher asked, needing to hear the words again.

Hunter took Asher's hands and met his eyes. "Absolutely. The kingdom's bylaws prevent anyone from interfering once the prince is engaged to be married—even my father. It keeps us safe in case he recovers."

Asher let go of the prince's hands. "Is this just another burden of leadership that's merely pragmatic?"

"No," Hunter whispered. "I want to spend the rest of my life with you. Nothing will change that. My father said I was raised carefree, like a wild foal, attending only to my own needs. For the first time, I have someone to care about—and someone who cares as much for me. You're beautiful. You're more of a leader than you know. Your kindness makes me want to be a better person to match some measure of your grace."

Asher looked away and blotted a tear with his sleeve. "In that case, I don't question your sincerity. But if you think I'm a leader, I question your judgment," he said with a playful smirk. "You're the leader. When you took the sword and rode toward an entire army, I knew then that you were the bravest person I've ever met. Well, aside from Gertrude. And Lattice, of course."

Hunter took Asher's hands once again. "If I was brave, it was only because I trusted you to have my back."

Together, they danced and laughed as they gradually bid farewell to their assembled guests. Once there were too few left to dance, the quartet delicately packed away their instruments. As the grand doors of the throne room swung shut behind them, the echoes of applause and cheers still resonated within Asher's heart, mingling with the warmth of newfound titles.

They returned to the veranda near their room, high in the castle. They spent the rest of the night laughing and recounting the past, their conversation filled with hopes for the future. With the Watchers passing above as their witnesses, Asher gazed out over the kingdom, blessed with the first rays of a rising sun. Despite the trials ahead, Asher took hope in love's guiding light, brighter than the sun.

To Be Continued . . .

THANK YOU FOR READING!

I HOPE YOU ENJOYED the first installment of *Asher and the Prince*. There's no better way to support this work and help others find it than to leave a review online. I will be eternally thankful if you would take a moment to do that.

If you're eager for the next installment, please let me know! Text the word Corbin to 55444 to join my mailing list.

www.ingramcontent.com/pod-product-compliance
Lightning Source LLC
Chambersburg PA
CBHW020334180626
46812CB00001B/205